MOLOGAN THE BOGGART
& THE GREEN LOBSTER

TO CLACHNACALA
CRANNOG
CRAIGMHOR LOCH
TURNIP FIELD
BIG SHED
TOOLSHED
SILAGE FIELD
MOLOGAN'S HILL
OLD BYRE
OUR CAMP
THE CLEARING
WHERE FIN FELL INTO THE BOGGART'S CAVE
STEEP SHORTCUT TO THE BEACH
SPOOKY ENCLOSURE
CREEPY WOOD
FAIRY PATH
THE TRACK
WATERFALL
BOATHOUSE
BIG BAY
TOR
MACHAIR
TATTIE FIELD
THE CUT
THE SOUND
CANOE KEPT HERE
SHEEP ISLAND
THIS IS WHERE WE GOT CUT OFF BY THE TIDE
BOAT BAY
EILEAN BODACH
(HOBGOBLIN ISLAND)
HERON ISLAND
SECRET ENTRANCE TO ROARY BOREALIS'S CAVE
RED BAY

Beth's map of
CRAIGMHOR
Isle of Shuma
BEN MHOR
SHEEP FANK
HENHOUSE
THIS IS WHERE WE SAW THE ADDER
DUNES
AEOLAIR TOR
RUINED VILLAGE
RABBIT GLEN
STANDING STONES
SECRET BAY
DUNES
THE SANDBAR
Craigmhor Bay
THE LAGOON
SALT PANS
OTTER ISLAND
THIS IS WHERE MOLOGAN FELL OVERBOARD
BROCH TOR
BLACK ISLE
ENTRANCE TO AGGIE HAG BOGGART'S CAVE
EILEAN NAN RON (SEAL ISLAND)
ROCKS

for Robert, Beth and Fin

MOLOGAN THE BOGGART & THE GREEN LOBSTER

WRITTEN & ILLUSTRATED BY
MAZDA MUNN

mercatpress
www.mercatpress.com

First published in 2004 by Mercat Press Ltd
10 Coates Crescent, Edinburgh EH3 7AL
www.mercatpress.com

ISBN 184183 0682

The publisher acknowledges subsidy from the Scottish Arts Council towards the publication of this volume.

Set in Veljovic Medium and Nueva Bold at Mercat Press
Printed and bound in Great Britain by
Bell & Bain Ltd

Contents

Boggarts and Bogling

This is a story about a Boggart. Perhaps you don't know what a Boggart is. That's not surprising. Most people never know of the existence of these solitary creatures. However, it is quite possible that a Boggart lives near you. If you have ever experienced a series of peculiar incidents such as things inexplicably breaking down or going missing (and often reappearing again unexpectedly) or if you have heard almost inaudible clanks, rattling and rustling sounds in the night, glimpsed an occasional lumpy silhouette against the moon or the glint of a green eye in the starlight, you may have been visited by a mischief-making Boggart.

Boggarts are canny and live by their wits. After hibernating all winter in their damp, hidden underground caves, Boggarts spend the summer sleeping during the daylight hours, and creeping about at night carrying out their traditional profession of 'bogling', which is Boggart-speak for making mischief, foraging for food and spiriting away discarded items. Since they are extremely secretive and as their skin and clothing resemble the colours and textures of their natural habitat, they are rarely seen.

Bogling is what Boggarts do. Boggarts have carried on this ancient and noble profession for centuries. It is bound by its own strict rules and regulations and is considered by Boggarts to be a valuable service to the community. Boggarts always leave tokens of their appreciation such as slimy, squirmy things, which are well intended, but not always noticed or appreciated by their recipients.

'Clamjamphrie' is the Boggart name for a collection of flotsam and jetsam, unwanted rubbish or discarded items collected and hoarded by Boggarts. The extent of their collection of clamjamphrie is regarded as a sign of their status and professional abilities.

The highlight of the Boggart social calendar is the Grand Bogling Competition which is held every ten years. Boggarts travel from their secret caves all over the country and congregate in one place to compete for the ultimate honour of winning the trophy for 'Champion of Mac-champions'. There are also stalls for Boggart snacks and competitions for crafts and unusual livestock. This event has, for centuries, been an important meeting place for solitary Boggarts.

The Boggart in this story is called Mologan. He has lived a peaceful, lonely and uneventful life in his cave at Craigmhor on the Hebridean island of Shuma for a hundred and forty-seven years. But as he wakes from his hibernation one midsummer evening, things begin to change...

CHAPTER 1

Dried Slugs and Treacle

Deep in the dark, damp caves of Craigmhor on the Isle of Shuma, Mologan the Boggart was suddenly awakened from his long winter hibernation by a loud, echoing THUMP.

THUMP, THUMP, THUMP, THUMP!

Dusty crumbs of peat, dislodged from the lofty ceiling of the cave, trickled down onto Mologan's bed.

THUMP, THUD!

'Humph, snort... ach-oo!'

Mologan the Boggart sneezed loudly. Still half asleep he pulled the grubby, moth-eaten potato sack over his head and listened.

Silence.

He peeped out into the gloomy cave with one beady,

sleep-encrusted eye, sniffed the air with his large snout, and sighed.

Mologan the Boggart groaned and turned over, closing his eyes tightly, trying to return to his favourite dream.

'Where was I? Mmm, aye, snuffle.' He drifted off to sleep again.

In his dream Mologan took the massive trophy and held it aloft in triumph. The golden quaich glinted in the moonlight highlighting the inscription:

NATIONAL BOGLING COMPETITION
GOLDEN QUAICH TROPHY
FOR CHAMPION OF MAC-CHAMPIONS

Mologan cleared his throat and clutched the cup to his chest. He was dazzled for a moment as the reflected moonlight lit up his proud, beaming face.

'Fellow Boggarts', he began, surveying the crowd of cheering Boggarts, 'I would like to take this mac-opportunity', Mologan paused to wipe a tear from his eye, 'sniff, to thank...'

His dream was interrupted again.

THUMP, THUD, THUD!

There it was again. The loud echoing sound which shook the very bedrock, vibrating the stalactites and stalagmites. Something in the cavern fell over with a clank. Mologan sat up, now grumpy and half awake.

He yawned, rubbed his eyes and scowled. A shaft of dust-speckled sunlight streaked through a crack high in the rocky cavern wall, illuminating the Boggart's untidy and cluttered cave. Mologan leaned back on his pillow of dried seaweed, putting both hands behind his head, and surveyed the cavern which had been his home for more than a century. From the high vaulted ceiling stalactites hung like huge, glossy, dripping fangs. Five doorways of different shapes and sizes, some hidden behind stalagmites or rocky outcrops, opened onto a series of subterranean tunnels and passages which led to various secret entrances on the Craigmhor cliffs. A spring bubbled up from a tiny crevice in the rock and trickled noiselessly into a mossy stone trough.

The remains of Mologan's last meal lay on a cluttered and cobwebby driftwood table surrounded by three chairs made of a skelfy packing case, an upturned rusty metal pail and a tractor seat precariously balanced on an old cracked flower pot. Shelves built of barnacled planks on rock ledges bent under the weight of their tightly packed contents. Mountains of junk were piled and strewn in every conceivable corner, hung on the walls, heaped on every stalagmite and suspended from every stalactite.

Piles of tangled rope mingled in a muddle of rusty bedsprings, tent pegs, plastic bottles and packing cases. Heaps of decomposing magazines mixed higgledy-piggledy with broken plates, dented dustbins, fishing lines and strangely shaped lumps of driftwood. A miscellaneous assortment of curious items poked out of confused and formless mounds of unrecognisable junk – a worn rubber wellington boot, an ancient wooden airplane propeller, half a stepladder, mis-shapen wheels, the skeleton of an umbrella, a brass porthole frame and a battered cork lifebuoy.

A broken camera was perched on top of a chaotic mountain of jumbled tins of dried-up paint, coat-hangers, frayed and crumbling baskets, rods, reels and balding brushes. There were building bricks, nylon shrimping nets, headless hammers, broken tools, mouse-traps, anchors, and fankled balls of baling twine.

Battered lobster pots tumbled in chaotic heaps amongst corroded chains, ancient black cannonballs, odd chair legs, mouldy coconuts, oil cans and a vast array of brightly coloured fishing floats.

This magnificent array of items was the result of Mologan the Boggart's tireless commitment to his ancient profession of bogling.

Mologan proudly scanned his vast collection. He smiled to himself, pondering how fortunate he was to be a Boggart of such means and to have so many useful and valuable possessions.

'Ah'm so mac-lucky,' he said out loud. 'This must be the most mac-wonderful collection o' clamjamphrie in the whole o' the Western Isles.'

THUMP, THUMP, THUMP!

Now he was wide awake. Realisation dawned.

'Wiggley mac-wurums,' he said out loud, 'It's the mac-visitors!'

⌘

THUMP, THUMP, THUMP!

'It *is* hollow.'

'No it *isn't.*'

'It *is,*' said Fin, jumping up and down on a grassy mound next to their caravan, which was parked on the cliff top beside the ancient and dense woodland. 'Doesn't it sound hollow? Beth, listen.' Fin jumped again.

THUMP!

'Oh, come and give us a hand, Fin, Robbie can't manage that bag on his own,' said Beth, struggling to carry a box of groceries into the caravan.

Reluctantly, Fin left the mound and went to help the others to unpack the car.

'Here's Mum,' called Robbie excitedly, as Mum approached, carrying a box of eggs. 'What took you so long?'

'Well, I couldn't be rude and dash off with the eggs,' she replied. 'Anyway, Iona and I had lots of gossip to catch up with.'

'So you've been gossiping over a coffee at the croft while we've struggled to unpack the car and get organised,' said Beth indignantly, hands on hips and a broad smile on her freckled face.

'You've done a great job, kids,' said Mum, picking up a stray trainer which had been dropped in a cow pat.

'Just look at this view,' she sighed, and walked round the caravan to the edge of the cliff.

The Douglas family's holiday caravan was perched on a flat grassy ledge close to the edge of a steep, densely wooded slope above the machair at the north end of Craigmhor Bay. Small but ancient gnarled oaks, tiny birch trees and twisted hazels clung stubbornly to the hillside. All the trees in this miniature forest were small and wizened, stunted by centuries of long cold winters and strong winds.

From this high ledge they overlooked the tidal sound between the mainland and the island of Eilean Bodach to the west and a dramatic and rugged landscape stretching to the south. A series of large sandy beaches surrounded the Bay, each enclosed by craggy pink granite cliffs. A pattern of small islands spread out to the south. Each summer Euan the crofter took a few sheep by boat to graze on each of these small islands. Beyond the shelter of the bay were the Serpent Rocks. This line of jagged rocks stretched for several miles into the Atlantic Ocean in what was one of the most treacherous stretches of water around the west coast.

'It's so beautiful here,' Mum said softly. 'I dream about this place. Listen.'

Beth, Robbie and Fin listened.

'What are we listening for?' Robbie asked after a few seconds of hearing nothing.

'The silence, the perfect silence,' Mum said dreamily.

The children looked at each other quizzically.

Mum turned away from the view, smiling, and went into the caravan. She put the eggs into the fridge. 'Anyone fancy a bacon roll?'

'Yeah!' they all chorused and piled into the caravan.

⌘

Meanwhile, in his cave directly below the grassy mound, Mologan was still lying in bed admiring his magnificent collection of clamjamphrie and contemplating getting up. A faint, pleasant smell of food seemed to be in the air. It was reminiscent of something, and he couldn't quite remember what, but it did smell good.

'Slimy-mac-slugs, I'm hungry,' he thought, and heaved himself out of the creaking fish-box bed.

After the long winter hibernation Mologan was sensitive to the merest glint of sunlight. He shielded his eyes against the shaft of light with his hand as he picked his way through the piles of clamjamphrie towards the spring. He tripped over a broken boat-hook, stumbled and stubbed his toe on the trough.

'Mac-ouch!'

He hopped up and down on a tiny, uncluttered spot holding his toe and muttering Boggart oaths.

When the pain subsided he took a deep, wheezy breath and peered into the dark, still water, squinting at his reflection.

'Another year older an' I'm jist as mac-handsome,' he said to himself, unsuccessfully attempting to smooth the wiry, heather-like tuft of hair on his large, pointed head.

He pulled his wide mouth apart at each corner with long mottled fingers, exposing two sharp fangs.

Closing one eye he examined them in the watery reflection, then stuck out an enormous blue tongue for inspection. He was pleased with what he saw.

Mologan was handsome, for a Boggart. He was about average Boggart height with big feet and hands, and a hump on his back. He had a large head with a wide jaw, gaping mouth, two marvellous fangs and no chin to speak of. His nose had a rather squashed appearance with big, sensitive nostrils – Boggarts have a well developed sense of smell. His small, beady eyes were close together, topped by rather expressive eyebrows resembling dark, hairy caterpillars, which sat high on his narrow forehead giving him a permanently quizzical expression. His ears were small and frilly like delicate tree fungus.

Mologan bent his knobbly knees a few times, birled his long arms around and then touched his toes stiffly.

'In perfect mac-workin' order,' he grinned, rubbing his face and casting another admiring glance into the trough.

Mologan's flaky skin was mottled in tones of grey, orange and sludgy green and resembled the lichen-covered rocks on the island. He wore a threadbare, grubby kilt made of drab green and faded purple plaid. Dusting himself down, bits of flaky skin and oos rose up, visible in the shaft of sunlight. He straightened his kilt, tightening the belt and re-positioning the rusty pin. Tying on his favourite old and smelly toadskin sporran, he smiled again at his reflection.

Having now forgotten his painful stubbed toe, the Boggart whirled round, danced a few steps of a jig, then burst into tuneless singing in a deep, gurgly voice which sounded like mud swirling down a drain.

'It's mac-summertime, it's boglin' time, an', it's grand to be...'

He punched high in the air with one hand, stamped his foot on the floor, disturbing a small cloud of dust, and cried joyfully at the top of his voice, 'UN-MAC-HIBERNATED!'

Mologan laughed a croaky, hoarse laugh, took a deep breath and scanned the cave with bright green, piercing eyes, peering at the overcrowded shelves and the cluttered table. Rubbing his tummy he said to himself, 'I must have some mac-food somewhere.'

The snacks which he had carefully prepared to sustain him throughout the long, cold months of his winter hibernation were all finished. There wasn't a crumb left of the dog biscuits, dried sea anemones, whelks in brine, dried banana skins and crispy cockroaches. He was hungry, so hungry he could eat... well, anything!

Mologan looked around vaguely, grunting to himself, 'Mac-food, mutter, mutter, mac-somewhere, got to be mac-somewhere,' in a deep, unintelligible mumble which sounded like a giant's tummy rumbling. He sniffed the air. He could still smell a wonderful aroma filtering down through air shafts from the world above. Something cooking. Something nice. It reminded him of summer and made him feel even hungrier.

He rummaged around among the miscellany of accumulated junk, pushing aside boxes, jars and piles of clamjamphrie, scattering the junk behind him and tossing things over his head. After a few moments of frenzied activity he had gathered a selection of breakfast food. A jar of dried slugs, a chunk of green and mouldy bread, a rusty tin without a label, and several live worms from his worm trap.

'I'll open this tin, there might be something mac-nice in it, peaches in syrup, creamy mac-custard, spaghetti hoops, cat food?' His mouth watered in anticipation as he searched for a can opener. The can opener was nowhere to be found among all the piles of clamjamphrie.

'I know I've got one somewhere,' he grumbled, his tummy rumbling. 'I bogled it from a camper in 1976.'

This was the year when Mologan had found a wooden crate washed up on the beach which had contained 48 cans of pineapple rings in syrup. Luckily there were campers at the croft at the time so he had crept into their tent that night and bogled a can opener. Being unused to modern technology it had taken him several nights before he worked out how to use it and finally tasted the delights of this new and delicious treat. Having opened all the cans in the excitement of learning this new skill, Mologan ate the whole lot at once and was very sick.

As he delved under a bundle of old ropes, Mologan discovered another old tin. He blew off the dust and cobwebs and rubbed it with the hem of his kilt.

'Mouldy mac-maggots, it's treacle,' he thought, and forgetting his quest for the can opener he picked up an old, rusty screwdriver and prised the tin open.

'Half full. Grunt, snort.' He poked a long grimy finger into its black stickiness and shoved it greedily into his mouth, dribbling a thin black trail over his chest.

'Breakfast!' he exclaimed, and was soon sitting on the edge of his bed tucking into a huge bowl of dried slugs and treacle with some live worms on top.

⌘

'Let's go exploring,' said Fin, swallowing a last mouthful of bacon roll.

'Wait for me,' cried Robbie, jumping up from the table with his half-eaten roll in his hand.

'Don't rush, finish eating first,' said Mum. 'Drink your fruit juice, Fin. Besides, there's no hurry, we're staying for three weeks, and you've been here before. I'm sure you've already explored the whole of Craigmhor.'

'I know, but it always seems new and exciting. We find new things to do every time we come. Anyway, it was raining for the whole week last time,' Fin mumbled through a mouthful of bread and bacon and tomato ketchup.

'The only things we explored last year were the books on how many games we could play with a pack of cards and a set of dominos,' laughed Beth.

'And the tearoom in Clachnacala,' added Robbie. 'Do you remember those wonderful chocolate and toffee shortbread cakes?'

'Trust Robbie to remember what we ate!' said Beth.

'Well, the sun's still shining,' said Mum. 'I suppose you should make the most of it. Off you go. I'll tidy up a bit. Come back soon and we'll put up the tent.'

Fin quickly slurped the rest of his orange juice and headed for the door, followed by Beth and Robbie who shuffled out more carefully from behind the table.

'Be careful on the cliffs,' Mum called.

Outside, Fin was jumping on the mound again.

THUMP, THUMP, THUMP!

'I'm sure it's hollow! I bet there's a secret cave under here.'

'Yes, and it's full of smugglers' treasure,' said Beth sarcastically.

'Let's go and find it then,' said Robbie.

'OK, follow me,' said Fin, disappearing into the woods through a clump of tall foxgloves, scattering a few pollen-laden bumble bees.

There was a narrow sheep-worn path through the wood. Winding through a patch of gnarled oak trees it led down a rocky incline onto a pleasant grassy ledge. Sunlight filtered through the trees with a green flickering light and there was the smell of honeysuckle in the air. The children could hear grasshoppers, bees humming around the honeysuckle and the faint honking of Iona's geese in the distance. Further on, where the ledge became boggy and the flag irises were beginning to show their yellow heads, the path sloped more steeply between lichen-covered rocks. In some places they had to duck to avoid low branches and in other places they climbed down through bracken which grew high above their heads.

On their left was a sort of enclosure formed by a tumbled down drystone wall on three sides, and by the cliff face on the north side. The stones and the rocks were green and mossy and the sunlight didn't seem to penetrate the gloom.

'Look, I can see our caravan up there,' said Beth squinting upwards through the trees. A small fragment of white was visible at the top of the cliff.

'Kinda spooky here,' said Robbie. 'I don't like it.'

'Don't be daft,' Fin said, breenging on through the bracken. 'We'll soon be at the bottom.'

But it was gloomy. Even Fin, trying to be the brave and intrepid explorer, felt a chill creep up his spine. He stopped, and the place seemed suddenly silent. No bird noise, no grasshoppers, no bees, no honking of geese.

The silence was broken by a distant call from the top of the cliff.

'BETH, FIN, ROBBIE!'

It was Mum.

'Perhaps we'd better go back and put up the tent,' Beth suggested in a broken whisper.

'Yes, s'pose so,' chorused the boys and they all headed back up the steep path as quickly as they could, reaching the top breathless and glad to be back in the sunlight.

CHAPTER 2

Squinky Mac-sookers

Fin woke early. He felt very hot. The sun was already shining through the canvas roof of the tent.

He heard the geese honking at the croft, and a dog barked. Robbie was still fast asleep but Fin was wide awake, although he had no idea what time it was as he had left his watch in the caravan. He slipped silently out of his sleeping bag, and bundling together his clothes and boots he crept out of the tent.

The sky was cloudless apart for a slight haze over the horizon, and the tide was so far out that a couple of the small islands in Craigmhor Bay were no longer surrounded by water. He heard a seal snort far out in the bay and a yellowhammer chirping in the clump of trees behind the caravan.

Fin began to get dressed. Picking up his trousers upside-down, the contents of his pockets spilled onto the grass. There was a penknife, a key, string, several elastic bands (Fin always picked these up if he saw them, because you never knew when they might come in handy), a pocket torch, coins, a lucky wishbone, a plastic soldier, sweetie papers, a quartz chuckie, a chewed pencil stump, a compass, a plastic film container containing a dead beetle, Grandpa's old army hat badge, a bus ticket, one of Beth's guitar plectrums he had found in the car and had meant to give her back, a piece of bark shaped like a duck's foot, and nine brightly-coloured, round hard sweets.

He picked everything up, stuffed it into his pockets, and, wiping a bright yellow sweet on his jumper, popped it into his mouth.

'Mmm, breakfast!' he said out loud, feeling quite naughty. The giant sweets had a swirly, marbled pattern on the surface and came in a selection of outrageous flavours and bright colours. They were bursting with flavour, lasted for ages and changed colour at least five times when you sucked them. Fin had discovered the sweets when they came to the Isle of Shuma for their caravan holiday last year. Before boarding the ferry to the island they had stopped in Invernoddle to buy last-minute groceries, and while Mum was in the supermarket the children had wandered around the shops spending some of their holiday pocket money.

There was a wonderful sweet shop called McSwiggan's in the main street, and it was here that

Fin first discovered and bought some squinky sookers. He had never been able to find them elsewhere. His parents didn't like him to eat McSwiggan's squinky sookers. Their words echoed in his head, *'They'll break your teeth! Artificial flavours! Full of additives! Chemical nightmares! They'll make you turn green!'* This year Fin had secretly bought a large packet of the forbidden sweets with his holiday pocket money and had hoped to make them last at least a week.

However, on day two, he only had nine - well eight now - left.

The fluorescent yellow sooker tasted wonderful.

'Yum! What an excellent breakfast!'

Fin sat on a rock and tied his boot laces. He took the sweet out of his mouth to examine it. Yes! It had turned from lurid yellow with white swirls to magenta pink with blue speckles.

He felt excited. No-one else was awake. Fin had Craigmhor all to himself. He shivered and buttoned up his camouflage jacket.

'I'm going exploring,' he thought, and crept past the caravan towards the woods, happily sucking the squinky sooker.

He followed the sheep path through the wood, down to the next level on the cliff and headed along the ledge in the opposite direction from yesterday's expedition. The ledge became narrower and Fin had to press himself against the cliff wall to make progress. He came to a damp clearing where lots of different ferns grew and the rocks were green and spongy with moss. He could hear water dripping and it became wet and slimy underfoot. Looking down, he realised that he was directly above the gloomy old enclosure they had discovered yesterday.

'Then I must be just below the caravan,' he thought. Turning to look up, Fin lost his footing on a mossy rock and slipped. Unable to get a foothold he tried to grab ferns and branches but they broke in his hands and he slid down the mossy slope smoothly and quickly on his bottom. He saw that he was heading straight for a large boulder which blocked his path.

'Oh no...o...o,' he cried, as he slid towards the boulder, covering his head with his hands, unable to change direction or stop.

Suddenly he was no longer moving in the same direction but falling downwards as though the earth had swallowed him. He landed with a soft thump at the bottom of a narrow, dark hole.

Recovering his breath took a few minutes. Fin was shocked and stunned at first. Looking around, he couldn't see much but he was conscious of a pungent, foosty smell. By a combination of squinting and feeling he could tell that he had landed on a pile of old ropes and fishing buoys. They felt damp and rough, but had been soft enough to break his fall. He stretched his arms and legs. No pain. He wasn't hurt. Good. That was a relief.

Some light penetrated the hole which Fin had fallen through and when his eyes became more accustomed to the dimness he guessed that he was in a cave. Feeling around with his foot he found a solid floor and tentatively stood up. He pulled his wet and muddy trousers away from his bottom with thumb and forefinger. 'Yuch!' Fin shivered. He felt very cold and damp. Never mind, if he moved around he'd soon warm up. He could explore the cave.

Fin remembered his torch and pulled it out of his pocket. Clicking it on, he shone it around the cave and was astonished to see that he was in a fairly large cavern which was piled high with the most amazing collection of junk. Ancient rusty petrol cans mingled with a heap of broken thermos flasks. A bit of iron guttering, a holed teapot, and a pile of mouldy shoes and boots in all shapes, styles and sizes were heaped in a corner. Fin looked closely, and there didn't seem to be any pairs of shoes. They were all different.

Fish boxes and milk crates were piled as high as the roof, and a ship's clock with the springs hanging out, a pile of old batteries, several rubber tyres and some oily engine parts were strewn around the floor.

'Wow,' said Fin out loud, 'I wonder who left all this junk here? And how did they get it in? Surely not through the hole I fell through.' He kicked a small plastic barrel out of the way and shone his torch up at the gap in the roof. 'No, definitely not, no way. There must be another way into this cave.'

Further exploration revealed a rocky niche which hid a wide doorway. Fin cautiously stepped through the door into a long, dark and drippy tunnel and shone his torch left and right into sooty blackness.

He thought there might be a glint of light visible which would guide him to the open air, so he switched off his torch and peered in both directions. Pitch dark. Fin felt a shiver up his spine. He quickly clicked the torch on again and stood still and indecisive in the gloom. He shone the torch upwards towards a rough and jagged ceiling, then pointed it at the ground. The tunnel floor was flat and sandy. He peered at it intently. The sand was rough and disturbed and there were scuffled indentations all over it. Fin shone the light further along the tunnel floor. Yes, more marks. Were they, could they be... footprints? On further examination they seemed to be going in both directions.

'If these are footprints then there must be a way out,' he thought, positively. 'Now, which way shall I go?'

Fin fingered the contents of his pocket and pulled out a ten pence piece. 'If this comes up heads I'll go right, and if it comes up tails I'll go left,' he said, tossing the coin. He examined it in the torch light.

'Tails, left. Here I go.'

He slowly made his way along the tunnel. This was a real adventure. He remembered books he had read about children finding secret passages and smugglers' caves, and how they always found their way back by leaving a trail of bread, or torn paper, or chalk marks on the walls... Fin stopped dead.

He hadn't left a trail. What if he had to find his way back to the cave? He had a moment's panic. Then he laughed. 'I'll only need to mark the trail if the tunnel forks,' he thought, but he scraped a big arrow in the sand with his foot, just in case.

The passage twisted and turned and seemed to be going very gently downhill. Then it veered sharply to the right, almost doubling back on itself. Fin noticed the entrances to small caves on each side of the passageway, which was now becoming wider. He flashed his torch into each small cave in turn. Every one was crammed to the doorway with piles and piles of junk similar to the first cave. One larger cave was completely filled with hundreds of empty wooden crates. He took a closer look. Stenciled on each one it said clearly 'SCOTCH WHISKY: FOR EXPORT ONLY.'

Fin shivered and his heart began to beat faster. 'Smugglers! Wow, a real smugglers' cave. Hell's teeth!' he thought, feeling butterflies in his tummy. 'I'd better be careful.'

He continued his exploration, walking very cautiously and listening for anyone else in the tunnel, but he could only hear an occasional drip and the sound of his own breathing.

Suddenly the passage became very narrow, and squeezing through the gap Fin found himself in a huge, vaulted cavern. He gasped, then sniffed. There was a distinct smell of rotting wood, fungus, and smelly feet. He looked around. This cave was also full of junk, but it was different from the others. It was more... well, lived-in. Fin scanned the cave again in case anyone was there, hiding behind a stalactite or a large piece of junk. He couldn't see anyone. He took a few tentative steps into the cave. There was a water trough against one wall which seemed to be filled from a small spring which trickled out of a crack in the rock. Almost hidden by all the junk there was a rough, cluttered table, some untidily packed shelves, and in one corner was a crumpled, unmade bed, or, to be more exact, a blue plastic fish-box with foosty old hessian potato sacks on it. A grubby bowl lay on the bed. It contained the black and sticky remains of a rather disgusting meal. A creepy thought entered Fin's head. 'Somebody lives here.'

Fin suddenly felt very scared and vulnerable. Believing that he had stumbled into a smugglers' hideout he imagined, with an uncomfortable sinking sensation in his stomach, that a band of rowdy and ill-tempered smugglers might return to the cave at any moment and discover him. He was an intruder in their secret place. Now conscious of a cold, creepy tingling up his spine Fin glanced over his shoulder to check that no-one had crept up silently behind him. Nothing there. He sighed with relief and immediately decided to get out of this cavern as fast as he could. Fin instantly formed a plan to go back to the cave he had fallen into, make a pile of fish-boxes and milk crates and climb out. He turned back towards the tunnel and froze on the spot. He could distinctly hear a noise in the tunnel. He listened carefully. Yes, it was getting nearer and nearer. A swashy, shuffling sound and a strange low humming, and could he hear words? Someone singing?

Panicking, Fin looked around quickly, scanning the cavern for somewhere to hide. Oh, no. Where? Behind these lobster pots? His heart pounding, Fin quietly shifted the dilapidated lobster pots forward and crouched behind them, pulling an old tattered sail partially over his head.

'Drat, my torch!' he thought. Switching the torch off, he realised that it was fairly light in the cave. Shafts of pale sunlight filtered in from a crack in the roof.

He could hear singing, well, singing of a sort, a monotone humming and a few mumbled words in a deep, gurgly voice. The hairs stood up on the back of his neck and he began to tremble. He felt cold and alone and wished fervently that he was back in the tent with Robbie.

⌘

Mologan was returning from the first night's bogling of the season. After a long winter spent hibernating underground he was glad to get back to his familiar bogling routine again. He had enjoyed himself so much that he had lost all track of time and the sun was already up by the time he returned to the secret entrance. He hummed a tune to himself and found himself singing an old bogling song.

'Bogling home and a song in the air...' He walked in time to the rhythm of the tune, his bogling bag clinking cheerily on his back.

As Mologan shuffled along the tunnel he hummed half-remembered snatches of 'Boggart Boogie-

Woogie.' His first foray had been very successful. He had let down a tyre on the crofter's Land Rover and had dropped green slime into the well. He'd tipped out a dustbin and put green snot on the door handle of the holiday cottage. He had collected a bent spoon, a dog's lead and a rather smart ballpoint pen with a glittery barrel and pictures of dolphins on it, a plastic bottle, a polystyrene ball and half a wellington boot.

Since there was a very low tide he had been able to dig up some razor shells and collect some mussels on the beach, which would make a delicious supper.

Reaching the entrance to his living cave Mologan noticed a strange, unfamiliar smell.

'Mac-poo!' he exclaimed, 'What's that smell?' He sniffed again, putting down his bogling bag and peering into the cave. 'Mmm, sniff, snort. This is gey macqueer!'

Mologan stood on the small patch of clear floor space beside his bed sniffing the air with his large nostrils, grunting and twitching his nose.

Desperately trying to remain still, Fin crouched behind the lobster pots, shivering with fear.

'Smells like unco fowk,' Mologan mumbled to himself.

Fin edged closer and closer to the cave wall and covered his head with his hands, shutting his eyes tightly.

'Who's mac-there? Who is it?' the Boggart grunted, now quite frightened himself at the thought of an intruder, or worse, a burglar in his home. It suddenly crossed his mind that someone was trying to rob him. Didn't he have the largest and most valuable collection of clamjamphrie this side of Ben Mhor?

'Come oot! Ah ken ye're there. Ah can smell ye,' he cried in a burst of bravado, picking up a small anchor and brandishing it menacingly. 'Come oot or Ah'll come an' get ye!'

Fin huddled silently beneath the damp and musty folds of the old sail. He could hear the creature wheezing and snorting. He shuddered and pressed his back tight against a lumpy lobster pot.

'Ah've got a mac-weapon,' Mologan the Boggart rasped, trying to affect his scariest, most intimidating voice. He gripped the anchor more tightly and waved it about fiercely.

Fin opened his eyes. Peeking through his fingers he could see the huge, threatening black silhouette looming nearer and nearer. He held his breath.

Determined to expose the intruder Mologan was feeling unusually courageous. Following the strong and unfamiliar scent of the concealed burglar the Boggart boldly kicked a fishing float out of his way, propelling it into a battered budgie cage and dislodging a precarious heap of clamjamphrie which toppled onto the cave floor with an almighty clatter. Undeterred by the sea of junk he continued to move towards Fin, wading steadily through the tumbled objects, wheezing and grunting noisily.

Fin's heart was pounding. He gasped. The immense anchor-brandishing shadow towered over him.

'Dae Ah huv tae drag ye oot or dae ye gie up?' the Boggart growled.

Fin's throat was dry. He thought he'd better reply to the creature but when he tried to say something no words came out, only an almost inaudible squeak.

'Let's be seein' ye then, ye clamjamphrie-rastler. Show yersel.'

Fin poked his head nervously from beneath the canvas.

Mologan could only see Fin's eyes in the gloomy corner.

'Who is it?'

'Fin. It's Fin,' was the muffled reply.

'Fin? Did you say Fin?'

A whispered, 'Yes.'

'Fin MacBogle? Fin, whit are you doin' here? Fur why are you hidin' in Mologan's cave? Are ye spyin' on Mologan?' Mologan moved menacingly towards Fin. 'That's it, ye're mac-spyin' on me. Ye think ye'll see what I wis plannin' fur the boglin' compie-mac-tishun!'

Fin MacBogle, the Clachnacala Boggart, and Mologan, the Craigmhor Boggart, had been arch-rivals in the Grand Bogling Competition for the past century.

'No, no, I fell through the roof,' gasped Fin, who was now within reach of the irate creature. He could smell the Boggart's fishy breath.

'Git oot here, Fin MacBogle,' Mologan said in a gruff, assertive tone, now confident that he knew the intruder and that he had the upper hand. Waving the anchor fiercely above his head he kicked away the nearest lobster pot. 'Oot, oot, oot!'

Realising that he had no option, Fin emerged reluctantly from his hiding place, shaking like a leaf.

Getting to his feet he was surprised to see that although this creature had a huge, menacing shadow, he was only the same height as Fin himself. He couldn't see clearly what the creature looked like. In the gloom of the cave he could only make out a rather lumpy silhouette and he was conscious of a very musty smell, like fungus in damp woodland, and the sound of snuffly, wheezy breathing.

'Wigguly-mac-wurums!' exclaimed Mologan, 'It's no Fin MacBogle at aw! It's a mac-visitor!'

'Of course I'm not Fin MacBogle,' said Fin, 'I'm Finbar Douglas!'

'So ye're another Fin aw-the-mac-gither?'

'Yes, I'm here on my holidays and I went exploring and I went along this slippery path and I slipped and I fell down a hole and I was in a cave and I couldn't get out and I heard you coming and...'

Fin stopped to draw breath. He was now conscious that the creature was wheezing and hiccupping loudly. He looked up. The great lumpy silhouette was shaking visibly and taking great gasps of breath. Fin realised that the creature was laughing. Holding his tummy and doubling over, Mologan had dropped the anchor and was obviously finding the situation extremely funny. Fin felt hurt. The creature was laughing at him and didn't seem in the least bit interested in his explanation.

'Why are you laughing at me?' he said crossly.

'Uch, snort, snort, Ah thought ye' were, hic, grunt, wheeze... Ah thought ye were old Fin MacBogle, snort, hic!'

Mologan lifted one leg, then the other, turned around in a circle and sat down on a large, rusty oil can. Covering his face with his hands he rocked back and forth, overcome with mirth. 'Fin MacBogle, Fin Mac-visitor!' he kept repeating to himself.

Mologan was now clearly visible to Fin in the shaft of sunlight. This strange creature was different from anything Fin had ever seen, even in books. He stared at Mologan's extraordinary features, his beady eyes, his mottled skin, his long pointed head, his hump. What on earth was he?

Mologan continued to laugh. It occurred to Fin that he could escape now, make for the doorway.

One, two, three, he darted quickly towards the cave entrance, then crash, bang, clink, splat! He fell over the lumpy, grimy bogling bag which Mologan had dumped on the floor.

'Mind ma supper!' the Boggart growled, still sitting on the oil can. He had now stopped laughing. 'There's clabbydhus an' spoots in that boglin' bag.'

He grinned from ear to ear, exposing two large fangs and wrinkling his blotchy forehead. Standing up, adjusting his kilt and wiping the tears from his eyes with his huge, scaly hands Mologan stomped towards Fin, who backed up against a pile of old plastic ice cream containers, a gramophone horn and a roll of chicken wire. Mologan snatched up the bogling bag, and clearing the clutter from the driftwood table by sweeping it onto the floor with his arm, he emptied the contents of the bag onto the table top. The Boggart pointed to the smelly pile of mussels and razor shells mixed with a dog's lead, a pen, part of an old boot and other assorted rubbish.

'Supper,' he said. 'You'll stay?'

Delighted to have some company Mologan had become quite cheery. It had been years since he had entertained. He racked his brains to remember who and when it was. Was it old Uncle Hector MacWhistle who stayed with him when the Bogling Competition was held on the island in nineteen hundred and thirteen? Or was it his cousin Mucus 'Mouldy' MacSnot? Yes, Mouldy had visited him in 1961, just before he was betrothed to Daphne Puddock-Stuil. What fun they had had that summer. What great bogles they had done together. Then poor Mouldy had set up cave with that snobby Boggart wifie. Daphne came from an old Boggart family who lived in the dungeons of an ancient castle and who had, it was rumoured in Boggart circles, the most extensive and valuable collection of clamjamphrie in the country. The Puddock-Stuils thought themselves rather posh and a cut above the cave-dwelling Boggarts. Mologan and Mouldy had never been allowed to see each other again, except at the Bogling Competition every ten years, and when they did Mologan had to remember to call him by his proper name, Mucus. What a mac-shame!

Mologan shook himself out of his reverie. Fin shuffled in his corner.

'Well, Fin Mac-visitor, sit yersel' doon.' Mologan patted the old tractor seat balanced precariously on a broken flower pot.

Fin sat down carefully, beginning to feel bemused. He had stopped shaking and was looking around the cave in amazement. The Boggart sorted out the shellfish from the other items he had bogled, pushed them all aside and wiped the table with the hem of his kilt. He skittishly darted off and returned with a cobwebby bottle of whisky and a dusty jar of dried caterpillars. He took the lid off carefully and placed the jar reverently on the table then scooped all the raw shellfish into a rusting First World War tin helmet.

'Wire in,' he said, pouring whisky into two small tin cans.

'It's very kind of you, but I've had my breakfast,' said Fin politely, eyeing the food suspiciously and the tin helmet enviously. He had recently started to collect First World War memorabilia.

'Aye, Mac-visitor, so have I... this is a wee bitty mac-supper.'

'But I've *just* had my breakfast.'

'Have ye? Ye're fur eatin' at strange times, Fin Mac-visitor. Ah always huv' ma supper when Ah feenish ma night's boglin.'

'Er, yes, I'm not exactly hungry. I had such a good um, mac-breakfast,' Fin continued.

'Whit did ye have? Sure, it couldnae be as guid a mac-purvey as this?' Mologan swept his hand proprietorially over his tasty spread.

'Oh, it was,' answered Fin. 'It was really good.' He rummled about in his pocket and pulled out a couple of round, brightly-coloured sweets and placed them carefully on the table.

Mologan's eyes widened.

'Squinky sookers,' said Fin.

Mologan touched one tentatively with an outstretched finger and rolled it carefully around the table. Its bright blue and orange marbled surface seemed to glow in the gloomy light.

'Squigglemint,' said Fin. 'My favourite. Try it.'

Mologan picked it up between thumb and forefinger and held it up to the light.

'A squinky mac-sooker?'

'Yes. You have to suck it. Don't crunch it or you'll break your fangs. It'll change colour.'

Opening his large, gaping mouth, Mologan stuck out his big blue tongue and placed the sweet on it carefully. As he sucked, a broad ecstatic grin grew on his face.

'Mac-scrumptious!' he mumbled through a dribbly mouthful of coloured stickiness.

Mologan the Boggart had never tasted anything so good. His normal diet consisted of slugs, raw shellfish, toadstools, grubs and leftover food bogled out of bins.

'This is even better than honey fungus,' he gurgled.

Feeling more relaxed, Fin decided to join him and popped the other squinky sooker into his mouth and the pair of them sat companionably in the gloom, silently sucking their sweets.

'It'll have changed colour now,' said Fin, taking his sweet out of his mouth. Mologan followed suit, peering at his sweet and taking it over to the shaft of light for closer inspection.

Holy mac-moly, it's purple and greenichy now!' gasped the delighted and amazed Boggart.

'Look, mine is fluorescent yellow,' said Fin, and they both popped the sweets back into their mouths, sucking hard to reveal the next colour.

'Bet I can get mine to change colour before yours,' said Fin, between bright yellow teeth.

'Bet you mac-can't,' said Mologan, sucking furiously and noisily through purple fangs.

'Do you live here?' Fin asked when his squinky sooker had become a manageable size and had changed to brown with white spots.

'Aye, Ah do that, young Mac-visitor,' said the Boggart, as a long green slaver dribbled down his chin.

'Ma name's Mologan.' He made a loud slurping noise.

'Sorry? Mo...what?'

'MO – LO – GAN,' the Boggart repeated, loudly, as if Fin was hard of hearing.

Fin nodded. 'And, um, *what* are you? I mean, I don't want to be rude but I've never met anything, er, anyone like you before.'

Mologan laughed with a snorty, wheezy laugh. 'There's no many o' us Boggarts aroon' so Ah dinnae suppose ye wull huv' met one afore.'

'So, you're a Boggart?'

'Aye, Ah huv the ancient boglin' rights to the whole mac-area.'

'Bogling?'

'That's whit Boggarts dae, did ye no ken? Whit sort o' mac-education huv ye had, Fin Mac-visitor?

'And, what, um, how do you bogle, Mologan?'

'Uch, ye just go oot at night an' weel, bogle things. Mind, it's no jist onybody could dae it. It takes years o' trainin', so it does. Mac-centuries o' experience.'

Fin looked puzzled.

'The art o' boglin',' Mologan continued, 'is to collect a bit o' clamjamphrie here and crack a few eggs or rattle a few windows there, or bogle a sock off a washin' line or tip oot a mac-dustbin or...'

'So you go out at night and do things to annoy people and steal things?' Fin interrupted, intrigued.

'Fin Mac-visitor! Wash yer mooth oot wi' squid ink!' exclaimed the Boggart. 'We Boggarts don't *steal* things!'

'I don't need to wash my mouth out with squid ink,'

said Fin, opening his mouth and sticking out his tongue which was now a deep, purply blue.

They both laughed. Mologan stuck out his tongue. It was bright orange. They laughed again, Mologan with a wheezy, snorty, infectious sort of laugh.

'I must be turning into a Boggart,' said Fin. 'My tongue's the right colour already!'

They laughed again.

Mologan sniffed deeply and rubbed his eyes. He took a sip of his whisky, burped loudly and sighed.

'Boglin' is an ancient an' noble profession,' he continued, 'providin' a mac-valuable service to the community.'

Fin was still puzzled. 'How?' he asked.

'Well, we collect all the clamjamphrie that's lyin' aboot.' He gestured towards the contents of the bogling bag scattered on the table, then to the contents of the cave.

'What's clamjamphrie?'

'Rubbish to you, Mac-visitor!'

Fin nodded.

'An' there's aw these important wee jobs we do,' Mologan continued, 'like fanklin' ropes, pokin' holes in things, loosenin' light-bulbs, makin' things slimy, lettin' doon airbeds – that's a special service fur the holiday mac-visitors – and um, pittin' spiders in beds and hidin' things, and that's jist fur a start.'

'But, WHY, Mologan?'

'Why?' said Mologan, throwing up his hands in an exasperated gesture. 'WHY? Who else wid dae it?'

There was no answer to this. Or if there was an answer Fin couldn't think of it. They sucked the very last tiny fragments of their sweets in silence.

'But what if you get caught when you're bogling?' asked Fin thoughtfully.

'Get caught?'

'You know, what if someone sees you?'

'They dinnae see me. Ah kinda look like the rocks an' things.' Mologan held up a mottled arm.

'Look.'

'Oh, like camouflage? I see.' Fin examined the Boggart's flaky arm, poking it with his finger.

'Aye, like cammy... like whit ye said.'

'Camouflage. You sort of blend in with the landscape. Like mine.' Fin pulled out the front of his camouflage jacket and gestured to his trousers.

'Cammy-mac-flag, aye, cammy-mac-flag, Fin Mac-visitor,' he smiled, 'an' years o' creepin' aboot macstremely quietly!'

Fin suddenly realised that he had been away from the tent for some time.

'Crumbs,' he said, 'I must go, Mologan, they'll be wondering where I am.'

'An' Ah've got ma boglin' books to write up afore Ah turn in.'

'Bogling books?'

'Aye, we keep a mac-record o' all the boglin' that we do.' Mologan pointed to a pile of huge, mouldering, old-fashioned leather-bound books stacked on a sagging shelf. 'Ah tell't ye we take oor work mac-seriously.

Every bogle that's ever bin carried oot at Craigmhor is listed in they boglin' books an' it's mac-valuable evidence fur the Boglin' Compie-mac-tishun.'

Fin was intrigued, and was about to ask Mologan to tell him more, but the Boggart cleared his throat hoarsely.

'It's bin a pleasure mac-talkin' to ye, Fin Mac-visitor,' he said, standing up. 'Ah'll show ye oot.'

They made their way along a wide passage and turned into a dark tunnel which spiralled steeply upwards.

The Boggart moved very fast and Fin had difficulty keeping up with him. He couldn't see very well in the dark and he kept tripping over steps and outcrops of rock.

'Noo, Mac-visitor,' said Mologan as they climbed, 'ye must remember that ma profession relies on absolute mac-secrecy, so Ah depend on yer mac-confidentiality.' They reached the top, slipped through a gap in the rock and they were standing in a clearing in the wood only a few metres from the caravan.

'Do mac-visit again soon,' said Mologan politely.

'Oh yes, when?' said Fin, anticipating the event.

Mologan thought for a moment, pondering how soon would be appropriate to ask a guest to return.

'In aboot a hunner' mac-years,' he said, and disappeared.

Fin was stunned by the Boggart's quick disappearance. He examined the rock where they had emerged from the tunnel but there was no sign of a hole or a door.

'FIN! FINBAR! WHERE ARE YOU?'

He heard his Mum calling.

'I'm here,' he called back, emerging from the wood.

Mum was hanging a towel on the makeshift washing line which she had stretched between two trees.

'Where have you been?' she said, smiling as she snapped a peg onto the rope.

'Oh, I woke early and went exploring,' he grinned, exposing bright blue teeth.

'You've been eating these squinky thingumyjigs again, haven't you? Look at your teeth! Go into the caravan and brush them immediately, and then have some proper breakfast.'

Fin turned to go.

'My goodness, look at you. Where have you been? Your back's all covered in mud and slime... and look at your hair! Get into some clean clothes before you sit down in the caravan.'

She began to fuss around Fin. He squirmed as she examined his matted hair.

'What a mess,' she continued. 'Your nice new holiday clothes, filthy already. I'll have to take them up to the croft and get Iona to put them in the wash.'

Mum sniffed.

'You smell a bit strange. Yuch... kind of, sniff, mouldy. Just as well we're going swimming today... at least you'll get a wash.'

Fin scowled. He didn't like washing. It was such a waste of time. But a swim would be fun.

CHAPTER 3

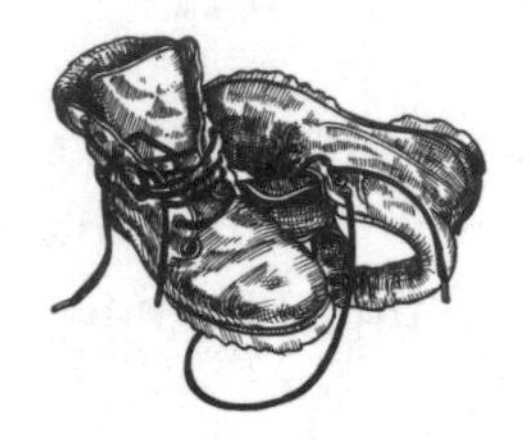

Things Get a Bit Greenichy

Fin was ravenous after his adventure and had soon changed into clean clothes and was tucking into some breakfast. Mum was bustling around finding swimming things and preparing a picnic to take down to the beach.

'Absolutely mac-scrumptious,' said Fin, his mouth full of the last bit of toast and chocolate spread. 'I was starving!'

'How long have you been up?'

'Oh, ages, Mum. I couldn't sleep any longer.' Fin made his way to the door hoping Mum wouldn't begin an interrogation about where he'd been. 'I think I'll go and see what Robbie's doing.'

'Ask him to give you a hand to take your bedding outside to air, then find the beach towels,' said Mum over the rustle of tin foil as she wrapped a huge pile of egg sandwiches.

'Pack lots of drinks, Mum,' said Beth, squeezing past Fin in the caravan doorway. 'It's going to be a very hot day.'

Eventually, after what seemed like endless preparation they finally set off down the main cliff path laden with all the paraphernalia necessary for a full day on the beach.

'Which beach shall we go to?' Mum asked.

'Dunno,' the children chorused.

'We could go to the sand dunes,' Robbie suggested. 'The tide is still out so we could walk there by the beach and the two big coves, and come back by the cliff path.'

'Yes, that would be great,' said Beth, shading her eyes from the sun with her hand and squinting towards Big Bay. 'We can watch the seals from there and swim out to the islands in the lagoon.'

'I saw an otter there last year,' Robbie began, but no-one was listening. They had hurried on, in anticipation of reaching the beach and cooling down in the sea.

The day was perfect. It was hot and sunny and they had the whole beach to themselves. Several seals were in the lagoon but they kept their distance when the children swam in the cold blue water.

The children built sandcastles, hunted for otters, skiddled in rockpools and lay on the sand dunes. They argued, sang, ate and drank. It was the most wonderful day. By three-thirty they were tired, had no food left and had begun to bicker about the silliest things.

'Stop saying that, Fin. It's stupid.' Beth snapped.

'Saying mac-what?'

'Saying "mac" before every word.'

'What do you mac-mean?'

'THAT! You said MAC-mean!'

'Mac-why?'

'Because it's irritating. Mum, tell him to stop. He thinks he's being funny.'

'He's just doing it to wind you up, Beth,' said Mum, taking off her reading specs and looking up from a fat romantic novel in which she had been engrossed for most of the afternoon. 'Where did you learn to say such silly things, Fin?'

'I dinnae mac-ken,' Fin replied mischievously. 'Come on let's pack up. I'm starving. What's for mac-supper?'

Mum tutted, and they began to shove their belongings into bags. 'Is that everything?' she said, 'no litter left?'

They all looked around to check.

'Alright then, last person at Big Bay is the mac-cook!' she laughed, and they headed home, running.

⌘

That evening the weather became overcast and the midges were out in full force, so any exciting outdoor activity was curtailed. The family were all happily exhausted, and after supper elected to amuse themselves indoors, playing games and reading.

Mum listened to her favourite radio soap at seven o'clock. This involved the farce of continually moving the radio around the caravan trying to get a reception, and lots of, 'Ssh, I can't hear for you talking,' and, 'Damn, it was OK there a moment ago... Watch out Robbie, I'll try putting it on that shelf above your head... Beth, if you could just move a little to the right that'll help the reception... perhaps if you stand there, Fin. No, to the left a bit, yes, stand on one leg and hold the radio in the air... that's better.'

The children were glad when it was over. The radio reception was always so bad at Craigmhor they didn't understand why Mum bothered to bring the radio at all.

'What'll we do now?' said Mum. 'Scrabble?'

'Scottish scrabble,' said Fin.

'What?' chorused the others.

'Well,' said Fin, making it up as he went along, 'you have to get as many words as you can beginning with m-a-c and you get extra points for these.'

'Why are you obsessed with this "mac" stuff, Fin?' Beth asked, clearing the table and unpacking the scrabble board and tiles.

'Well, it would make it different,' said Robbie. 'It sounds fun.'

'But you can't have proper names in scrabble,' Beth argued, 'MacDonald, MacGregor, MacKay are all *proper* names!'

'Ah,' said Fin, 'this game is different. You can have mac-trousers, mac-cornflakes and um, mac-sandwich...'

'And, guess what?' said Beth. 'You can mac-play it yourself!'

During the evening the weather became more muggy and by bedtime thunder rolled in the distance and occasional flashes of lightning lit up the horizon. In bed in their tent, Fin and Robbie lay listening to the rain, and counting the seconds between flashes of lightning and rolls of thunder.

'One - and - two - and - three - and... it's only three miles away. It's getting nearer.'

'Do you think it will be overhead soon?'

But if it was, the boys missed it as they were soon fast asleep.

It was still dark when Robbie woke with a jump. Perhaps a crash of thunder had wakened him, for soon afterwards a flash of blue lightning suddenly and briefly illuminated an enormous shadow on the tent, like a gigantic hunched figure with a huge head. Robbie sat up, afraid. There was nothing there. He must have been having a nightmare. He snuggled down again, pulling the sleeping bag right over his head. It was definitely a dream... but it was so vivid.

Fin slept soundly, dreaming of Boggarts and caves and swimming with seals and eating slugs and raw shellfish and squinky mac-sookers.

Next morning the storm had blown over and the sun was shining again although the sky was still cloudy in patches. Fin and Robbie slept late and Beth had to come and waken them around ten o' clock.

'Don't hang about. Breakfast is ready and Mum's in a bit of a mood,' said the disembodied head poking through the tent door.

Grumbling, the boys climbed out of their sleeping bags and dressed quickly.

'Yuch,' said Fin, emptying something squidgy out of his left boot. 'Robbie, did you put slugs in my boot?'

'Don't be daft. You wouldn't catch me touching slugs, never mind putting them in your boots. Why should I do that?'

As Fin rubbed the squelched-up slugs off his sock onto the grass he had to admit that his brother had a point. Robbie hated creepy-crawlies of all kinds and would do anything rather than touch one. Curious, though, that three or four slugs should slither into one boot overnight. Just as well it wasn't Robbie's boot! Fin grinned to himself, imagining how cross Robbie would have been if he had squashed slugs on his sock. He wiped the inside of his boot with a face flannel and put it on.

'Fin, hurry up.'

'I'm coming.' Leaving his laces undone Fin ran to the caravan.

Mum was rattling about in the caravan, banging down plates and being rather snappy.

'Here's your cereal,' she said, dumping the corn-flakes down on the table.

'Why are you in a bad mood, Mum?' asked Robbie.

'I'm not in a bad mood,' she snapped, thumping down a milk carton and spilling some of the contents in the process. After mopping up the milk she sat down to finish a cup of tea.

'Mum's lost her specs,' explained Beth.

'You were wearing them when I went to bed,' said Robbie.

'Yes, I remember. You were reading,' Fin added, through a mouthful of cornflakes.

'We've looked everywhere,' said Beth.

'I put them down beside my bed when I put the light out,' Mum added. 'They can't be far away, but we've hunted high and low.'

'Even emptied the bin,' said Beth, laughing.

'I'm sure you'll find them Mum,' said Fin giving her a hug. 'They must be somewhere in the caravan.'

Robbie cut some bread and put it under the grill to toast. 'I read an article once,' he said, bending down to check if the toast was ready, 'in one of these folklore and earth mysteries magazines that Auntie Morag gets. It was about things going missing.' He turned the toast. 'This woman who wrote it reckoned that there are these creatures called Boggarts who...'

Fin suddenly choked on his cereal.

'Are you alright, petal?' said Mum, patting his back.

'Y-yes Mum,' he managed to whisper.

'What about these Bogles, Robbie?' Beth asked.

'Boggarts,' he replied.

'Don't you swear at me!' Beth laughed.

'Very funny. Ha, ha. If you don't want to hear about Boggarts, I needn't tell you.'

'Go on then,' Beth sighed, 'I know you're dying to tell us.'

Robbie threw a cushion at Beth.

'Come on Robbie, we're all desperate to know now. What did it say about these Boggarts?'

'Well, they're sort of mythical creatures who creep around at night hiding things and stealing stuff and making mischief.'

'What sort of mischief?'

'Oh, upsetting animals and putting sand in shoes and cracking windows, scaring people and pinching things.'

'What do they look like, these Boggarts?' Fin asked, greatly amused.

'I think they're small, like dwarves with slimy skin, webbed feet and bad breath,' Robbie went on, creatively, 'and they're invisible to humans. They live in secret caves and only come out on the first night of the full moon.'

'And it said all that in this article you read?' Fin asked.

'Yes, well, kinda,' Robbie answered. 'It was along those lines anyway.'

'Nonsense,' said Mum, 'I've never heard such rubbish. I wish your Auntie Morag wouldn't fill your heads with such nonsense.'

'But it was in the magazine, Mum!' Robbie protested.

'It would explain your lost specs,' said Beth, 'and didn't you say the Calor gas was turned off this morning, and you could have sworn you left it on?'

'That's just the sort of thing a Boggart would do,' agreed Robbie, now fancying that he was a bit of a Boggart expert. 'I bet there's one round here. Was there a full moon last night?'

Fin was dying to say something, to tell them all about the real Boggart. But he bit his tongue. After all, Mologan had asked him to tell no one. It was so hard to keep the secret, but he'd better not tell.

'That's enough about Boggarts,' said Mum, getting up. She started clearing the table. 'There are no Boggarts around here, no such thing. I've just misplaced my specs, that's all.'

She squirted washing-up liquid into the sink with some force.

'This water's got green slimy bits in it,' she said, 'We'll have to get a water filter. Now, what'll we do today? Any ideas?'

They decided to go to the Secret Bay, a favourite swimming place which was about forty-five minutes' walk from Craigmhor, so preparations were soon in progress for picnicking and swimming.

'It's going to be hot later. I think you kids should change into your shorts,' Mum suggested, trying to cram a bottle of sun cream into an already jam-packed rucksack.

Fin found his shorts, discarded on the tent floor since their return home from the beach the previous day. He put them on then proceeded to transfer the contents of his trouser pockets into the pockets of his shorts. He couldn't go without any of his possessions:

the torch, the key-ring, the lucky chuckies, the elastic bands, the two beautiful arctic cowries which he had found on the beach yesterday.

'Very rare,' he said to himself, admiring the cowries. He shoved them into a pocket. The army hat badge, the plectrum, the squinky sookers... hold on! Where were the squinky sookers? Fin looked on the tent floor, inside his sleeping bag, under his pillow. Then he turned his trousers upside-down and shook them.

'Strange,' he thought. 'I didn't eat them, and they were there last night. I was saving them in case I saw the Boggart again.'

'Come on, Fin, we're leaving,' he heard Mum calling, so he gave up the search and headed for the Secret Bay with the others.

⌘

Mologan was sleeping cosily in his cave dreaming of burglars and pineapple rings and squinky macsookers. He woke with a start. What had disturbed him? It was still fairly light in the cave, too early to get up. He turned over and grunted. Suddenly he became aware that there was something green and glowing lying on the pillow beside his head. He tried to focus on it for a second then,

'Aargh!' he jumped out of bed in fright.

Mologan stared at the pillow. He looked under it, and then, tentatively, under the grubby potato sack. Nothing.

'Must have been a mac-dream,' he mumbled, and shuffled over to the spring for a drink of water. As he bent over the stone water trough he saw a strange unearthly green glowing creature. He jumped back, startled, then peeked again. Part of a green, blotchy face with fangs peered back at him from the trough. He picked up a broken walking stick and poked it into the water, pushing it to the bottom of the trough and moving it around, feeling for something in the water. Distorted green ripples were now visible on the surface.

Puzzled, Mologan pulled the stick out of the water. Throwing it aside, he glimpsed his hand and arm. Then he realised. They had changed colour. His skin was bright green!

Thinking quickly, he searched for a proper mirror, throwing piles of clamjamphrie in his wake. Plastic bottles, broken teapots, a punctured lilo, clumps of heather, feathers, a paraffin lamp...

'Where is it?'

Plant pots, bin lids, a garden hose, a tap and a rubber tyre piled up behind him.

'Ah, here it is, mutter, mumble.'

He pulled out a long, blotchy and cracked wardrobe mirror and dragged it over the piles of rubbish to be nearer the light.

He propped the mirror against a stalagmite and took a step back to see the complete reflection of the rest of his body, revealing a bright green and luminous Boggart from head to toe.

'Boils and mac-blisters!' he choked and recoiled in horror, stepping on a punctured squeaky rubber toy which emitted a loud raspberry noise. Alarmed, Mologan turned quickly, kicking a lump of driftwood which was supporting an ancient iron bed-head. The bed-head fell over with a deafening crash, dislodging a mountain of junk which had been jammed behind it, and an avalanche of clamjamphrie tumbled noisily on top of him.

He poked his head out from a hotch-potch of damp cereal boxes, discarded clothes and lampshades. Pushing aside bottles, crab shells and electrical cables he emerged dazed, muttering to himself grumpily. He squinted again at his luminous reflection in the mirror.

'Stoorie mac-spiders, Ah've turned greenichy!'

CHAPTER 4

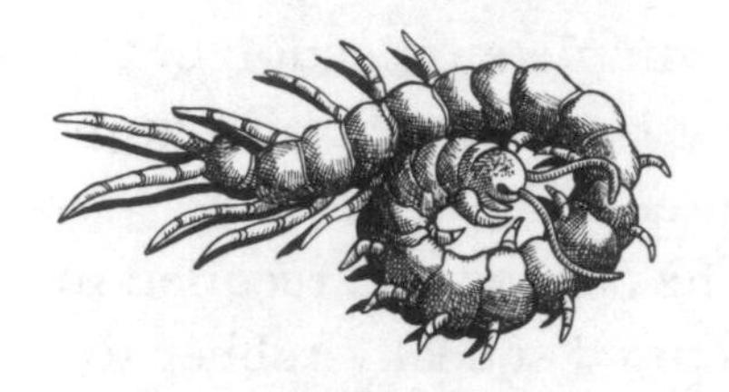

Common Boggart Ailments and Simple Remedies

Leaving a trail of luminous footprints behind him, Mologan crept quietly from the secret tunnel entrance towards the camp. The moon-light cast long, eerie, glowing shadows as he listened by the door of the tent. He heard the sound of deep, sleepy breathing and slipped silently inside, casting a green glow on the roof of the tent. He found Fin's bed and shook him lightly.

'Fin Mac-visitor, wake up.'

Fin groaned, sighed and turned over.

'Fin, Fin Mac-visitor,' Mologan whispered again.

Fin opened his eyes. 'What is it?'

'Shoosh, dinnae make a mac-noise,' the Boggart hissed. 'Wake up quietly, Mac-visitor.'

Fin blinked, dazzled by the green glow from the

large head peering down at him. 'Mologan, is that you?'

'Aye, of course it's me.'

'But, why...?'

'Shoosh. Get up, get up.'

'But...'

'Ah need yer help, Mac-visitor.'

Recognising the urgency in the Boggart's voice and mindful that he mustn't wake Robbie, Fin slid out of his sleeping bag. Grabbing the pile of clothes heaped beside his bed he followed Mologan out of the tent.

Horrified at the sight of the green, glowing Boggart, Fin stared open-mouthed for a few seconds before he was grabbed by a large, luminous hand and led into the wood. Out of sight of the camp they sat down on big rocks in a clearing. Fin pulled on his clothes and boots.

'I thought all Boggarts were camouflaged,' was all he could think of to say.

'Cammy-mac-flagged? Cammy-mac-flagged? Does this look like cammy-mac-flag tae you, Fin Mac-visitor?' Mologan whined, holding his shining arms out in front of him.

'But why...?' Fin began.

'Ah'm feenished, done fur. Ah cannae dae ony Boglin' noo. They'll *see* me. Ah'm vusible!'

'Not half,' Fin laughed.

'It's no mac-joke,' said the Boggart, sliding off his rock. He began to pace up and down, leaving an ever-increasing pattern of shiny green footprints on the mossy ground. 'How can Ah carry oot ma mac-noble an' mac-portant profession if fowk can see me?'

Fin noticed a very neat green luminous bum-print on the rock.

A green tear rolled down Mologan's face.

'Whit am a tae dae? Ah've bin a Boggart aw ma life. Ah've aw these folk dependin' on me. Ah've a repu-mac-tation tae keep up.'

'Hold on, Mologan,' Fin interrupted. 'Listen to me. *Why* have you turned green?'

'Ah dinnae ken.' The distraught Boggart twisted the hem of his kilt round a long finger.

Fin squinted at him. 'When did it happen?'

'Ah jist woke up and there it was. Mac-greenness.'

'So you were a normal colour, er, colours, when you went to sleep?'

'Aye.'

'Mmm, are you ill? If I'm sick or something Mum sometimes says I've gone a funny colour, or if you're seasick or mmm...' Fin scratched his head. Mologan continued to pace distractedly.

'I heard my Gran talking about her neighbour being green with envy when Grandad won the garden make-over competition.'

Mologan pricked up his ears at the mention of 'competition'.

'Are you envious of anyone, Mologan?' Fin continued.

'No, fur why wid Ah be mac-envious?'

'Not even a wee bit jealous of someone?'

'No, Fin Mac-visitor,' said Mologan, indignantly. 'Well, no really. Ah wis wance a wee bitty jealous when Fin MacBogle won the National Boglin' Competition in 1963.' He rubbed his chin, thoughtfully. 'An' when old Hector Bog-Snot found thon cases o' tinned pilchards on the beach in nineteen-seeventy-twa, an...'

'No, Mologan,' Fin was becoming exasperated, 'I mean, are you jealous just now? Did you get jealous between going to bed and getting up?'

'Och no, Ah wis mac-sleepin'.'

Fin had now begun to pace up and down. They were both silent in thought when they were startled by the crunch of a breaking twig, and they turned to see Robbie entering the clearing.

'Fin, there you are, I've been following these weird green footprints.' He stopped suddenly, his mouth still open. He tried to speak but no words came out.

Mologan snorted loudly in surprise.

Robbie took a quick, involuntary step backwards, sliding slightly on a patch of sheep poo. He gasped and regained his balance. 'Oh, whew, um, gulp!' Robbie now appeared to be rooted to the spot, mesmerised by the strange green glowing apparition. His face turned white and he began to tremble.

He swallowed hard, his mouth dry. 'Em, gulp, Fin is... is that an a-a-alien?'

Mologan shrugged his shoulders and looked at Fin.

'Fin, Are you OK? Um, don't worry, I'm here now.' Robbie's voice was weak and shaky. 'Back off slowly.' He stared at the Boggart with as fierce an expression as he could muster. He picked up a stick from the ground. 'I'll keep you covered, Fin, make a dash for it.'

The Boggart flinched and took a step back.

Fin grinned, then with a strange glazed expression on his face said in a low monotone, 'I-cannot-understand-you. Who-are-you? You-must-only-speak-to-my-master-Mo-lo-gan-of-the-planet-Slugg. He-has-taken-over-my-mind.'

'Fin, come over here, it's Robbie.'

'Mo-lo-gan-of-the-planet-Slugg-is-all-powerful.'

'Get back, you won't take over my mind,' said Robbie, bravely moving towards the bemused Boggart brandishing his stick. 'I'll...'

The Boggart backed up against a birch tree.

Fin couldn't hold back his amusement any longer and burst out laughing.

'It's no' mac-funny,' Mologan moaned miserably.

⌘

Realising that Fin had played a scary trick on him Robbie didn't think it was funny either. He scowled crossly at his brother. Taking Robbie's arm and guiding him a little way into the woods, out of earshot of the Boggart, Fin attempted to calm him. He explained that although it was now obvious to Robbie that this strange green-glowing creature was not a dangerous and mind-robbing alien the real explanation was equally weird.

'He's a Boggart, Robbie. An ordinary Scottish Boggart. His name's Mologan and he lives in a cave in the cliffs under our caravan,' Fin whispered. 'Honest. Would I kid you on?'

Robbie glared at Fin. Unsure whether to believe his explanation Robbie looked through the trees at Mologan sitting sadly on a mossy rock, engrossed in picking his large green-glowing nose. The Boggart now appeared quite small and harmless.

Robbie remembered their conversation the previous day when Mum had lost her specs, and recalled the article he had read about Boggarts in Auntie Morag's magazine. This creature could be a Boggart. If it wasn't, what else could it be?

'It's true,' said Fin. 'Cross my heart. He wants me to help him because he has mysteriously turned green.'

'Ach, that explains my mistaking him for an alien,' said Robbie ironically. 'I'd have known he was a Boggart if he hadn't been such an unusual and untypical colour.'

Mologan began pacing impatiently around the clearing.

Fin told Robbie how he had met Mologan and quickly explained about Boggarts and bogling.

'I told you that there was a Boggart at Craigmhor, Fin. Nobody believed me. But I was right,' Robbie whispered. 'I knew it all along.'

'I believed you,' Fin said.

'You didn't say you believed me,' Robbie grumbled.

'I couldn't. I'd promised Mologan I'd keep his secret.' Fin looked his brother in the eye. 'You won't tell anyone, will you, Robbie? Mologan relies on secrecy and anon, anonym...'

'Anonymity?'

'Yes. No one must know he exists or he won't be able to carry out what he calls his ancient and noble profession successfully. He needs to creep furtively about in the dark and bogle things and collect his clamjamphrie undisturbed. He has to work in total secrecy.'

The boys looked over at the luminous Boggart who had wandered over to a tree and was now engrossed in picking grubs from a piece of loose birch bark and popping them into his big mouth.

'He'll hardly be able to creep about unseen now he's all glowing and bright green,' Robbie observed.

'Mmm, that's the problem,' Fin said, scratching his head. 'But I don't know how Mologan expects me to help him. I'd better introduce you properly now. Since you're here you might be able to think of a way to solve his problem.'

⌘

Some time later Fin, Robbie and Mologan were sitting on the moss-covered rocks, heads in hands and deep in thought. Robbie had forgiven Fin for scaring him and could now appreciate the humour of his brother's joke. He felt smugly vindicated that he had been right about there being a resident Boggart at Craigmhor.

Mologan was still morose and slightly grumpy. As he sat in the clearing with Fin and Robbie, a strangely uncomfortable feeling began to creep over him. He shuddered, suddenly concerned that in his panic he had acted rather hastily. Contacting a human mac-visitor and asking for help seemed extremely fool-hardy. He had lived all his life at Craigmhor in perfect seclusion and secrecy and now, within the first couple of days of his hundred and forty-seventh bogling season he had become known to *two* unco fowk. Not just one mac-visitor. That was bad enough. But *two* mac-visitors? He felt butterflies in his tummy. Now his secret was out things might never be the same again. But what should he have done? He was bright green from head to toe. Who else could help a poor suffering solitary Boggart? He felt miserable. Even his small snack of grubs and maggots had not cheered him up. A green tear rolled down his knobbly green cheek.

'Don't cry, Mologan. Things can't be that bad,' said Fin, patting the Boggart's hump kindly.

Feeling sorry for himself the Boggart lamented again at some length about how his working life was finished and how there was no future in bogling now he was un-cammy-mac-flagged.

'Cheer up. We'd help if we could,' said Fin.

'Nuthin' wid cheer me up,' the Boggart grumbled.

'If I had any more squinky mac-sookers you could have them,' said Fin, kindly.

'Uch, they're aw feenished noo. They were gey mac-tasty,' said Mologan wistfully.

'What do you mean... finished? How, er... I thought I'd lost them,' said Fin, puzzled.

'Naw. Ah bogled them last night.'

'You *bogled* them?' Robbie was mystified.

'Aye, while you were mac-sleepin'.'

'And you ate them *all*?' Fin was shocked.

'Ah did that.' Mologan said proudly.

'How many?'

Mologan held up six fingers.

'SIX?' the boys chorused.

'They were supposed to last me all holidays,' Fin growled. 'You're a very greedy Boggart.'

'Never mind, Fin,' Robbie grinned, 'Mologan's done you a favour. They're not good for you. Full of additives, synthetic flavouring and chemicals.' Robbie imitated his Mum's voice, '*and they'll make you turn green*!'

'THEY'LL MAKE YOU TURN GREEN!' the boys chanted in unison, slapping their right hands together. Beaming, they turned to Mologan. 'It's the squinky mac-sookers!'

Mologan looked mystified.

'THE SQUINKY MAC-SOOKERS,' Fin shouted at him, 'THEY'VE TURNED YOU GREEN!'

'Mac-how?'

'It's all the additives and stuff,' Robbie began to explain. 'You see, these sweets are not made of natural ingredients, they're full of chemicals and additives.'

Mologan stared blankly at the boys.

'YOU KNOW, MAC-CHEMICALS,' said Robbie, shouting at Mologan as if he was hard of hearing.

'He doesn't understand,' Fin mumbled, tearing an oak leaf distractedly.

'But Ah'm still mac-luminous,' said Mologan, glowering at the boys. 'Whit are we goin' to do?'

'WE?' Robbie and Fin looked at each other quizzically, then turned to Mologan.

'Weel, it's your mac-fault.'

'*Our* fault?'

'It wis your squinky mac-sookers!'

'But I didn't ask you to bogle them... and eat them all in one go,' Fin said, indignantly.

'Calm down. Let's just think about it for a bit,' Robbie rubbed his nose thoughtfully. 'What we need is an anecdote.'

'You mean an antidote?' laughed Fin.

'Well, you know what I mean,' said Robbie, huffily.

'Don't be huffy.'

'I'm not, but you're such a know-it-all, Fin.'

'I am *not*.'

'You *are*.'

'I'm...'

'Wheesht. Wait a mac-minute,' Mologan interrupted, feeling left out.

'Sorry, Mologan,' Robbie said, turning to face the Boggart, 'we were just saying that you need an anec..., em, antidote.'

'An' whit's a mac-antidote when it's at hame?'

'A kind of, well, a sort of stuff that, well, if you were poisoned, for instance, it would stop you being poisoned and you'd be cured,' Robbie tried to explain.

'So Ah've been mac-poisoned? Ye're tellin' me that

Ah've been mac-poisoned. Mouldy mac-maggots, Ah'm really done fur noo. Ah'm goin' tae die. Ah'm goin' tae die.' Mologan covered his big green face with his hands and wailed loudly.

Robbie and Fin didn't know what to do. Fin patted Mologan's hump reassuringly.

'No one's saying that you're poisoned or going to die. We were just giving you an example of what an antidote might do.'

Mologan moaned pathetically and covered his face with his hands.

'It would also work if you'd eaten something which turned you green. An antidote would turn you back to normal,' Fin tried to reassure him.

'What *is* normal?' Robbie asked.

'Oh, sort of mottled, like the lichen on the rocks,' Fin explained.

'I see... mmm.'

'An' whit's wrang wi' that, young MacRobbie?' Mologan's indignation made him forget that he was upset.

'Nothing, nothing, just wondered.' Robbie glanced at Fin and shrugged.

'Well, how do we find this mac-antidote then?' Fin asked, sitting down again on a rock.

'Dunno, I've no idea.'

Mologan shuffled over to a rock, leaned against it and wiped his nose with the ragged hem of his kilt.

Fin scratched his head and Robbie screwed up his face in concentration.

'Mum has a sort of medical dictionary. There might be something in that,' Fin was thinking aloud.

'But it's at home,' said Robbie.

'Yes, em, but someone might have one.'

'At this time of night?'

Fin looked at his watch. 'Half past one.' He shivered. 'I'm cold.'

'And I'm tired,' said Robbie.

'Have you ever seen any medical dictionaries while you've been bogling, Mologan?'

'No,' Mologan replied glumly.

'Do you know what we mean?'

'No.'

'Well, it's a big, fat book with lists of all sorts of diseases and illnesses and it tells you how to cure them.'

'Aye, Ah've got wan o' them,' said Mologan quietly, absent-mindedly picking small white grubs from a piece of birch bark and stuffing them into his sporran.

'You've got one?'

'Aye.'

'Where, how?'

'Ben the cave. Ah've hud it fur years.'

'Well, there you are, Mologan, all you have to do is look it up when you get home,' said Fin, standing up and turning towards the camp.

But Robbie's curiosity was aroused.

'Where's your cave, Mologan? Is it far.'

'Ma cave? It's jist ablow here.' Mologan pointed downwards towards the ground. 'It's no far.'

'We'll come with you and look up the book, won't we, Fin?'

'Uch, Robbie, I'm tired.'

'Go on, it's the least we can do. After all it was your squinky mac-sookers that turned him green.'

'I didn't ask him to steal them,' Fin whined, rubbing his eyes and fidgeting from foot to foot.

'Aren't you keen to see the Boggart's cave?'

'Na, I've seen it.'

'Go on, Fin, it won't take long.'

'You're just nosy, Robbie. You just want to have a good look around Mologan's home.'

'Well, I'm kinda curious. I wouldn't mind a wee look.'

'Well, if it's not too long...'

'Great, lead on mac-Boggart!'

Smiling, Mologan the Boggart led them to a large mossy rock which was leaning against the lichen-covered cliff face. He beckoned them to follow as he slipped into the gap between the rock and the cliff and disappeared.

The boys followed, and found themselves in a damp, gloomy tunnel which led downhill. Occasionally, at particularly steep bits of the passage, there were rough stairs cut into the rock. As the path became steeper it became a long flight of rough-hewn steps. The roof was very low in parts, and sometimes the tunnel so narrow that they had to squeeze through.

The boys could see where they were going by following the glowing footprints and the radiance of the

Boggart himself as he moved silently down the dark passageway at great speed.

'Wait for us, Mologan,' Fin cried, slithering down some crumbling, slimy steps. 'You're going too fast!'

'Ouch!' exclaimed Robbie, bumping his head on a stalagtite.

The damp, musty air seemed to smell stronger as they descended. The passage twisted and turned and the boys lost all sense of direction. Suddenly they found themselves in a a larger tunnel and Fin recognised it as the one with all the storerooms leading off it. Mologan disappeared into a cave at the top of the tunnel. As they caught up with him he was lighting a candle. It seemed quite bright and inviting, in a homely, cluttered way.

Robbie and Fin stood in a small clear area of floor surrounded by all Mologan's clamjamphrie. Robbie was speechless. He gazed open-mouthed at the piles of junk and the fish-box bed and the green-glowing Boggart.

'I must be dreaming,' he thought.

A few CDs suspended between stalactites on a fishing line reflected the candle light. As they twisted in a slight breeze from an air vent, light sparkled and flickered all over the cave. There was a slightly unpleasant odour of mouldy leaves, old fish and smelly feet. Robbie clamped his hand over his nose and mouth but was too polite to mention the peculiar smell. Fin hardly noticed it at all.

'This is it,' said Mologan proprietorially, 'Whit dae youse mac-think?'

'Um... cool,' Robbie mumbled.

'These are all the things that Mologan has bogled,' said Fin, gesturing with an exaggerated arm movement.

Not *all*,' Mologan interrupted, 'Ah've a muckle collection of clamjamphrie. Wid yees like to see the rest o' it?'

'Perhaps another time, thanks,' said Fin.

Robbie was fascinated, but was almost wishing that he had not come. The cave was cold, smelly and untidy. And suppose this Boggart turned nasty and didn't let them go. Suppose they were trapped in here... forever. He made a slight move towards the entrance, bumped an old rusty oil can with a loud dull clink and a pile of mouldy ropes and an old-fashioned telephone slid noisily to the ground, making the standing space somewhat more cramped.

Mologan the Boggart jumped.

'Mind ma guid clamjamphrie, Mac-Robbie. It's the maist valuable collection this side o' Ben Mhor.'

'Show us the book,' said Fin, changing the subject.

'Aye, aye, Ah wull.' Mologan began moving piles of clutter from a far corner of the cave, throwing it over his shoulder onto another precarious heap. A picture frame, an old shoe, mouldy coconut shells, a chain, a chair leg, a gardening glove, old magazines and assorted hunks of driftwood piled up behind him, revealing an old shelf constructed solidly from worm-eaten and barnacled wood. It bent under the strain of several old-fashioned, heavily-bound books.

Mologan stood aside, gesturing with one hand towards the shelf and dusting cobwebs off his chest with the other. A few very large black spiders scuttled off the books into the shadows.

'The mac-library,' said Mologan, proudly.

Robbie forgot his apprehension.

'Wow, they're ancient,' he cried, wading through the clamjamphrie towards the books. 'Where did you get these, Mologan?'

'Ugh, Ah've had them fur years. Let me mac-think.' The Boggart scratched his head thoughtfully. 'Ah think Ah got them frae ma cousin Peely Wally when he got a job wi' Boggart Books. Ah think it was aboot nineteen hunner an' mac-fifteen or thereaboots. Boglin' times were hard. There wis some sort o' big stramash on and there wur'ni many humans aroon'. Them that were, were muckle canny wi' their possessions. Peely Wally took a wee part-time job sellin' speci-mac-ality books. Ah felt mac-sorry for him as nae-Boggart wis interested in books in them days. Ah ended up buying the whole set.'

Mologan picked out a dusty volume from the shelf and blew off the dust.

'Guid yanes tae, cough, not the bog-ordinary birch bark covers, ATISHOOOOO!!!' He wiped his nose on his flaky green arm. 'Real toadskin, wi' tooled gold letters. See? It's a braw, cough, choke, big book, is it no'?' He passed the book to Fin.

'*The Boggart's Companion*, volume five,' he read aloud, '*Best-loved Bogling Songs.*'

'And this one,' Mologan enthused, passing another damp, crumbling book into Robbie's hands.

'*Cooking the Boggart Way* by Ella Fang? A cookbook, wow, I must have a look at this.' Robbie, whose hobby was cooking, took the book enthusiastically from Mologan's hands. He cleared a space on the cave floor and carefully opened the cover. It creaked, and several bits of mouldy toadskin flaked off. He turned the first damp page, revealing a contents page. The book was not printed, but written in an old fashioned grey script. The page was surprisingly clean and bright, only browning slightly towards the edges.

'Crumbs, I've never seen recipes like these before. Look, Fin.'

Fin fetched the candle and leaned over Robbie's shoulder.

'Hotch-potch of old Clabby-Dhus, Slug Surprise, Sea Slug Cocktail, Seaweed Salad, Worm Soup. Yuch! And wait for it... Pickled Sea Anemones, Anemone Jujubes, Boiled Bladder Wrack, Black Beetle Bites, Toadstools on Toast. Have you ever made any of this stuff, Mologan?'

'Aye, Ah used tae be a guid mac-cook. Ah could dae maist o' these homely type recipes. There's a gid yin there fur Maggots Stir Fried wi' Bluebell Bulbs an' Sea Slaters. It's a wee bit compli-mac-cated but it aye went doon well when Ah wanted tae impress. Ah prefer puddin's maself. Ony-thin' sweet an' mac-sticky.'

'Why did the monster eat a sofa and two chairs?' Fin asked, suddenly remembering a joke Beth had told him.

Mologan shrugged quizzically.

'Because he had a suite tooth!'

'Shoosh, Fin,' Robbie whispered and nudged his brother. 'That's a bit near the bone.' He nodded towards the Boggart. Mologan was looking thoughtful and scratching his head. Suddenly he beamed widely, exposing his fangs.

'A suite tooth! A sweet tooth! Chairs an' sofas! Funny craiturs these monsters.' He chuckled loudly. 'A sweet tooth. Jist like me! Have you any more guid jokes, Fin Mac-visitor?'

'I can't think of any just now. My sister's good at jokes, though.'

Robbie was still concentrating on the Boggart cook book.

'Look at this,' he babbled excitedly. 'Bean-weed Broth, Sea Sorrel and Oyster Stew, Sea-noodles. This is very trendy stuff, Fin. Some of this is cool food.'

'You'd better check the actual recipes,' Fin cautioned. 'You'll probably find the sea-noodles are fried in slug fat and garnished with crispy wood-lice.'

Robbie closed the book carefully. 'Yes, you're right. But maybe I could look at the book another time, Mologan.'

Mologan the Boggart was not listening. He was absorbed in a small grubby volume, flicking through the pages delicately with his large green fingers.

'Ah forgot Ah had this,' he said, dreamily engrossed in the pages of *The Bumper Book of Bogling*. 'Just listen to this...'

'Hold on, we're supposed to be looking for the medical book,' Fin interrupted. 'We'll be here all night if we read them all.'

'Ah suppose you're right, Fin Mac-visitor. Give me a hand to wipe the stoor off this lot and we'll see what we've got.'

They rubbed the cobwebs and dust off the spines of the remaining books and Robbie held the candle closer to illuminate the faded titles.

'Mmm,' said Fin, '*The Modern Cave Dweller: One Hundred Ways with Clamjamphrie*.'

'Next!' said Robbie impatiently.

'*Bogling for Fun and Profit*. Em,' Fin peered at another faded cover, '*The Baby Boggart's First Book*?'

'Ah,' sighed Mologan, a daft smile on his big lumpy green face, 'that wis ma first mac-book. Wait till Ah have a wee keek.'

'No, later, Mologan,' said Robbie, pulling the Boggart back by his plaid. 'Keep your mind on the job. What's that one, Fin?' He pointed at a large fat tome with mouldy, moth-eaten edges.

Fin pulled it out. 'Gosh, give me a hand, someone. This weighs a ton.'

Fin and Robbie lifted out the heavy book and laid it carefully on the cave floor.

'It's, um, *Common Boggart Ailments and Simple Mac-remedies* by...' – Robbie rubbed a rather nasty sticky brown blotch off the cover – 'by Aggie Hagg-Boggart.'

'That's it. That's the mac-one!' Mologan sang out excitedly, jumping up and down on a very small clear spot amid the clutter. 'Ah ken't Ah had it somewhere.'

All three leaned over the book jostling to have a close look. As they opened the first page a huge black moth flew out, brushing Robbie's face.

'Arghhh.'

'Wow. It's old,' said Fin, ignoring Robbie's shock. '1872.'

'Seems like mac-yesterday Ah got that book. Ah remember...'

Mologan was about to go off on one of his long reminiscences. Fin nudged the Boggart.

'Look, here's the index. Let's see if we can find your problem.'

Robbie slid his finger down the extensive list of Boggart ailments.

'Boils and blisters, bad breath, creaky bones, cracked ribs, chilblains... Stop me when you think I've found what we're looking for. Where was I? Coughs, colds, colly-wobbles, excessive bogies, exposure to sun-light, fangs (care of), flaky skin. Is your skin flaky, Mologan?'

Mologan shrugged his hump. 'Aye, mac-usually.'

'How about fungus in feet, eyes, head or oxters, flatulence, hump disorders, hibernation (preparation for).'

'Let me see. You don't need to read it all out,' said Fin impatiently, pushing Robbie out of the way. He scanned the list. 'Mmm, snuffling, collecting ear-wax. Have you ever tried any of these remedies, Mologan?'

'Aye, when Ah was ill in nineteen hunner an' fifty three Ah mixed up Aggie's potion for mac-ingrown toenails. It worked a mac-treat, so it did.'

'Ingrown toenails! That's not being ill!' Fin retorted.

Mologan grunted loudly, stirring up more dust. 'Jist you try climbing all these secret passages an' creepin aroon crofts wi' sair feet, young Fin Mac-visitor. Then ye'd ken whit ill is!'

'Sorry, Mologan,' Fin said. 'But to get back to the point, I can't see anything here which describes your problem. Have you any other books?'

'No, that was the only one,' Mologan replied, disappointment choking his voice.

Robbie closed the book with a thud and as he did so a small card flew out, twisted in the air on the draught from the closing pages, and landed on the cave floor.

Fin picked up the fragile card and squinted at its faded text.

'What does it say?' Robbie asked.

'It's kind of hard to read. The writing is strange and squiggly.' He handed it to Mologan.

'Ah canny make it oot. Ah'll get ma specs.' said the Boggart, and rummaged around by his bed. He came back squinting through a small pair of rather smart gold specs which he held about twenty centimetres from his face. With one eye closed and an expression of concentration he focused on the card and read slowly:

> *The author has striven to cover all possible Boggart ailments in this volume. However, she offers personal consultations on request for unusual or complex complaints.*
> *—Aggie Hagg-Boggart, the Cavern, Eilean Nan Ron.*

'That's the answer,' Fin cried. 'You can go and see Aggie Hagg-Boggart!'

'Aye, she's a right clever auld Boggart wifie,' Mologan grinned.

They all cheered up. They had forgotten it was the middle of the night. Robbie absent-mindedly tidied up the the books and Fin and Mologan danced around the cave stepping carefully over assorted junk and debris.

'Hold on,' said Robbie suddenly. There's one big problem.'

Fin and Mologan stopped dancing and looked at Robbie.

'What's that?'

'Well, if the book was written in eighteen–seventy two then this Aggie Hagg-what's-her-name won't be alive now.'

'Uch aye,' said Mologan. 'She was only aboot two hunner an' fifty years old when she wrote it.'

The boys looked dumbfounded.

'She's still goin' mac-strong over on thon island o' hers.'

'But she must be...' – Fin counted on his fingers – 'two hundred and fifty plus a hundred and thirty one is, em, three hundred and, um, eighty-one, I think. She's three hundred and eighty-one years old!'

'Aye, she must be. She's middle-aged noo. Still practisin' all her cures an' potions. She's a sea Boggart, auld Aggie. Comes from an auld line o' famous Boggart healers an' witches. A bit o' a hermit, ken.'

'What's a sea Boggart?' Fin interrupted.

'Ach, do they no teach youse wee mac-humans onythin' at school?' Mologan shook his head. 'There are fower kinds o' Boggarts. Sea Boggarts, like auld Aggie who collects all her clamjamphrie from the sea, and there's mountain Boggarts an' moor Boggarts an' machair Boggarts like me.' He poked his plaid-covered chest with a large index finger.

'Who pick up clamjamphrie from the machair?' said Robbie.

'Aye, the machair and thereabouts,' Mologan continued.

'Will you go and see Aggie Hagg-Boggart, Mologan?'

Mologan scratched his chin and screwed up his big face. 'Ah widnae be surprised if she put that wee card in the book an' kent fine that nae-Boggart wid make all the mac-effort to visit her. Thon island's a guid distance away. There used to be a mac-secret passage over to Aggie's island when Ah wis a Boggart bairn but it's fallen in noo.' The Boggart rubbed his nose thoughtfully. 'We'll need a boat!'

⌘

Later, as the sun was coming up Fin and Robbie slipped silently into their tent. Their heads were buzzing with all the things that had happened to them that night.

Mologan had led them back to the camp by a tunnel which had come out near the caravan. The Boggart, and the entrance to the tunnel, had disappeared as soon as the boys stepped out into a cool and drizzly dawn. As they ran quietly towards their tent Robbie noticed that the rain had washed away all traces of the luminous green footprints.

Fin kicked off his boots and dived fully clothed into his sleeping bag. Robbie wearily undressed and put on his pyjamas, then folded his clothes neatly before getting into bed. Fin didn't notice the two luminous hand-prints on his sleeping bag.

'Fin,' said Robbie, sleepily, 'You know those specs of Mologan's?'

'Mmm.'

'They looked a bit like Mum's specs.'

But Fin was fast asleep.

CHAPTER 5

Dabberlocks

It was midday when the boys woke up. The sun wasn't shining and it was very quiet. Robbie peered out of the tent. It was grey and drizzly. Mum's instructions to the boys earlier that morning seemed like a dream to Robbie.

'You don't have to get up now, boys,' she had said, poking her head into the tent, 'It's still early. Beth and I are going to the mainland to get a bit of shopping. Beth needs guitar stings. Take care, and don't do anything daft. I've asked Calum to keep an eye on you. He and his Dad are white-washing the byre, so they won't be far away. There's plenty to eat in the caravan. We'll be back before three. Kiss, kiss.' And she zipped up the tent door.

Robbie looked at his watch. Twelve-fifteen. They

would be back quite soon. Last night's adventures flooded into his mind.

'Gosh, we have a lot to do,' he thought, remembering the plans they had made with the Boggart. 'Fin, wake up, it's late. We have things to do.'

Fin grunted.

'Come on, Fin,' Robbie urged, dressing quickly. 'I'll get us some breakfast. I'm starving. Aren't you? Fancy some flaky Boggart corns and hedgehog milk?'

'Great,' Fin mumbled, still half asleep.

The boys were ravenous. While eating one of Robbie's delicious and substantial breakfasts they made plans.

'We've got to get everything in place before Mum and Beth get back,' said Robbie, munching a mouthful of toast and chocolate spread.

'Yup, we'd better start soon. What's first?'

'The canoe.'

'That's the worst bit. It's so heavy.'

'Best take it down to the beach first then make a couple more trips with the other gear.'

Dad's canoe was a large, old and heavy Canadian two-man canoe which was kept underneath the caravan. It was rarely taken down to the beach until Dad arrived for his holiday, which was usually a week or so later than the rest of the family. Sometimes it wasn't used very often as Mum was very nervous about the family paddling out to sea. She insisted that it was only used on very calm days. The children had learned to paddle the canoe around the bay and had been on a few 'expeditions' to some of the small islands and remote bays with Dad.

The boys dragged out the canoe and emptied it of all the accumulated paraphernalia, paddles, Dad's red plastic box of fishing lines, hooks and floats, balers, a dead vole and a mouldy apple left over from a picnic last year. They began to carry the canoe along the path towards the croft.

'Look, here's Laddie,' said Fin, breathless with the exertion of carrying the canoe.

They put the canoe down as a shaggy collie ran to greet them.

'Good boy, good boy. Hey, get your nose out of my pocket. Where's Calum? Is Calum with you, Laddie?'

Just then a tall, lanky, smiling figure appeared.

'Thought I'd see what you two were doing. Up to any mischief, then?'

'No, not much,' said Fin, rubbing Laddie's neck.

'What's this?' Calum gestured towards the canoe. 'Going fishing?'

'No, we thought we'd take it down to the beach before Dad comes on Tuesday.'

Calum grinned. 'A bit heavy for you two, is it no'?'

'We thought we'd take it slowly. We've got all day.'

'Don't be daft. You should have asked me. I'll take it down on the trailer.'

'Would you?'

'Aye, nae bother. Put all your gear inside the canoe. I'll be back soon.' Calum strode off. Laddie stayed with the boys, sniffing around the canoe and then following them back to the caravan.

The boys had to think quickly. What would they need for tonight's expedition? They began to make a pile on the grass. Life-jackets, a baler, paddles, rope, a torch, the tarpaulin to cover the canoe, a bottle of drinking water and a couple of packets of crisps. Laddie was sniffing around excitedly. He seemed to be following an interesting scent and was heading for the woods.

'Look at him. He smells rabbits,' said Fin, stuffing Dad's fishing cagoule and an old knitted balaclava helmet into a plastic bag.

'Boggart, more like!' said Robbie, ironically. 'Laddie, come! Here's Calum and the tractor. Good dog.'

Soon the canoe and all the gear were loaded and the boys climbed onto the trailer. The journey down the track to the Bay was slow and very bumpy. Generations of use and years of wild and wet weather had transformed what once would have been a passable track into a muddy, rocky and uneven path like the dried-up bed of a highland burn. They jolted and bumped along. The boys gritted their teeth and held on tightly to the shaking sides of the trailer. Fin and Robbie loved travelling on the back of the Craigmhor trailer. It reminded them of past summers when Calum was younger and had time to play with them. Calum had taken the children to watch the sheep shearing and sheep dipping and they had helped to round up the sheep which grazed on the small islands and bring them back to the croft in Euan's boat. They had raced around the beach at low tide on the back of Calum's 4 x 4 and spent many happy hours on rainy days helping him to renovate an old tractor in the toolshed.

Calum had always been great fun. Now he was working on the mainland and only came home at weekends. Even at weekends they didn't see him often as he was usually busy helping Euan on the croft or out socialising. Robbie suspected that Calum had a girlfriend!

The tractor soon reached the bottom of the bumpy track. It jolted past the boathouse, bounced through the cut and began to pick up speed as it reached the machair. It was a relief not to rattle about so much.

'Usual place?' Calum shouted over the noise of the tractor engine.

'Fine,' Robbie called, as the tractor turned into Boat Bay, scattering a flock of sandpipers.

The tractor came to a halt on the beach. The boys jumped down, rubbing bruised bottoms.

'I'll leave you to get sorted out,' said Calum as he helped them unload the trailer. 'I'd better get back to help Dad.'

'Thanks, see you later,' Fin called as the tractor trundled off.

The boys put the canoe carefully into the natural cleft in the rocks above the tide line where it was stored each summer. They piled all the gear inside the canoe and covered it with the tarpaulin just as it began to rain.

They ran across the machair into the shelter of the woods and climbed the steep shortcut back to the camp.

⌘

The moon was full that night and the sky had cleared of cloud and drizzle. Moonlight illuminated the calm sea as Fin and Robbie pushed the canoe out into Boat Bay. It was a strange sight. Three figures in a canoe heading out into Craigmhor Bay. Two boys paddling carefully, wearing hooded cagoules and padded life-jackets, while between them, in the middle of the canoe, sat a hunched figure dressed in a cagoule which was too big, a life-jacket which was stretched tightly over a humped back and a lumpy balaclava helmet which emitted a strange glowing light from gaps in the stretched knitted wool.

Phosphorescence dripped off the paddles as they silently passed Heron Island. It was going to take some time to reach Eilean nan Ron, which was the furthest island in Craigmhor Bay. The boys did not hurry. Dad had taught them that slow but sure, rhythmic paddling would get them there just as quickly.

Mologan the Boggart had been surprisingly nervous about the canoe trip. The boys were astonished that he had never been in a boat before. Earlier that night they had met in Mologan's cave to prepare for the journey. The Boggart had to be covered up entirely to hide his highly visible and luminous body and to prevent him leaving a trail of shiny green footprints.

Rummaging around the cave they found a huge old wellington boot, a damp and holey fisherman's sock and an enormous battered old trainer which Mologan forced onto his lumpy feet with much complaint. Huffily, he put on the strange assortment of clothes and footwear and forced his hands into mis-matched gardening gloves.

Down on the beach Fin and Robbie squeezed Mologan into Dad's cagoule, the tight balaclava helmet and a life-jacket. Then they helped him climb clumsily into the canoe.

'Ah dinnae mac-like this,' he whispered, 'It's aw mac-wobbily.'

'Hold tight, Mologan,' said Fin, pushing the canoe into the bay. 'You'll be fine.'

'Ah dinnae mac-like this at aw,' Mologan said, standing up.

The canoe rocked dangerously.

'Mologan, sit down. You'll capsize us!' hissed Robbie. 'Sit still. You're OK.'

'Ah'm no. This is mac-...'

Robbie pulled Mologan down.

'Sit down, keep still and hold on tight or you'll have us all in the water.'

Mologan sat down. He gripped the sides of the canoe tightly as the boys paddled off. All three soon relaxed into the rhythm of the paddling and they moved smoothly and rapidly through the calm water towards Aggie Hagg-Boggart's island.

They were silent for a long time. The canoe slipped past Black Island into the lagoon.

'Alright, Mologan?' Fin asked.

'Aye,' the Boggart croaked, in a husky whisper.

'We'll soon be there. You'll have to guide us when we reach the island. Do you know where we should land?'

A seal suddenly appeared beside the canoe and somersaulted out of the water with a loud SPLASH!

'Aargh! What the mac-stoorie is that?' Mologan turned round quickly, unbalancing the canoe.

'Just a seal, Mologan. Relax.' Fin reassured him, balancing the rocking canoe with his paddle. 'Look, there's the island.' The dark shape of Eilean Nan Ron loomed up ahead.

A seal's head appeared again, then disappeared as the animal dived under the canoe and reappeared at the other side. It bobbed up again and snorted loudly.

'Gosh, he's coming in close.' Robbie grinned. 'He doesn't seem to be afraid of us.'

The seal made another dive under the canoe then somersaulted right out of the water three times.

'Wow, what a performance,' Fin exclaimed. 'Do it again, seal.'

The seal obliged with a back somersault and another dive under the canoe.

'Dinnae encourage him.' Mologan grunted, 'He's jist showin' aff.'

The seal swam alongside the canoe and barked softly at Mologan.

'Aye ye are so, Dabberlocks. Ye're the mac-biggest show-off in Craigmhor Bay. Away an' leave us alane. We're on a mac-portant mission.'

The seal snorted and blew a few bubbles.

'Dabberlocks?' Robbie said. 'Is that the seal's name, Mologan? Do you know him?'

'Aye.'

The boys had stopped paddling and the seal poked his head high out of the water next to the canoe. He barked softly and at length to Mologan.

'Uch, ye should huv said, Dabberlocks. That's mac-fine,' Mologan said, patting the creature's head.

'You can understand what the seal is saying?' Fin was incredulous.

'He's bin sent tae mac-guide us. He's Aggie's familiar. She mac-sent him.'

Dabberlocks grunted and barked again.

'He says tae throw him yon wee mac-rope at the front an' he'll tow us,' said Mologan.

The seal swam to the prow of the canoe and Robbie threw him the painter. Dabberlocks caught it deftly, snorted and swam off at speed.

Fin gasped as the canoe began to speed through the water. The boys laid the paddles along the length of the canoe and held on with the same tight, white-knuckled grip as the Boggart.

They crossed a choppy stretch of water and followed the rugged coastline of Aggie's island. Soon they came to a rocky bay and Dabberlocks turned into it so suddenly that Fin, Robbie and Mologan were very nearly tipped into the sea.

'Oi!' Mologan grunted, 'take it mac-easy. We're no in a race.'

Disturbed sleepy seals, wakened by the Boggart's loud booming voice, slid into the water from rocks on all sides. An oystercatcher flew up, its eerie cry echoing spookily from the cliffs which now towered above them. Dabberlocks had towed them into a deep, dark, water-filled cleft. It seemed as if the island had been broken in two and the sea had flooded the gap. It appeared darker now as the cliffs cast long moon shadows on to the water.

Dabberlocks continued more slowly along the edge of the cliff.

'Ah think we're nearly there,' Mologan whispered, as if in awe of this strange place. The canoe came to a stop and bumped gently against the silvery damp rockface. Dabberlocks snorted and the sound echoed scarily. He dropped the rope and barked at Mologan. The canoe drifted towards a large rock which stuck out from the cliff face. They were almost touching the rock when they realised that it stood slightly apart from the cliff and there was a gap behind it.

'He says we're on our own noo,' said Mologan. 'Paddle ahint the big rock, Mac-Robbie.'

They carefully manoeuvred the canoe through the tight space and into a narrow high-sided watery passage.

'Torch, Fin,' hissed Robbie.

Fin was already searching his pocket. He switched it on as they drifted quietly into the drippy, seaweed-covered tunnel. It was too narrow now to paddle, so they began to pull the canoe along by grasping the clumps of shiny brown seaweed which hung from the walls. Their breathing and Mologan's wheezing echoed strangely in the tall thin cave.

Suddenly they entered a large cavern. Fin shone the torch around the walls. They were wet and shiny and covered in a myriad of different coloured seaweeds: green, purple, grey, yellow and many shades of brown, like a great slimy patchwork. At the far end of the cavern there was a large horizontal slab of rock and a dark opening beyond which lay what looked like the entrance to another passage.

They pulled the canoe in beside the rock slab. The boys noticed a large seaweed-covered hump. On closer inspection it was in fact an ancient coracle made of willow and seaweed. Robbie tied the canoe to a rusty iron ring beside the coracle and gingerly climbed out of the canoe onto the slippery slab. The boys manoeuvred Mologan out of the canoe, Fin pushing the Boggart's stiff body from behind. Mologan wheezed and grunted as the boat rocked dangerously.

'Ups-a-daisy, Mologan,' Robbie laughed, as he heaved him onto dry land. Mologan was shaking all over.

'Wasn't that bad,' said Fin, undoing Mologan's life-jacket and helping him out of it. 'Come on, there's a passage. That must be the way. Careful you don't slip.'

The passage was dry. Their feet scrunched on a sandy, gravelly floor as their route led upwards and around a sharp bend. Mologan's green shining face cast an unearthly glow on the rock walls and the sound of his heavy steps seemed oddly uneven due to his mismatched footwear. After climbing about a hundred metres they were aware of a dim light at the end of the tunnel and a faint smell of boiled fish.

Mologan stopped and sniffed and pricked up his small frilly ears.

Clickity click, clickity squeak, squeak.

'Listen! Aye, she's there right enough,' Mologan whispered.

The strange clicking and squeaking sounds got louder as they approached the light.

Fin, Robbie and Mologan emerged from the tunnel into a huge cavern lit by candles and filled with steam from a cauldron which was bubbling and gurgling on a fire in the centre of the cave.

Beside the fire was an old Boggart woman rocking back and forward in a squeaky old rocking chair made out of a barrel. She was clad in a green and brown knitted dress, a bobbly knitted hat, a lacy knitted shawl, knitted slippers with purple pom-poms and fine fingerless gloves. She was deftly knitting a long green and gold scarf from a large ball of spun seaweed. She slowly put her knitting needles on her lap and looked up.

'Uch, here ye are. Ah wis mac-spectin' you,' she said in a crackly voice and smiled fanglessly.

Robbie and Fin suddenly felt sick. There was an overpowering stench of decomposing seaweed, sooty candles and rotting fish. Robbie was trying politely not to gag, and Fin zipped his jacket right up over his nose.

'Sit ye doon, sit ye doon,' said the old Boggart in a croaky voice. 'My, it's gid tae huv mac-visitors. Ye're maist mac-welcome.'

The boys looked around for something to sit on. Aggie Hagg-Boggart gestured with a long mittened hand towards three knobbly lumps on the other side of the fire. All three shuffled obediently towards the lumps which appeared to be rocks covered in bobbly knitted seaweed. They sat down. The rocks were surprisingly comfortable, if a little damp.

The boys looked around. They were in a high, vaulted cave. All round the walls were well-worn stone ledges, driftwood shelves and piles of old boxes. The shelves were stacked with jars, tins, bottles and rusty cans. Each one had a neatly written label tied on to it.

They could read some of the labels from where they were seated. Sea-lice, Squid Ink, Octopus Eyes, Dead Man's Fingers, Earwax, Bog Myrtle, Bladderwrack, Warty Venus, Furbellows. Bunches of herbs and flowers hung from the ceiling, dusty and mingling with cobwebs and unmentionable stoory things. Dried jellyfish and an assortment of fish in various states of decay were suspended from a long pole which was tied between two stalactites. A pile of stained and crumbling books was stacked neatly in a corner next to a heap of driftwood and several large bubbling wine jars.

In a gloomy niche in the rock there was a small comfortable bed covered in a colourful patchwork quilt of knitted seaweeds. Seaweed scatter cushions were carefully placed along the back of the bed (perhaps tidied and plumped-up to look neat for guests) and a row of knitted seaweed dolls like miniature Boggarts with ugly little faces lay propped up against the cushions.

Everything in the cave was knitted. Aggie Hagg-Boggart was an avid knitter. There was a knitted curtain which screened off the entrance to another passageway. An old teapot sported a nifty purple and green tufted cosy and the floor was strewn with assorted knobbly rugs.

A sudden SPLASH and a loud grunt distracted the boys from their silent gawking at the cave interior. Turning round, they noticed a small inky-dark pool behind them.

'Snort, splish.' A seal's head appeared in the pool. He made a soft barking noise and winked at Fin and Robbie with a large liquid eye.

Aggie Hagg-Boggart rose slowly from her old creaky rocking chair, steadying herself with a knobbly stick.

'Ach, Dabberlocks, here ye are, ma boy. Aye, they got here safely alright.' She shuffled towards the table and uncorked a large stone jar. Thrusting her hand into the jar she pulled out a rough grey biscuit. Dabberlocks barked loudly and splashed excitedly. Aggie Hagg-Boggart threw the biscuit to the seal and he caught it deftly, crunched it twice and swallowed it before disappearing under the water.

'He's a guid boy is wee Dabberlocks,' said Aggie Hagg-Boggart, resuming her seat by the fire and picking up the knitting which had fallen on the floor. 'He loves his fishy mac-bannocks.'

'Aye, he helped us tae find ye, Aggie Hagg-Boggart,' said Mologan. 'We widnae huv mac-managed withoot him.'

The old Boggart wifie smiled a toothless smile. 'Noo, where's ma mac-manners? Ah huvnae offered youse a drink. Bring over that tray, Mologan,' she instructed, pointing to a small metal disk that looked like an upturned wheel trim. Mologan fetched it and put it on the floor beside Aggie. The boys' stomachs turned in unison.

On the tray was a dusty green bottle with a label written in Aggie Hagg-Boggart's neat script. It read, 'Seaweed and Limpet Cordial'. Aggie deftly uncorked the bottle and poured small amounts into four assorted cups.

'There youse are noo,' she said, passing Fin a small glass eyebath of cordial. Robbie received his in a chipped tumbler which seemed to have moss or seaweed growing inside. Mologan picked up a handleless cup with the worn gold crest of the Western Steam Packet Company on the side. Aggie had a tin can with a peeling paper label on it. Fin could make out the faded picture of a cat and, in partly torn-off blue lettering, '...ITTY ...UNKS'.

'Slangey mac-var!' said Robbie raising his glass, digging Fin in the ribs with his left elbow.

'Oh, slangey mac-var!' Fin echoed, pretending to drink from the blue eyebath. Both boys were glad that they hadn't got the '...ITTY ...UNKS' tin.

Aggie and Mologan solemnly raised their glasses.

'Noo, said Aggie, glancing pointedly at Mologan, and downing her drink in one gulp, 'Ah huvnae been properly intro-mac-duced.'

'These are ma twa friends, Aggie, Fin Mac-visitor and Mac-Robbie.'

The old Boggart wifie smiled. 'Drink up Fin Mac-visitor and Mac-Robbie. This is a grand mac-cashun. Youse are the first mac-humans ever tae visit the auld Hagg-Boggart cave.'

'Th... thanks, Mrs... um... Hagg-Boggart,' Fin mumbled, lifting the eyebath again to his lips. He inadvertently tasted a drop of the cordial. It actually tasted quite nice. He smiled.

'Don't be so formal, wee Mac-visitor,' Aggie Hagg-Boggart replied kindly. 'Call me Aggie.'

'We used to call her Haggie Aggie when we were Boggart wains,' said Mologan, laughing.

'Mologan! Ah'll hae none o' that. Behave yersel',' Aggie reprimanded. 'Don't pay ony attention tae him, mac-humans. He wis always the cheeky wan, wis Mologan.' She looked at Mologan fondly and reached over to pat his large green hand. 'But a very kind and considerate sowel, aw the same.'

Robbie and Fin were now feeling more comfortable. They had become used to the smell and had unzipped their jackets down from their faces. They sipped some of the seaweed and limpet cordial and relaxed a little. Aggie Hagg-Boggart was a very nice Boggart. She had made them feel very welcome.

Aggie handed round a small bowl which looked like half of an old fishing buoy.

'Crispy sea slug, anyone?'

The boys declined politely. Mologan took a large handful.

'Mmm, ma mac-favourite, Aggie.' He shoved them all into his big mouth and chomped noisily.

'Noo,' said Aggie, in her raspy, gravelly voice, 'let's get doon tae mac-business. Ye're no here fur a social call, are youse? Is it somethin' to dae wi' yer health, Mologan? Ah can see yer a wee bit off-colour.'

CHAPTER 6

Aggie Hagg-Boggart's List

'Take aff that daft bunnet an' let me have a look at ye, Mologan,' said Aggie Hagg-Boggart.

Mologan pulled off the tight balaclava with difficulty, still chewing crispy sea slugs.

'Aye ma boy, whit have ye done to get intae this state?' said Aggie, staring intently at Mologan's green face, now indented with the pattern of the knitted balaclava. 'Is it like this all over?' She poked him with her knobbly stick.

'Aye,' Mologan mumbled, biting his nails in embarrassment.

'Ah'll take yer word for it. Ah'm sure ye're no wantin' a mac-zamination.'

'No, Ah umnae.' Mologan squirmed in his chair and his big cagoule rustled and creaked.

Aggie sat back in her chair rubbing her hands together. 'An' how do you think this happened to you?'

Mologan explained, with help from Fin and Robbie, all about how he had bogled the squinky sookers from the tent and eaten them all. And how he had turned green as a result, possibly due to an allergic reaction to the artificial additives and colours in the sweets. As she listened Aggie poked the fire absentmindedly. She said nothing for some time. The cave was silent apart from the 'plop, plop, plop' from the jars of fermenting seaweed wine. The boys began to feel warm and, now more used to the smell, they unzipped their jackets completely.

'Well,' said Aggie, eventually, 'Ah've never seen the like o' this afore. Ah'll have tae consult the chuckieboord.'

Aggie got up slowly from her chair, supporting herself on her stick, and hobbled over to a shelf near her bed. She picked up a piece of well-worn driftwood, almost rectangular in shape with uneven but smooth edges. There were five small holes on the board. As Aggie brought it into the firelight and laid it on a small box between herself and Mologan, the boys could see that it was also decorated with grid lines and swirls and strange symbols. Aggie untied a small knitted drawstring bag from her belt and carefully emptied seven smooth shiny green pebbles into Mologan's hand.

'Rummle the chuckie-stanes aboot between twa cupped hands,' she instructed. 'Shut yer een an' macconcentrate.'

Mologan closed his eyes. His big green face wrinkled in concentration. He shook his cupped hands up and down.

'Guid,' said Aggie, 'Noo, very mac-carefully, mind, drap the chuckie-stanes onto the boord.'

As Mologan did this Aggie hummed a strange, eerie tune and rocked to and fro in her barrel chair.

The pebbles rattled onto the wooden board and Aggie, still humming, leaned over it, peering intently. Then, moving her hand slowly above the board she began to sing softly a strange haunting song.

A cold shiver ran up Fin's spine. Robbie felt slightly uneasy.

Aggie's song sounded like a spooky mixture of Gaelic and the sound of the waves on a pebble beach. It was mesmerising. A cloud of blue steam rose from the cauldron, filling the cave with a warm fish-smelling mist. For a couple of minutes the boys could see nothing in the blue fog. Aggie's queer, repetitive song echoed softly in the cavern as if coming from no one place. Robbie pinched himself and touched Fin to check that this wasn't a dream. Yet, here he was in this strange underground cave on a tiny island in the middle of the night with two Boggarts, one of them singing in a strange language and creating blue steam from a fishy old cauldron. It must be a dream.

Suddenly Aggie stopped singing and the steam disappeared. Fin sighed loudly, relieved. Mologan opened his eyes and blinked a few times. Aggie carefully turned the board around towards her and stared at it intently, her nose almost touching the wood. Two of the pebbles had fallen through the holes in the board leaving five, which she studied carefully.

'Aye, aye,' she mumbled to herself. She stared into Mologan's eyes and croaked, 'There's muckle strange on thon chuckie-boord, young Mologan. Ye've three chuckies on the cusp line and a flype cross. Yer life's all tapsulteerie.'

Mologan nodded sagely as if he understood completely.

'Ye're going to travel above water an' ablow water.'

Fin and Robbie winked at each other.

'There's a mac-creature here, aw covered in fernitickles. Aye this mac-creature will help ye, Mologan. Look oot for the fernitickles, aye, mmm.' Aggie scratched her chin and tapped the board lightly with a long bony finger. 'It says here ye're going to be a great mac-chieftain.' She cackled to herself and looked Mologan up and down. 'Are ye sure ye mac-concentrated mac-properly when ye threw the chuckie-stanes?'

'Aye, Aggie, Ah did ma best,' Mologan bristled indignantly, then puffed out his chest. 'A mac-chieftain? Me?' He smiled.

'Weel, weel, ye neever can tell whit the mac-future holds.' Aggie continued. 'Noo, let's look at yer health.' She tutted and screwed up her eyes. 'Yer health chuckies are on the flype cross. That's aye mac-complicated. Ye need a mac-mixture, that's fur sure. The grossart stane has gone doon a hole, so ye'll need somethin' for that an' aw.'

Mologan clasped a hand to his left side. 'Ma grossart?'

'Aye, it's been affected by thon squinky mac-thingummygigs an' it's no workin' mac-properly. That's why ye've turned green.'

Aggie raised herself stiffly from the chair and hobbled over to the pile of books. Choosing a very large tome she bent to pick it up.

'That looks very heavy,' said Fin, moving towards the old Boggart, 'Let me help.'

'Thank you, wee mac-visitor. Jist put it oan the boorden,' Aggie said gratefully, pointing at the table.

Fin stood beside her as she carefully opened the huge book. It was very old and appeared to have been well-used. The pages were made of a thick, brittle substance like pale translucent seaweed, and they were stained with coloured blotches and sticky smears.

Aggie's long index finger ran down a list of indecipherable words.

'Ah, here we are,' she mumbled to herself. 'Grossart, page six-hunner an' three.'

Fin turned the pages for her. 'Five-hundred and ninety-nine, six-hundred and one, six-hundred and three. There it is, Aggie,' he said, turning to a page full of squiggles, strange anatomical diagrams and a picture of a Boggart pointing to his left side.

'That's a grossart,' said Aggie, pointing to a scratchy drawing of a hairy yellow organ resembling a cross between a sea urchin and a gooseberry.

'What exactly is it?' asked Robbie, who had come over to look.

'Ah dinnae suppose mac-humans have a grossart,' Aggie said, pointing to a diagram of Boggart anatomy on the opposite page. 'It's here.'

'Sort of like our appendix?' Fin asked knowledgeably. Fin's friend, David Dobbs had had appendicitis last year.

'Aye, jist like it, Fin Mac-visitor. Its function is tae keep Boggart skin so wonderfully flaky and to keep its distinctive colours. Youse can see fur yer mac-sels what can happen if it's no workin' mac-properly.' Aggie nodded towards Mologan who was absentmindedly poking the fire.

'Noo, haud yer wheesht while Ah work this oot.' She scrutinised the page and mumbled to herself. 'Flype, flype? Yes, mmm. Tut tut, mmm. Oh, aye, mmm.'

She pulled out another old book. This one was very small and battered and held together with frayed seaweed laces. Aggie undid the laces and carefully opened the book. Turning to a blank page she began scribbling furiously with a bony quill pen. Fin and Robbie looked over her shoulder.

'Ye're crowdin' me oot, wee mac-humans,' she said, distractedly. 'Awa' an' sit doon jist noo. Ah need tae mac-concentrate. Help yersels tae mair crispy sea slugs. Ah jist need a wee bitty mac-peace tae work this oot.'

The boys sat down on the seaweed-covered rocks again. Mologan smiled at them and silently offered them more sea slugs. They shook their heads in unison. No one said anything. The cauldron bubbled gently and the wine jars plopped rhythmically. Aggie scribbled in her notebook with her old sea-quill, occasionally sighing and muttering quietly to herself.

Fin and Robbie peered at the shelves of jars on the cave walls. They could make out more of the labels. Pickled Lugworm, Dried Sea Mice, Horn Wrack, Bubble Shells, Squilla Mantis, Preserved Piddocks, Salted Sea Hares.

Aggie had completed a very complex diagram in her notebook and was flicking through the pages of the gigantic book.

'That's it,' she cried triumphantly. 'Ah've got it!'

A few minutes more of frantic scribbling, then Aggie shuffled back to her seat by the fire brandishing a piece of paper roughly torn from her notebook.

'Jist a simple mac-mixture,' she said, 'and you'll be as right as rain, Mologan. If ye can jist get me these mac-gredients afore the half moon Ah can brew up the mac-mixture in nae time.'

Aggie handed the list to Mologan.

'Make sure that aw the mac-gredients are properly bogled, mind. It willnae mac-work if they're no bogled.'

Mologan was staring open-mouthed at the list of ingredients.

'Ah've marked the mac-gredients that Ah've already got but there are wan or twa that Ah'm clean oot o',' Aggie began, 'Ah've already got the...' She was interrupted by a sudden SPLASH and Dabberlocks appeared in the pool.

'Uch, wee Dabberlocks, is it time already? Whit a shame.' Aggie turned to the boys. 'It's time fur youse tae go, afore the tide changes. It can be mac-dangerous oot there in the lagoon. Dabberlocks will guide youse back. Ah, time flies, does it no, when ye're havin' a guid time?'

As Robbie and Fin got up to leave and were helping Mologan to squeeze into the tight balaclava, Aggie took a stone jar from a high shelf. She proffered it to the boys.

'Choose one each,' she said, shaking the jar.

They peeped into the jar. It contained small round polished stones of many colours.

Not unlike the squinky sookers, thought Fin.

'Fib-stanes,' said Aggie. 'Very useful charms.'

'Fibstanes?' Robbie asked, choosing a pink stone mottled with pale green.

'Aye,' said Aggie, shaking the jar again and offering it to Fin. 'Jist pop yin in yer mooth an' people will believe whatever you say withoot question if ye tell a lie, an' disbelieve ye when ye tell the truth. Ah've a feelin' that ye'll need a fibstane afore ramorra's oot.'

'Thanks Aggie,' said Fin, choosing a pale blue fibstane with swirly purple lines on it. 'We've had a lovely time. Thanks for entertaining us in your beautiful cave and making us feel so welcome. If only we could repay the hospitality.'

Robbie glared at Fin, thinking he was being a bit too creepy, but Aggie Hagg-Boggart beamed with pride and happiness. Fin had a charming personality which always went down well with old ladies, and obviously with old Boggart wifies!

'It wis a great pleasure tae huv youse here,' Aggie smiled fanglessly. 'Do come back wi' Mologan when he brings the mac-gredients for his mac-mixture.'

Mologan coughed discreetly from the entrance to the passageway. 'Dabberlocks will be mac-waitin',' he said, adjusting the balaclava.

'Come back in eight nights at the neep tide an' Ah'll have the base mac-mixture furmented, aw mac-ready,' Aggie called after them as they made their way down the passage to the cave where they had left the canoe.

⌘

Dawn was coming up as Beth watched the canoe gliding effortlessly and surprisingly quickly into Boat Bay. Three silhouetted, hooded figures disembarked onto the beach. There was a barking sound and a great splash in the bay.

'I wonder what they've been up to,' she thought, as she climbed back into bed. 'And who's their chum?'

⌘

Robbie and Fin wearily dragged the canoe up the beach and secured it in the cleft in the rocks.

'I'm glad Dabberlocks towed us back,' Fin whispered. 'I'm exhausted. It's been a long night.'

'And a strange one,' said Robbie.

'Ah'm gey glad tae be oot o' yon boat,' Mologan sighed.

In the bay Dabberlocks barked and jumped high out of the water, returning with a great SPLASH. Then he swam off underwater like a torpedo.

Back in Mologan's cave Fin shared out the potato crisps he had brought as emergency rations.

'Plain crisps, Mologan, no additives,' Robbie munched.

Mologan nodded and smiled, revealing a mouthful of half-chewed crisps. He peeled off the tight balaclava and sighed with relief. Robbie helped the Boggart to pull off his mis-matched shoes. 'Phew!' a shower of half-chewed crisps sprayed over Robbie's head.

'Mologan!' Robbie said, disgustedly, flicking off the damp crisps. 'Yuch!'

Mologan didn't notice. He was rummaging in his sporran. He retrieved several white grubs, a couple of earwigs and a handful of whelks and placed them on the table.

'Ah, here it is,' he grunted, pulling out a damp fragment of seaweed parchment. 'The mac-list.' He held it up and squinted at it.

'Well, all you've got to do now is bogle the ingredients for the mixture. Then we can take you back to Aggie's and she can mix it up, and you'll be fine,' said Fin, zipping up his jacket, ready to go back to his tent.

Mologan frowned.

'Look at this,' he said, handing the list to Fin.

Fin peered at the spidery writing trying to decipher it. Hesitantly he read, 'Ten puggie nits, nine sting winkles, herr o' a birsie dug, hen pen. There's a cross beside that one. Do you think she's got some of that?'

Mologan and Robbie shrugged.

'Em, three greenichy kail wurums, five yella' fingers,' Fin continued, trying his best to read Aggie's queer instructions. 'Twenty-five sea lice - another cross at that one - four roosty caddles?'

'Rusty nails,' Mologan translated.

'There's more,' said Fin. 'A wee shoo rid biddie, one goose yowk, seven grossets and a gizzard or a wee shoo orange goo. That's it.'

'Looks simple enough,' said Robbie taking the list from Fin. 'Did you understand what all these things are, Mologan?'

'Of course,' Mologan snorted indignantly.

'Well, let us know when you've got it all and we'll help you deliver it,' said Robbie, handing the list to Mologan. The Boggart wasn't paying attention and the list fluttered to the floor.

'Look,' said Fin. There's something written on the back of the list.'

Mologan picked up the seaweed parchment. He groaned loudly. 'It just gets mac-worse,' he said, sitting down with a thump on the end of his bed. 'There's mair!'

'Read it then,' Fin encouraged.

Mologan screwed up his eyes and read slowly, 'Fee fur consultation and mac-muxture: return of bogled green lobstur. Answers to the name o' Horace. Payable on receipt o' remedy. AHB.'

'A lobster?' Fin asked. 'A lobster called Horace?'

'Aye,' Mologan sighed, 'it's her pet. She was right fond o' Horace. Aggie wis goin' tae enter him fur the livestock compie-mac-tishun at the next Boglin' Show.'

'And what happened to him?' Fin asked.

'Ach, he wis a real braw beastie. A right prize-winner o' a lobstur. Bright green an' spreckled wi bright blue spots.' Mologan sighed a wheezy sigh. 'Horace wis bogled frae right under Aggie's neb by that nasty yun frae Eilean Bodach. Uch, it was a right shame.'

'Who bogled the lobster, Mologan?' Robbie asked.

'Yon Roary Borealis. The Boggart frae Eilean Bodach. Ah tell't ye.'

'Why?' Fin asked.

'Weel,' said Mologan in a throaty whisper. The boys had to come closer to him to hear properly. 'Roary Borealis is the meanest maist mac-nasty Boggart this side o' Ben Mhor. He's evil and bad temper't an' has a roar like thunder. Ah've heard,' Mologan lowered his voice even more, 'that if he's in a rage his roar can knock a Boggart aff his feet at twinty paces.'

'And this nasty Roary Boggart stole, um, bogled Aggie's lobster.'

'Aye, Mac-Robbie, oot o' her own sea cave.'

'But why?'

'Roary Borealis aye wins the green lobstur section o' the livestock compie-mac-tishun at the Boglin' Show. He couldnae thole Aggie havin' a better lobstur than ony o' his.'

'Valuable then, these green lobsters?' said Robbie.

'Aye, Mac-Robbie, that's why Aggie wants him back – worth a mac-fortune. She's probably got her eye on the Golden Creel Trophy!'

'Well, good luck then, Mologan. You're going to be busy with all that stuff to find,' Fin said. 'We'd better be off now. I'm really tired.'

Mologan put his green head in his green hands and snorted. He wheezed a great sigh.

'What's up, Mologan?' Robbie said. 'We've got to go. We'll be missed if it gets any later.'

'But it's aw got to be bogled,' said Mologan in a soft, pathetic voice. He gulped, then snorted. 'Bogled! Aw thon mac-gredients *an'* the green lobstur hav' tae be *bogled!*'

'So, what's the problem?' Robbie asked.

'*This*!' Mologan said, dramatically pointing to his green luminous face, then his arms, then his legs and big feet.

'Well, you could wear the cammy-mac-flag again,' Fin suggested. 'It worked OK tonight.'

'Could Ah noo?' Mologan was indignant. 'How do ye s'pose Ah could creep aroon the croft mac-quietly in thon rustly mac-jacket and they nimpit shoes?'

'You could practice, or... um... you could find better clothes,' Robbie began, feeling too tired for this kind of discussion.

'... An' that daft bunnet,' Mologan continued huffily, 'it wilnae mac-work. Ah canny mac-compromise ma mac-professionality. Ye ken that!'

The Boggart drew himself up to his full height and strode over to the spring. He examined the watery reflection of his face in the water trough. Squinting with one eye then the other he whined, 'It's just the mac-same. Ah'm still un-mac-cammy-flagged.' He turned to Fin and Robbie, 'Ah canny work like this.'

'But you've got to bogle the ingredients if you want to get better,' Robbie reasoned.

Fin yawned and rubbed his eyes. 'C'mon Robbie. I'm tired. We can sort this out tomorrow.'

'Wait,' Mologan pleaded. 'Ye've got to help me.'

'But, Mologan, what could we do?' Robbie asked.

'You could bogle the stuff for me.'

CHAPTER 7

The Fib-stanes

'Us?' Robbie spluttered. 'Us? Me and Fin bogle the ingredients for you?'

'Aye, it's mac-obvious.' Mologan stared at them, hands on hips.

'But we couldn't. We... ' Robbie began.

'Of course ye mac-could.' Mologan folded his arms.

'But we don't have the, um, expertise, Mologan,' said Fin. 'You said yourself it was a skilled job and takes years of practice.'

'Aye, that's true, Fin Mac-visitor.' Mologan scratched his chin. 'But Ah could train youse.'

'No, Mologan, we couldn't do it. It's impossible. We don't really have the time,' said Robbie gently.

'Aye youse could. Ah'm dependin' oan ye both.'

'We'll have to think about it,' Fin said.

'There's nae time. Ah could mac-starve in the meanwhiles,' Mologan snapped.

The boys looked at each other. Fin shrugged.

'Look Mologan, we're too tired to decide just now,' he said.

'Ach, go on. Think of it as um, learnin' a new skill. A career mac-move, so to speak.'

'Mmm, I'm not sure.'

'It's mac-citin'.'

'No, I don't think... '

'Youse'll be helpin' a friend. Youse'll be savin' ma mac-life. Ah might die o' starvation otherwise.'

Fin and Robbie looked at the Boggart. A green tear rolled down his cheek and he sniffed loudly. They looked at each other, shrugging.

'You're a real drama queen, Mologan,' Robbie said.

'A clever and devious manipulating old Boggart, more like,' said Fin.

'What d'ye mean, OLD?' Mologan growled.

The boys laughed.

'OK, we'll help you a bit,' said Robbie. 'But only a bit, when it's really necessary.'

'OK-mac-dokay,' said Mologan, cheering up. 'Boglin' the mac-gredients AN' getting' the green lobstur?'

'Oh, alright,' said Robbie, now too tired to argue.

'Tomorrow?'

'No, we've got something on tomorrow night,' said Fin, remembering that they had been invited to a ceilidh at the croft. The night after?'

'But whit'll Ah eat in the meanwhiles?'

'Don't worry,' said Robbie, 'we'll leave you something at the tunnel entrance. We really must go. It must be light by now.'

Fin yawned. 'Night, Mologan.'

'Nighty mac-night, fellow Boggarts,' Mologan grinned, as he left the boys at the tunnel entrance.

The boys headed sleepily for the tent.

'Wait a minute, Fin. Look.' Robbie whispered, pulling something from his pocket.

'Mum's specs?' Fin grinned

'Yes, just hold on.' Robbie held the specs up to the watery dawn sunlight. They were covered in green smudges and fingerprints. 'Won't be a tick.' He cleaned the specs carefully on a towel that was hanging on the washing line then silently slid them through the open window onto the sink draining board.

Fin smiled sleepily. 'That'll cheer Mum up. How did you get them?'

'Oh, I was just mac-practisin' my boglin' skills,' Robbie grinned.

⌘

'And where were you two last night?' Beth stood at the tent door, a mug of tea in each hand.

'Go away, it's the middle of the night,' Fin groaned, pulling his sleeping bag over his head.

'No it isn't. It's after ten. I've brought you some tea.'

Robbie's tousled head appeared from his sleeping bag. 'What is it? I need my sleep.'

'You obviously didn't need it in the middle of the night. Out canoeing in the bay with your friend. I saw you,' said Beth accusingly, squeezing carefully into the tent, trying not to spill the tea.

'You must have been dreaming,' said Robbie, stretching out a hand for the mug.

'No I wasn't. I saw you,' said Beth indignantly. 'I had to get up in the night. I stopped to look at the dawn coming up and there you were, bringing the canoe into Boat Bay.'

'It must have been someone else, Beth,' said Robbie reasonably.

'You think I can't recognise my own brothers?' Beth was annoyed.

Robbie sipped his tea thoughtfully. Fin sat up.

'You've still got your clothes on!' Beth pronounced. 'You've definitely been up to something.'

'No, I often sleep with my clothes on... Well on holiday I do.'

'True.' Robbie nodded.

'And why are there three life-jackets here?' Beth asked, prodding the discarded articles with her foot.

'Em...'

'You can't answer that one, can you?'

'Well, um...'

'If you don't tell me I might have to mention it to Mum,' said Beth.

'But that's blackmail,' Robbie whispered, spilling tea on his sleeping bag.

'Mum would like to know what you were getting up to. You know how nervous she is about canoes and water and...'

'Shoosh, Beth,' Fin hissed. 'We can't tell you. It's a secret.'

'So it *was* you. I knew it.'

'Boys, Beth, breakfast.' Mum's cheery voice interrupted their argument. 'It's on the table now.'

'Tell me after breakfast,' Beth whispered. 'We'd better go. Mum's made scrambled egg and sausages.'

'Scrambled eggs and sausages?' said Robbie. 'Mum never makes a cooked breakfast. What's the celebration?'

'She's in a good mood,' said Beth climbing out of the tent. 'She found her specs.'

⌘

'I can't understand it,' said Mum. 'I'm sure I would have seen my specs on the draining board. After all, I wash up every day. They couldn't have been lying there unnoticed for two days. More tomato ketchup, anyone?'

'Have you any brown sauce, Mum?' Fin asked, prodding a sausage with his fork.

'Here you are, dear. Pass it to Fin, Beth.' Mum retrieved the bottle from a cupboard, absentmindedly wiping the excess glutinous sauce from around the cap with a tea towel. 'I feel as if I've been the victim of a practical joke. How could a pair of specs just reappear like that?' She sat down at the table.

'You boys are very quiet. Do you know anything about this? Have you been playing tricks?'

'We're just enjoying our breakfast, Mum,' Robbie mumbled through a mouthful of toast.

'Mmm,' Mum said, 'There's something very odd about this. I just can't see why...'

'Coo-ee!' A loud call interrupted Mum's wondering. 'Can I come in?' Iona's head poked in through the half-door of the caravan. 'Still at your breakfast?'

'Yes, we've moved onto Craigmhor time,' said Mum, making room for Iona on the bench seat. 'We've put our watches away, and we do things whenever we feel like it. No more timetables for the whole holidays!'

'Yeah, and we threw our alarm clock off the edge of the cliff to see if time flies,' said Beth.

Iona smiled. 'You should be quite rested then,' she said, 'Apart from you two,' she added, glancing at Fin and Robbie. 'You look as if you've been up all night.'

The boys fidgeted guiltily.

'I hope you've got energy for the ceilidh tonight?'

'Yes, Iona, I was going to pop over later to see if you needed some help to prepare the food,' said Mum, pouring tea into a mug.

'Thanks, I was hoping you'd offer. There's quite a lot of people coming. I thought I'd do the usual buffet.' Iona sipped her hot tea. 'Would three o'clock suit? Craigmhor time, of course. Anyway, what's new at the Douglas encampment? What have you all been up to?'

'This and that,' said Beth.

'Did I tell you that I'd lost my specs?' said Mum.

'Aye, I knew. Euan said you'd been over at the croft to phone Bob an' ask him to bring your spare ones up on Tuesday. Must be awkward though. Can you still read?'

'Well, actually,' said Mum, taking her specs from her pocket and rubbing them on her jumper, 'I found them.' She rubbed harder, then pulled a tissue from another pocket. 'There's some strange green stuff on the bridge.' She rubbed vigorously. 'In fact, I was just saying to the kids how weird it is they just turned up. They were lying on the draining board this morning. And they definitely weren't there last night.'

'Spooo-kee,' said Beth.

'Sounds like you've been a victim of the Craigmhor Boggart,' Iona laughed. 'It happens all the time.'

'That's strange,' said Mum. 'Robbie said it could be a Boggart. 'He'd read about it in some book or other.'

'So I was right,' said Robbie. 'There *is* a Boggart at Craigmhor.'

'Ach, there's a legend about a Boggart that lives in a cave in the Craigmhor cliffs,' said Iona, and paused for a sip of tea. 'When we were wee, if anything got broken or disappeared my Granny used to say, 'It's yon Boggart up tae his tricks again!' It's a good excuse to blame all these annoying wee unexplainable things on something else. It's always been like that in the islands.'

'What kind of things does the Boggart do?' Beth asked.

'They say he creeps about at night annoying animals, putting the hens off laying, stealing things and scaring folk. Another one of the Boggart's tricks is to make something disappear, then mysteriously appear again sometime later.'

'Have you ever seen this Boggart, Iona?' Fin asked, chomping toast.

'No, he's invisible and creeps around at night when everyone's asleep. I remember when I was a wain, on dark winter nights I used to think that all the noises of the wind in the chimney and the clattering of the slates and the creaking of the byre roof were the noises of the Boggart moving about outside. And the Boggart was always used as a threat to make us behave. If we weren't good, the Boggart would come and get us.' Iona screwed up her face and wiggled her fingers in front of Fin in an attempt to impersonate a scary Boggart.

'You don't believe that, really?' asked Beth.

'Well, I canny say aye and I canny say no,' said Iona thoughtfully. Mum topped up Iona's mug with tea. 'There's all sorts of things we don't know about, and sometimes odd things happen and there's no explanation. Ask Shona at the other caravan when they arrive tonight. Last year her wedding ring went missing. She looked high and low for it and couldn't find it anywhere. A few days later it suddenly turned up in the morning, on top of a book beside her bed.'

'Just like my specs,' said Mum thoughtfully.

'Well,' said Iona, standing up, 'I can't keep gossiping all day. I've got a hen house to muck out. Oh, I left your clean clothes by the door, Finny Boy.'

Fin winced. He hated Iona calling him Finny Boy.

'See you all later. Thanks for the tea, Lizzie.' Iona bustled out of the caravan.

'What nonsense,' said Mum, still poking at a green sticky blob lodged in the bridge of her specs with a screwed up tissue. 'I wouldn't have thought Iona would believe such things.'

'Remember last year I lost a rubber out of my art box and we couldn't find it?' said Beth.

'Mmm,' said Mum, who had given up trying to clean her specs and was clearing the table.

'And I went to Clachnacala and got a new one.'

'Yes, pass me Fin's plate, please.'

'And when I opened my box to put it in, the old rubber was sitting on the top after all.'

'That must have been the Craigmhor Boggart,' said Robbie. 'Definitely.'

'Yeah, definitely,' Fin agreed. 'No mac-doubt about it!'

'Don't be so daft, all of you. What are we going to do today?' said Mum, changing the subject.

Sleep, thought Fin and Robbie, simultaneously.

⌘

Beth didn't manage to see Fin and Robbie on their own until the afternoon, when Mum went over to the croft to help Iona with the preparations for the ceilidh. Robbie was rooting around in the food cupboard looking for something to leave Mologan for his supper. Fin was stretched out reading a comic.

'Now,' she said. 'I want the truth, no fibs. Just tell me what you were doing.'

Robbie rattled a few cans and pretended not to have heard. Fin engrossed himself in his comic, re-reading a story he had just read.

'Come on. I won't tell,' she said encouragingly. 'I'm interested, that's all. You always leave me out of your games. I'm fed up being the oldest. You two are always plotting and planning schemes for yourselves. You never involve me.'

'Uch, it's a boys' thing,' said Fin. 'You know, having adventures and exploring and stuff.'

'That's OK at home, Fin, but I'm bored here. We're on holiday as a family. We should do things together. Come on, what are you up to?'

Fin stood up and searched his pockets for something. 'Promise you won't tell?' he said.

'Of course.'

'Well, Robbie and me...' he began.

Beth glanced at Robbie.

'Robbie and me met the Craigmhor Boggart and he ate so many of my squinky sookers that he turned green.'

Robbie was staring open mouthed at Fin and shook his head vigorously.

'And?' said Beth.

'And we had to go over, under cover of darkness, to Seal Island to consult an old Boggart witch about how to turn him back to his normal colour.'

Robbie put his hands over his eyes.

'That's why you saw the three of us being towed back from the island by a seal. Dabberlocks was his name...'

Beth began to laugh. 'You should write stories, Fin. You have a wonderful imagination. You were just out fishing with Calum, weren't you?'

'Of course we were. We went fishing for mackerel and we didn't catch a sausage,' laughed Fin.

'Well, let me know next time you go. I'd love to come with you.' Beth picked up her trainers and sat down to put them on. 'I'm going down to the beach. Are you coming?'

Robbie saw Fin spitting something into his hand. Fin winked as he wiped his fibstane on his T-shirt and slipped it back into his pocket. Robbie grinned. He popped his own fibstane into his mouth.

'I'll come with you in a minute, Beth. I'm just looking for something nice for the Boggart's supper.'

'Very funny, Robbie. Stop winding me up.' Beth tied her laces and stood up. 'What does a big nasty carnivorous Boggart call human beings?' she asked.

Robbie turned from the cupboard. 'Dunno.'

'Breakfast, lunch and dinner!'

Robbie groaned.

'Come on, I'll race you both down the shortcut,' Beth called, heading for the woods.

⌘

The ceilidh was great fun. Iona's parties always were. The children enjoyed meeting the locals whom they had not seen since last year and they also met up again with some regular campers who had just arrived at Craigmhor for their annual holiday.

As they made their way back to the camp they felt tired but happy, stuffed with wonderful food and still laughing at some of the amusing stories and antics of the guests. As they climbed into their beds they could still hear the faint sound of accordion music and laughter from the croft. They guessed that the party would go on for most of the night. Iona's parties always did.

Next day the croft was quiet, as everyone slept even later than usual. It was wet and windy and no one felt like doing much. Beth read a book from cover to cover. Mum drank lots of coffee and listened to the radio even though the reception was patchy. Fin studied his *Training with the SAS* book, trying to pick up hints about night raids which might be useful when he and Robbie helped Mologan to bogle the ingredients for Aggie's potion. Robbie was engrossed in a cookbook which Iona had lent him and was fantasising about Boggart equivalents for the recipes. Crispy Caterpillar with Red Anemone Jus. Stuffed Jellyfish with Cockroach Croutons on a Bed of Knotted Wrack. Puddocks in Oatmeal and Sautéed Potato Peelings Flambéed with Seaweed Liquor.

He had just decided to cook some supper (Limpets au Gratin and Tree Fungus on Toast?) since no one else seemed to be bothered, when Calum knocked at the steamed-up window.

'Could you use some leftovers?' he called. 'Hope you can. Otherwise they'll be thrown in the bin. Mum always makes too much,' he said, handing Robbie two large baskets.

Robbie peeked under the tea-towels which covered the baskets. In one basket there were spicy chicken legs, prawns, slices of ham and beef, potato salad, rice salad, pasta salad, quiche, pickled herrings and garlic bread, and that was only the top layer. In the other there was a selection of cakes.

'Wow, Mologan'll love some of this stuff,' Robbie mused to himself.

'Must dash. I've got to catch the boat to Invernoddle. I'm working tomorrow,' said Calum. 'Cheerio. See you next weekend.'

'Thanks Calum,' they all chorused, rousing themselves at the thought of a feast.

CHAPTER 8

Mologan the Red

In his cave, below the Douglas's camp, Mologan was preparing for the first stage of the bogling training. As soon as he was awake and out of bed he had shuffled up the passageway to retrieve the food which the boys had left for him at the secret entrance. His tummy was rumbling.

'I hope they've left me mair than yesterday,' he mumbled to himself. 'Ah need mac-sustenance fur the trainin'. Thon broon mac-slug thing Ah had wis gey dry, an' beans aye gie me windy-wallets. Ah dinnae ken why campers aye eat beans.'

Mologan picked up the plastic bag which Robbie had left for him and rushed back down the tunnel in anticipation. He tipped the contents onto the table. His eyes opened wide and his mouth watered.

'Wiggily mac-wurums, what a mac-feast!'

There were juicy prawns, a piece of salmon, a chicken leg, buttered crusty bread, a plastic tub of rice salad, a squashed tomato, a baked potato, pasta salad, a slice of fruit tart, some creamy trifle, jelly and a slab of gateau. Mologan reached beneath the table and brought out a large rusty iron pot. He scooped all the food into the pot and stirred it with rusty spoon. Licking his lips in anticipation he delicately sprinkled some dried woodlice on the top to season his meal. He sat down on the upturned bucket and tucked in heartily.

Scraping the last vestiges of cream, rice and pasta from the sides of the pot, Mologan belched loudly.

'That was mac-nificent,' he said out loud, rubbing his tummy dreamily.

Happy, and full up, Mologan bustled around the cave collecting bits and pieces that he would need for tonight's bogling training and piled them on the bed. Then he dressed very carefully in his new cammy mac-flag outfit. He glanced at his reflection in the water trough. Pleased with his clever improvisation, and content that his green-ness was reasonably concealed, Mologan stuffed two ancient mouldy books into the plastic bag which had contained his supper, put Aggie's list carefully into his sporran, picked up his bogling bag and set off.

The boys were ready when Mologan reached the tent. They had already dressed and climbed back into their sleeping bags to wait. Fin was wearing his newly washed camouflage trousers and jacket and was also wearing a camouflage baseball cap, back to front. Robbie was dressed in black, from woolly hat to black boots. In true SAS style they had smeared mud on their faces.

Mologan crept silently into the tent.

'Are youse mac-ready then?'

The boys sat up. Fin flicked on his torch, illuminating Mologan in his new outfit.

'Yeah, we're ready.' Fin hesitated. 'Mologan, what are you wearing?' He began to laugh.

Robbie giggled. They couldn't help it. Trying not to make too much noise, Fin put his head under his sleeping bag, Robbie stuffed the corner of his pillow into his mouth.

'What are youse laughin' at?' hissed Mologan, indignantly. 'What's so mac-funny?'

Mologan had spent most of the previous night perfecting his camouflage outfit. He was wearing the same knitted balaclava helmet but had cut out holes for his ears, which stuck out like flourescent green flowers. He had added a cracked green plastic sun visor, tied around his head with a piece of old fashioned grey knicker elastic. (Where had he bogled that from? And when?) He thought this eye shade added a cool and sporty touch. Over his tattered plaid he wore an enormous khaki T-shirt which was so wide that the sleeves came down past his elbows, and so long it completely covered his kilt. A few moth holes here and there emitted a faint green glow. His sporran was tied on top of the T-shirt. He had cut the toes out of the giant welly and the huge trainer for comfort, as they had both been a tight fit. He wore the long fisherman's sock on the same foot as the trainer, secured above his knobbly knee with baling twine. He had then tied an old tea-towel jauntily around his neck. The mis-matched gardening gloves completed his spectacular outfit.

'It's you. It's your...' Fin dissolved into helpless laughter.

'What? My what?' Mologan asked, feeling a bit irked.

'Where did you get that outfit?' Robbie chuckled, wiping the tears from his eyes. 'Did you make it yourself?' He and Fin burst into another fit of laughter.

'Shoosh,' said Mologan, feeling a bit hurt, 'Youse'll wake everyone up. This isnae a guid stert tae yer boglin' career. Come on,' he said, huffily. 'We'll go to the clearin' an' make a mac-stert,' and he disappeared silently out of the door.

Still giggling, Robbie and Fin followed the Boggart into the wood.

'Mologan could start a new fashion in peep-toed wellies,' Robbie whispered.

'Or sling-backed trainers,' said Fin and the two boys exploded into silent laughter.

'Youse mac-visitors are no' takin' this trainin' mac-seriously,' Mologan admonished, as he sat down on the largest lichen-covered rock in the clearing.

'We are. We've dressed up in camouflage gear and we've blackened our faces,' said Fin.

'Aye, the dressin' up is mac-portant right enough,' said Mologan, adjusting the elastic on his eye-shade.

Both boys stifled giggles.

'But maist mac-portant is yer commitment,' he continued, 'to the craft o' boglin'. It's a gey serious job, an' Ah'm relyin' on youse.'

'OK, Mologan, sorry,' said Fin. 'We didn't mean to upset you. We were a bit taken aback by your, um... inventiveness.'

'Right. Nae mair mac-carryin'-oan then,' said Mologan, assuming an air of command. He stood up. 'Ah want to show youse the boglin' books.' He pulled two ancient books out of the plastic bag and laid them on the grass.

'What's that gooey thing on the cover?' Robbie asked. 'Looks like... yuch, is it a slug?'

Mologan picked the flaccid white thing off the book cover and popped it into his mouth.

'Mac-pasta,' he said, licking his lips. He opened the book.

'Bogling for Fun and Profit,' Fin read. 'What's the other one, Mologan?'

'The Boggart's Handbook,' he replied. The Boggart licked some cream and jelly off the cobwebby toad-skin cover. 'You have to know the rools of boglin' afore ye start.'

'Rules?' the boys chorused.

'Aye,' said Mologan, surprised, 'Did ye no ken that there wis rools fur boglin'?'

'No,' said Fin, 'I just thought that you went out and, em, bogled things.'

'Jist bogled things, willy-mac-nilly?' Mologan was indignant. 'Ye've got a lot tae learn, Fin Mac-visitor. Did Ah no tell ye that boglin' wis a craft that needed years o' trainin' an' mac-practice?'

'Let's get on with it then,' said Robbie impatiently, 'otherwise we'll never learn. What's the first thing we have to do?'

Mologan turned to the first page in *The Boggart's Handbook*, stood up and cleared his throat.

'The mac-rools o' boglin',' he read, in a croaky, yet important sort of voice. 'Every Boggart must sweareth an oath to follow mac-dutifully the rools o' their craft and never tae bring the ancient and mac-venerable profession intae disrepute.' He paused and looked at Fin and Robbie with a serious expression and continued. 'The rools are,' he cleared his throat, 'wan: if ye taketh ye must leaveth.'

'Sounds like the bible,' said Fin.

'Aye, it is a kind o' boglin' bible, young Mac-visitor,' said Mologan reverently, and took a deep breath. 'Twa: ye must never be seen by een o' the bogl't yin.'

'What's a "bogle't yin" Mologan?' Robbie asked.

'The buddie that's bin bogled!' said Mologan, exasperated by being interrupted again. 'Three: never bogle ablow the light o' the sun. Fower: harmeth not man nor beastie. Five: return wan percent o' all clamjamphrie, but...' Mologan pointed a gloved finger at the boys and grinned, 'an' this is maist mac-portant... aye return it to a mac-different place.'

Robbie and Fin exchanged knowing glances, remembering the incident of the disappearing and reappearing ring which Iona had mentioned and Beth's mysterious vanishing rubber.

'Six,' continued Mologan, glaring at them. 'Six: never passeth a guid bit o' clamjamphrie withoot pickin' it up. Seeven: aye mac-separate pairs o' things.'

'What happens if you bogle a pair of trousers, then, Mologan?' Fin asked.

'Or a pair of knickers?' Robbie added.

'Ah ken't youse wernie takin' this mac-seriously,' said Mologan.

'It is a serious question,' said Fin. 'How can I swear an oath to separate a pair of knickers?'

Mologan sighed and screwed up his face and the sun-shade sprung off his head with a 'thwang!' 'Aye, um, youse have got a point there.' He rubbed his chin.

'Maybe when the rules were written everyone wore kilts,' Robbie ventured.

'And knickers weren't invented,' said Fin.

'Ye're right,' Mologan grinned. 'Weel, Ah s'pose Ah could jist mac-change that rool. Up-mac-date it a wee bittie. Let me see... Seeven: aye mac-separate pairs o' things, except troosers an' mac-knickers. How's that?'

Robbie and Fin grinned and nodded.

'An' eight,' Mologan continued, 'obey the Boggart's oath.' He closed the book with a thump.

'Is that it?' Robbie asked.

'Aye.'

'Do we have to learn it by heart?' Fin asked.

'No, not mac-zactly. That wid take too mac-long,' said Mologan. 'Youse'll jist have tae be aware o' it. Ah'll keep youse mac-right.'

'OK-dokay, Mologan, we're aware of it. What's next?' said Robbie, impatient and keen to move on.

'Wait a minute.' Fin scratched his head thoughtfully. 'You know rule number one?'

'Aye, if ye taketh ye must leaveth.' Mologan quoted.

'What exactly does it mean? What does a Boggart leaveth?'

'Och, it's mac-simple,' said the Boggart sitting back down on his rock. 'If ye bogle somethin' frae a croft or a hoose or a tent ye always leave somethin' behind.'

'Like what?' Fin was confused.

Mologan sighed. 'Weel, if Ah came into your tent an' bogled, for mac-zample a sock... one sock, mind. No' a mac-pair! If Ah bogled this sock, Ah wid leave a wee bit o' slime on yer tent zip, or a bogie on yer pillow or a spider in yer boot. Or if Ah didnae have onythin to leave Ah wid leave, um...' he scratched his head thoughtfully, 'a mac-fert.'

'I see,' said Fin, grinning widely. 'Sounds like fun.'

'I'm not sure,' said Robbie remembering the slugs in Fin's boots the morning after the squinky sookers were bogled. 'Sounds a bit disgusting.'

'Ach, Mac-Robbie, it's only right tae leave a wee inpit in macs-change fur whit ye bogle. A wee shoo slaters or mac-wurums or a wee bit o' earwax is no much tae have mac-ready.'

'S'pose not,' said Robbie, 'but I'm not keen on carrying all these creepy-crawlies about with me.'

'Ah keep them in ma sporran.' He opened it to show them. In the dark depths of the sporran beneath Aggie's crumpled list lots of slimy things wriggled about. Mologan absent-mindedly flicked a black beetle which was making a bid for freedom back into the sporran and closed it carefully.

'Right mac-team,' he said, jumping up. 'Manoeuvres!'

Mologan led them out of the wood.

'Follow me,' he said. 'Stick to the shadows and move mac-silently.' He took a few hunched strides and disappeared.

Mystified, the boys followed, striding in the same direction and bumped noisily into the Boggart in the shadow of a large rock.

'Ouch! Watch where youse are mac-goin',' Mologan hissed. 'Ye stood on ma foot. Pay mac-tention noo.' He rubbed the glowing toes which were sticking out of his wellie boot.

Mologan shuffled along sideways with his back against a wall of smooth flat rock, then crawled, panther-like, to the shadowy cover of a birch tree. Keeping their eyes on him the boys followed.

'I can see his ears glowing,' Robbie whispered. 'Keep watching his ears.'

All three huddled in the shade of the small tree.

'Guid,' said Mologan. 'Ah'm goin' tae move mac-faster noo, alang the ledge to the byre. Try an' keep up. Use the bracken for cover.' And he was off.

Fin and Robbie were amazed at how silently and quickly Mologan could move. They couldn't hear a cracked twig or a rustle of bracken. When they moved it sounded like a herd of elephants.

'I think we need lots of practice,' Fin whispered breathlessly as the boys rested, face down in a clump of bog cotton. They had lost sight of Mologan but were heading in the general direction of the byre as instructed.

'Come on, head for the whins,' Robbie hissed, getting up slowly.

The night sky was cloudy and overcast. In the darkness it was difficult to see where they were going. The boys ran in a semi-crouched position towards the silhouette of the gorse bushes, carefully side-stepping a small rock and narrowly avoiding a patch of stinging nettles. A long straggly bramble caught Robbie's jumper, but he pulled himself free and made a last dive for the cover of the whins.

'Great, we've made i... aargh! Oh!'

Robbie tripped over something big and solid and woolly. Crump. He landed on his front in a bed of gorse needles and nettles.

'Ouch! Aaah!'

A frightened sheep which had been sleeping peacefully under the bush stumbled noisily to its feet and galloped off into the bracken. Cattle began to snort and shuffle around in the nearby byre. Then the croft dogs began to bark loudly.

Fin joined Robbie under the bush.

'Oh no, that's all we need,' he whispered. 'Mologan won't be pleased.'

The Boggart suddenly appeared beside them.

'Guid, guid. Weel done,' he grinned, his big green smiling face glowing in the dark.

'But the dogs, Mologan!' Fin began.

'Uch, it's a guid trick tae make the dugs bark. It wakes folk up. All pert o' the Craigmhor boglin' service fur the mac-visitors. Come oan, back to the woods. We'll go to the tap o' the hill. Try no' tae run ower a ridge when the moon's ahint youse.'

'What moon?' said Robbie, looking up to the dark sky.

But Mologan didn't reply. 'This way mac-Boggarts!' The Boggart dashed off through the bracken.

Fin and Robbie followed him as best as they could. Although their eyes had become accustomed to the gloom it seemed to have become even darker. They could barely see where they were going as they scrambled between massive boulders on the steep slope, trying to follow Mologan's glowing ears.

'Mologan must have good night vision,' said Robbie. He had stopped to rub his leg which he had grazed on a rough lichen-covered rock.

'I can't see him anywhere. I'm taking a rest,' said Fin breathlessly. He sat down heavily on a soft mound of grass, which immediately stood up and tossed him to the ground.

'Aaah!' Fin screamed as the sheep ran off. 'Another one of these damned sheep. That gave me a hell of a fright.' He stood up, his heart thumping. He rubbed his bum. 'That was sore.'

'Shoosh, it can't be as bad as the nettle stings I have,' Robbie said.

'These sheep should have luminous ears so that we can see them in the dark,' said Fin. 'Where's Mologan?'

'Ah'm here,' said a disembodied voice from a nearby clump of bracken and foxgloves.

'Didn't see you,' said Robbie, startled.

'No, but Ah can see and hear *youse*!' Mologan replied crossly. 'Can youse no keep mac-quiet and look whaur youse are goin'?'

'But that's the problem, Mologan, *we* didn't see the youse.'

Mologan shrugged and looked at Robbie, mystified.

'The youse! It's a joke. The *youse*. The *ewes*. The *sheep*! Get it? We didn't see the ewes. That's why we fell over them!'

Mologan grunted. He still didn't understand the joke.

'Come on, this way,' he said. 'We're near the tap.'

At the summit of the hill all three lay on their tummies and surveyed the landscape. The clouds cleared and the moon was reflected in the bay. The islands were inky blue against a silver sea.

'It's beautiful,' said Fin. 'We never get the chance to see this view at night.'

Robbie turned over onto his back. 'Look at the stars. There's the Plough, and the Milky Way.' He pointed upwards. 'This is definitely the place to see the stars.'

'Aye, it's Mologan's Hill,' Mologan murmured dreamily.

'What did you say?' Fin asked, engrossed in star-gazing.

'It's Mologan's Hill, this hill,' Mologan repeated.

'Called after you, Mologan?' said Robbie.

'Na, Ah wis called after it! There's always bin a Mologan here fur mac-centuries. This hill was named after the very first Mologan.'

'How long ago was that?' Robbie asked, rummaging in his pocket.

'Ah dinnae ken. The boglin' records only go back nine-hunner years. They didnae mac-bother wi' boglin' books afore that.'

Robbie found the chocolate bar he had been searching his pockets for. He peeled off the paper carefully. The chocolate was smashed into small fragments as a result of his fall over the sleeping sheep.

'Did all the Mologans live in your cave?' Fin asked, accepting some crumbs of Robbie's chocolate.

'Oh, aye,' said Mologan stuffing a handful of chocolate pieces into his mouth. 'It's bin, chomp, chomp, mac-stended a guid bit since then, mind, munch, tae mac-commodate all the clamjamphrie. My, that was guid. Any mair mac-chocolate Mac-Robbie?'

'What was this first Mologan like?' asked Fin, who loved history and stories about historical characters.

'Weel, his name wis Mologan Dearg, which is the Gaelic fur Mologan the Rid... an' he wis *cursed*!' Mologan threw a chunk of chocolate in the air and caught it in his ample mouth. Grinning at Robbie and Fin, he looked for congratulations for achieving this feat.

He couldn't miss with a mouth that size,' Robbie thought, ungraciously.

'Very good, Mologan. Nice trick,' Fin said, winking at Robbie. 'What did he do, this Mologan the Red?'

'Weel,' Mologan began in a conspiratorial tone, 'it wis gey quiet aroon these perts when Mologan the Rid lived here. Ony mair mac-chocolate, Mac-Robbie?'

Robbie shook his head. Mologan sighed.

'Ach weel! In them days Craigmhor wis almost deserted. Sometimes in the summer, shepherds wid bring their sheep fur a few weeks grazin' an' wid stay at the sheilin'. Ye can still see the ruin o' it doon there.' Mologan pointed to a rectangle of fallen stones in a clearing below them.

'Mologan the Rid maistly ate shellfish an' insects, but when the shepherds sterted comin' he learned how tae bogle a wee bit o' purridge an' tae draw a puckle mulk frae the sheep.

'Still, Mologan wis gey mac-lonely. Aye, there wisnae a Grand Boglin' Compie-mac-tishun every ten years in them days, only a puckle o' sma' events an' gatherin's every fifty years or so. Craigmhor wis so remote that nae-Boggart ever mac-visited him. He wis approachin' his hunner an fiftieth birthday. That's the comin' o' age fur Boggarts.'

'What's the coming of age?' Fin interrupted.

'Uch, it's the age when Boggarts can get mairrit,' Mologan explained. 'Ah'm a hunner an forty-seeven noo. Ma comin' o' age is in three years frae noo. Onyways, Mologan wid be a hunner an' fifty jist efter the next hibernation, so he wid be able to look fur a Boggart wifie and huv mac-company at last.

'Noo, everythin' wis dull in thon days. Everything wis kinna mac-natural. Like broon an' grey an' mac-beige an' darker broon. Mologan yearned fur a wee bittie mac-colour in his life. Ah s'pose his Boggart mac-hormones were stertin' tae work an' he had strange mac-notions o' findin' a Boggart wifie an' settlin' doon.'

Mologan screwed up his face and grunted. 'Boggart wifies,' he shuddered, 'Ah dinnae unnerstand the mac-traction.'

Robbie and Fin nodded in agreement. They couldn't see the attraction in girls either.

'Whaur wis Ah?' Mologan continued. 'Aye, he be-gan kinda' nest buildin' like the birds an' the animals dae an' spent weeks clearin' oot an' tidyin' the cave. Cleanin' an' dustin' aw the clamjamphrie an makin' it mac-comfy.'

He paused, thoughtfully. 'That wis the last time it wis cleaned oot, mind!'

The boys laughed.

'Go on,' said Robbie.

Mologan continued, 'As Ah said, everything wis dull in thon days. Mologan got so mac-keen on all this mac-terior design stuff that he craved fur a wee bittie colour tae cheer up the cave an' make it mair mac-tractive tae a prospective Boggart wifie. He dreamt of somethin' bright an' cheerfu' like the colour o' a robin's breast or the machair flowers. Some rid curtains, a blue bed cover, some pink cushions. He became obsessive!

'Wan evenin' jist afore the hibernation, Mologan wis makin' his way doon tae the shore tae bogle some clabbydhus fur his supper. He noticed a ship comin' intae the bay. It wis a huge ship wi' a dragon's heid carved at the prow. The crew were foldin' up a muckle white sail wi' a muckle rid mac-square oan it. He watched as the boat wis beached an' dragged up oan tae the machair by a wheen o' mac-visitors who were all dressed in leather an' had pointy bunnets wi' coos' horns stickin' oot o' them.'

'Vikings!' Fin whispered.

Mologan cleared his throat. 'The mac-visitors made camp oan the machair,' he continued, 'an' efter drinkin' an' eatin' a lot o' scran they fell asleep wrapped in haps, aroon the fire. Mologan waited until they were aw snorin' and crept doon tae their camp. He bogled some leftover meat an' a puckle o' scraps frae their meal an' a sherp knife which hud bin yased tae cut the meat. He mac-quietly climbed oantae the boat an' un-mac-folded the sail. Mologan then cut the rid square oot o' the middle o' the sail. Nice an' mac-tidy, mind. Then he mac-foldit it up again. Leavin' the knife in the boat he shoved the rid material intae his boglin' bag an' stertit back fur the cave wi' thoughts o' nice rid seat covers an' mac-frilly table clouts and other soft mac-furnishin's in his heid.

'At dawn, the mac-visitors wakened up an' packed up camp. They shoved the boat intae the watter an' rowed oot intae the bay. They were jist un-mac-furlin' the sail when a sudden squall broke oot an' the ship began tae toss lik' a cork in the watter. As Mologan watched frae the cliff the crew tried tae control the ship, but the sail noo had a muckle hole in it an' it wis nae use. As the ship approached the Serpent Rocks a right big wave turn't the hale thing ower and mac-smashed it oan a wappin' jaggy rock.'

Mologan stopped to take a big wheezy breath, but before anyone could interrupt again he continued, 'An' the hale lot sank withoot trace.'

'What happened next?' Robbie asked.

'Weel, Mologan wis mac-devastated. He had bin so preoccupied wi his mac-plans fur the mac-decoratin' o' the cave he hadnae thought o' the consequences o' his boglin'. He had broken the fourth rool!'

'Dae nae harum tae man nor beastie,' the boys quoted in unison.

'Did all the Vikings die?' Robbie asked.

'Mac-droonded, every yin,' said Mologan in a sombre tone. 'An' when the other Boggarts heard aboot whit had happened they cursed Mologan an' mac-ostracised him an' banned him frae aw the Boggart events an' gatherins. Efter that he wis mac-doomed to remain on his own, shunned by aw the other Boggarts an' cursed fur the rest o' his mac-days.'

'Did he ever find a Boggart wifie?' said Fin.

'No, nivver. He lived on in the Craigmhor cave himself, an' the rid material mac-moldert an' rotted in a heap in yane o the caverns an' wis nivver made intae mac-nuthin'. Efter that he wis aye call't Mologan Dearg, Mologan the Rid.'

'That's so sad, Mologan,' said Robbie.

'Aye it is that, Mac-Robbie,' said Mologan, and a large green tear rolled down his cheek.

Back at the clearing, Fin checked his watch. Ten past three. He thought it would have been later. They had done so much. Mologan stuffed the bogling books into the plastic bag.

'That'll dae fur tonight, boglin' mac-squad. Youse didnae dae too badly.'

Robbie and Fin grinned.

'Same time ramorra? Meet youse here. Mac-synchronise, um...' Mologan looked around.

'Watches?' Robbie ventured.

'Mologan checked his wrists. 'Naw, jist, um, mac-synchronise yersels,' he said, picking up his bogling bag. Dinnae forget ma mac-supper, mind. Somethin' alang the lines o' tonight's wee mac-purvey wid be fine.' Mologan disappeared behind a rock.

'That was fun,' said Robbie as they climbed into the tent.

'Yeah, Mologan's great. I wonder what we'll do to-morrow night.'

'What's that smell, Fin?'

'What smell?' said Fin, untying his boots.

'It's kind of... ugh. Look at yourself, Fin.' Robbie shone his torch onto Fin.

Fin squinted down at his trousers. 'Sheep poo! Oh no, it's all over me. Look, my jacket's covered in it as well. Mum'll kill me.'

Very carefully, Fin removed the soiled smelly clothes and dumped them on the floor.

'You can't leave them there,' said Robbie, 'They'll stink the tent out. I'm not sleeping beside stinking clothes.'

But Fin was already in bed.

CHAPTER 9

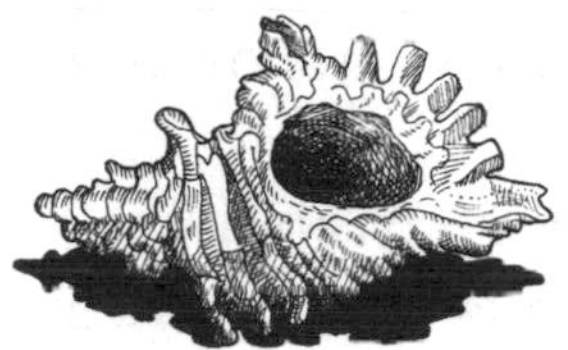

Sting Winkles

Monday was hot and sunny. Mum had already packed a picnic when Robbie and Fin got up.

'This is a good day to go to Eilean Bodach,' Mum said, while washing up the breakfast dishes. 'Have you finished with that mug yet, Fin? The tides are just right today. If we leave soon we'll get across the sound before the tide comes in and it'll have gone out again by the time we're ready to come back.'

Eilean Bodach was a tidal island which could be reached by walking across the sand at low tide. Beth was practising her guitar outside the caravan.

'Give Beth a shout, and pack your swimming things,' Mum said, as she folded up the breakfast table. 'Hurry up, we'll have to leave in ten minutes.' She looked at

Fin and Robbie and sniffed. 'Have you two washed? You look filthy.'

Fin glanced in the mirror. He rubbed his grubby face with his shirt sleeve. 'Have now!' he said.

The walk to Eilean Bodach was glorious. Under a cloudless blue sky everything was bright and clear. There were butterflies everywhere feasting on the wild orchids, and the island was loud with grasshoppers and humming bees. A buzzard soared overhead as they reached the summit of the island and took a short rest by a cairn of stones.

'The smell of bog myrtle on a hot day always reminds me of summer holidays,' said Beth, sniffing a freshly picked sprig. 'I'll take some back to the caravan. It's supposed to ward off midgies.'

'Egg sandwiches always remind me of holidays,' said Robbie. 'Can I have one now? I'm starving.'

'We'll soon be at Red Bay, Robbie. We'll have our picnic there. Come on, it's downhill all the way.' Mum picked up the rucksack containing the picnic and set off again.

Red Bay was rugged and magnificent. It seemed to be on a different scale from the rest of the world. High red granite cliffs towered on either side and great boulders the size of double-decker buses were strewn on the beach. This place made the children feel very tiny. The sea rushed into the bay through a narrow gap in the cliffs and waves pounded noisily on the red sandy beach. Seabirds wheeled and dived into the milky green water, their cries echoing off the monumental rock faces. A great jagged standing stone sited on the machair above the bay added to the splendid drama of the place.

The Douglases found a flat ledge to sit on and were soon tucking into their picnic.

'I wonder why this island is called Eilean Bodach,' Beth mused. 'What does it mean?'

'I think it means Hobgoblin Island,' said Mum. 'Iona told me once that there was a story about a hobgoblin who lived on the island and scared away all the inhabitants. That's why there's a deserted village. But then, in the Highlands and Islands, there are stories and folklore about every island and hill and loch. Doesn't mean you have to believe them all, though.'

'I think Iona does,' said Robbie.

'Maybe there's something in it,' said Fin, remembering Mologan's story about Roary Some-Boggart-or-another. The one who bogled Aggie Hagg-Boggart's green lobster. According to Mologan this nasty, evil Boggart lived on Eilean Bodach. 'Maybe there is something scary here. Maybe it lives under that standing stone.'

'And maybe you'll be believing in Boggarts next,' said Beth, standing up. 'Let's do a bit of beach-combing. I've brought my *Pocket Book of the Scottish Sea Shore*. We could have a look in the rock pools. Dad and I found a pipe-fish here last year.'

'Great,' said Fin. He loved pottering about in rock pools. Grabbing a small bucket he climbed enthusiastically down to the beach.

'Look at this.' Mum was kneeling beside a colourful rock pool. She prodded a knobbly, ridged shell with her finger. Fin, Beth and Robbie peered into the pool. 'They're odd. What are they, Beth?'

Beth turned the pages of her book importantly. Fin fished one of the shells out of the water and examined it closely.

'It's very sculptured,' he said, feeling the ridges with his pinkie. 'I haven't seen shells like these before.'

'Here it is,' said Beth. 'Does it look like this?' She showed the book to Fin. Fin held the shell next to the picture.

'Looks very like it,' he said. 'What is it?'

'Sting winkle or oyster drill,' Beth read, 'Muricid similar in shape to the common whelk. Grows up to sixty millimetres in length. Generally conical in shape with heavy transversal ridging. Like other muricids it feeds by drilling through the shells of its prey such as oysters, cockles and barnacles.'

'Are there many in this pool?' Robbie asked, poking aside some bright green seaweed. 'We need nine,' he whispered to Fin who was kneeling beside him.

Fin looked puzzled.

'Why?'

'Shoosh! They're on the list. Aggie's list. Nine *sting winkles*!'

'Yes, *yes*.' Fin grinned. He stared more intently into the pool. 'Do they have to be dead or alive?'

'Dunno.'

'We'll keep them in a bucket of water then,' said Fin, his shirtsleeves wet up to the elbow.

'You collect them and I'll hold the bucket,' said Robbie.

The boys spent the next half hour collecting the sting winkles. They were not as common as the other whelks on the shore but by the time Mum and Beth had wandered off to the headland and back, the boys had at least twelve in the bucket.

'Time to go,' Mum called. She was up on the ledge packing up the picnic debris.

'Aw, Mum!'

'Come on. Get ready. It'll take forty-five minutes to get back. We've got to remember the tides.'

'I'll have my book back please, Fin,' said Beth, snatching it out of his hand. 'You've got greasy fingerprints all over it.'

'You're not taking these awful winkle things back with you?' said Mum.

'Yes, the whole mac-bucketful,' said Fin.

'I hope you're not planning to cook them for us, Robbie. I couldn't bear to eat winkles. I wish Iona hadn't lent you that cookery book.'

'Oh, you never know,' said Robbie. 'Sting winkle curry might be nice.'

'I'm starving now,' said Fin.

Mum gave each of the children three chocolate digestive biscuits. 'These are all we have left, bar the sting winkles,' she said. 'Put them in your pockets to munch on the way back.'

⌘

'I thought I'd get some shopping tomorrow when I go to the mainland to pick up Dad from the station,' said Mum, looking up from the list she was writing. She took off her specs and rubbed the persistent green spot with a tissue. 'Can you think of anything I need to get?'

'Smoked haddock,' said Fin. 'It's my favourite. And Dad's.'

'Good idea,' said Mum, noting it down.

'Some decent cheese. Maybe a Dolcelatte or a Brie,' Robbie suggested, 'and some fresh herbs.'

'We're on a caravanning and camping holiday, Robbie. You can't be a food snob here. You'll have cheddar, and like it! Who's coming with me? Boys?'

'No thanks, we'll stay here,' they chorused. Fin didn't like shopping and Robbie was planning to have a lie-in to catch up with all the sleep he'd missed since they'd become involved with Mologan.

'Beth? Are you coming?'

'I think I'll stay here, Mum. I'll move my stuff into the tent and I want to practise my guitar.'

Fin and Robbie looked at each other, aghast. They had forgotten that Beth would be sharing their tent from tomorrow night. She'd be bound to hear or see them creeping out to meet Mologan.

'Fine,' said Mum. 'I'll leave early since I shan't have to wait for you to get ready. You'll be in charge, Beth.'

'Do they sell tinned snails at the supermarket, Mum?' Robbie asked thoughtfully.

'Snails? Is this for some fancy recipe you want to try out? Well, I have to say you'll not catch me eating snails. Yuch!'

Robbie sighed. 'It was just a whim,' he said, thinking of how Mologan would have enjoyed them.

There wasn't much left in the cupboard for Mologan's supper. A bowl of soggy cornflakes, two dried figs, an apple, three slices of dry bread and jam and some potato peelings out of the caravan bin were left by the secret door. There was a note lying on the grass, weighted down by a small stone. Fin read it with difficulty.

BRUNG A JAR AN
A BOGLIN BAG A
POK WID B GUD
ASWEL

'I think he wants us to be prepared to bogle some of the ingredients tonight,' Fin said. 'We'd better get a bag and a jar now and hide them for later.'

CHAPTER 10

Mologan's Boggarts

At midnight Robbie and Fin were at the clearing dressed in their somewhat smelly bogling gear. Armed with an empty honey jar, a margarine tub and some plastic bags they were ready for anything.

Mologan suddenly appeared between them.

'Aargh!' Robbie recoiled in shock. 'Don't do that, Mologan, you scared me to death.'

'It's just the Boggart way, Mac-Robbie. Youse'll huv tae get mac-used tae it. Huv youse onythin' tae eat? That wee bittie mac-breakfast youse left me wis a bit mac-scimpit.'

'It's all we had, Mologan, but Mum's going mac-shopping tomorrow and there will be plenty then,' said Fin.

'Uch, Ah s'pose Ah could pick up a few wee mac-nibbles whiles Ah'm oot,' said the Boggart. He poked at a small crack in the bark of an oak tree. 'Ah, here's mac-somthin'.' Mologan discarded his gardening gloves and pulled out a fat white grub. Delicately holding the grub between thumb and forefinger he put it to his lips and gently sucked out the gelatinous flesh, leaving a sack of translucent skin which he flicked on the ground. He poked at the bark again. 'There's another yin. Wid youse like tae huv it?'

'Yuch,' said Robbie, screwing up his face. 'No thanks.'

'We've already had our supper,' Fin added. He held up a small bucket. '*And* we've got the sting winkles.'

Mologan had a good sniff at the bucket of molluscs. 'The very mac-dab!' he chuckled. 'Guid work, mac-team. Youse'll mak guid Boggarts yet. How mony did youse bogle? They *are* bogl't?'

'Yes, we bogled them out of a rock pool at Red Bay. There are plenty,' Robbie said.

'Rid Bay? Near the mac-stane?' Mologan grinned.

'Yes. Just there.'

Mologan smiled broadly, exposing his fangs. 'So they're bogl't frae Roary Borealis's mac-beach! Very mac-propriate!' He took the bucket from Fin and stared at the contents. Mologan birled round and jabbed one arm in the air. 'Guid mac-boglin',' he said, almost falling over his un-aerodynamic footwear. He was obviously pleased.

Mologan went to the secret door and tucked the bucket inside, out of sight.

'Sit youse doon,' he said. 'We'll dae mac-theory first.' He picked a few more grubs from the tree and stuffed them in his sporran.

Mologan paced back and forward in front of the boys with an extended finger on his chin in the attitude of an eccentric professor deep in thought. His ears glowed strangely in the moon shadows.

'Whit's the first rool o' boglin'?' he said, suddenly stopping dead and staring at Fin and Robbie. If Mologan hadn't looked so daft in his cammy-mac-flag clothes he would have seemed very menacing.

'If you taketh, you must leaveth,' the boys chanted, in 'primary-one' sing-song voices.

'Guid.'

A long silence.

'Noo,' said Mologan, thoughtfully, 'If Ah bogl't, fur mac-instance, a broken flowerpot, whit wid Ah leave?'

'A spider in the sugar bowl,' said Fin.

'Or sand in wellies?' Robbie added.

'No mac-bad, wee mac-visitor Boggarty craiturs,' said Mologan. 'No mac-bad. Here's a harder yin. Whit wid ye leave if ye bogl't the last o' the toilet roll?'

'If it was from our house I'd leave the country,' Robbie chortled. 'Dad's got a terrible temper.'

Fin got a fit of the giggles.

'Youse are still no takin' this mac-seriously.' Mologan faced them, hands on hips, his green ears pulsating in annoyance and his wiry eyebrows puckered over his screwed-up eyes.

'You've lost your sense of humour, Mologan. It's only a joke,' said Robbie.

Mologan silently bit his lip. He looked hurt.

'Sorry,' Robbie said. 'I couldn't help it. I'll try to take it more seriously. What's the next question, since you're on a *roll*?'

Fin exploded with laughter again. Mologan glared at the boys then continued pacing up and down in silence.

'If,' he said, pausing to scratch his chin, a smug grin appearing on his face, 'If Ah had left snot on a doorhandle what wid Ah huv bogl't?'

'Is this a trick question?' Fin asked.

Mologan tapped his nose and winked.

'Well, um... is it... um... a box of tissues?' Fin stammered.

'A box o' mac-tissues?' Mologan repeated. 'A box o' mac-tissucs?' He snorted loudly. 'A box o'...' He held his tummy and wheezed and gurgled with laughter. 'Whit wid a self-respectin' Boggart want wi' a box o' mac-tissues?' He began to cough and choke. Robbie thumped him on the back.

'Are you OK?'

'Aye, snort, wheeze. Ah hav'nae had sich a guid mac-laugh fur years. A box o'...'

'Now who's not taking it mac-seriously?' said Fin. 'What's the answer then, Mologan?'

'A worn-oot scrubbin' brush, of course!' Mologan chortled.

The boys looked puzzled. Robbie shrugged. Fin shrugged. 'Yes, its obvious when you think about it.' Robbie said ironically.

Mologan wiped the green tears from his eyes and the snot from his nose with the hem of his T-shirt.

'Time tae go boglin',' he cried. 'Have youse got yer mac-quipment?'

'Yessir!' Fin saluted.

'Follow on, mac-Boggarts!' Mologan disappeared into the shadows.

'Where are we going Molo...' Robbie began. But the Boggart was gone.

After startling a few unsuspecting sheep and lambs and squidging through several boggy bits Robbie and Fin caught up with Mologan at the croft. They squatted in the shadow of the garden wall.

'Yer mac-mission tonight is tae bogle the grossets.' Mologan whispered.

'What?' Fin asked.

'The *grossets*. Ye ken? Thon wee green mac-birsie things on thon jaggy bushes yonder.' He pointed into the garden.

'Gooseberries?'

'Aye. We need seeven. Youse loup ower the dyke an' Ah'll wait here.'

Fin was overcome by a wave of excitement. Robbie suddenly felt nervous and wondered what they had let themselves in for. This was it. This was bogling for real. What if he was seen? What if they were caught? He'd never live it down.

'I think I'll go home,' he whispered. 'I can't do this. It's stealing.'

Mologan grabbed Robbie's arm. 'No if ye leave somethin', Mac-Robbie.' He held Robbie with a surprisingly strong grip. 'Ye cannae let me doon noo.'

'Come on,' said Fin, gripping Robbie's other arm. Iona won't miss a few gooseberries. The birds eat most of them anyway.'

'OK then,' said Robbie, almost convinced, 'but what'll we leave?'

'What have you got?'

The boys stuffed their hands into their pockets and rummaged around.

'Chewing gum,' said Robbie holding up a very crumpled stick of gum.

'A cowrie shell,' said Fin. 'Very rare. It's an arctic cowrie. I found it on the beach.'

'Leave the shell. I'll have this,' said Mologan, snatching the chewing gum out of Robbie's hand. 'Are youse ready? Over the dyke!' He shoved the chewing gum, paper and all, into his mouth.

The two reluctant trainees slid silently over the wall into the kitchen garden.

Holding their breath for most of their short burst of activity in the kitchen garden the boys returned breathless to the spot where they had left Mologan. He was not there. They sat in the shadows and counted the gooseberries into their plastic bag.

'Shoosh, stop mac-russlin'.' Mologan appeared beside them. 'Youse should ken better than tae bring yin o' thon plastic mac-pokes on a boglin' mishun. They're too mac-loud.' Mologan slurped and stretched the chewing gum right out of his mouth.

'We've got ten grossets,' said Fin ignoring Mologan's annoyance. 'Where have you been?'

'Uch, Ah saw this oan the windae sill ben the mac-holiday cottage.' He held up a small bottle of red nail varnish.

'Nail varnish?' Robbie asked. 'What do you need that for?'

'Youse'll see.' Mologan winked.

'It's to make him look smarter in his peep-toed wellies,' Fin whispered.

'I don't think it's his colour,' Robbie giggled.

Mologan didn't hear what they said. He had already headed off towards the ridge. 'Away mac-Boggarts!'

Robbie stuffed the bag of gooseberries into his pocket and they followed Mologan silently, imitating his strange hunched walk and his long strides.

Fin and Robbie were skirting round Shona and Donald's caravan when they heard a strange rustling sound accompanied by a soft squeaky murmuring. They stopped dead and ducked behind a large boulder. They felt Mologan beside them in the darkness.

'What's that, Mologan?'

'Look,' Mologan whispered, pointing beneath a table which was on a flat area of grass near the caravan. The Boggart's eyes were keener than the boys' but after a while they could make out a discarded crisp packet which was moving around in circles, propelled by a couple of small hairy back legs. As it rustled and squeaked its way closer to them they saw it was a packet of moon munchies propelled by a greedy hedgehog which had got his head stuck in the bag. The hedgehog licked the inside of the bag with a raspy tongue and squeaked excitedly as it moved around.

Fin moved and put his hand down on a stinging nettle.

'Ouch!'

The rustling stopped. The hedgehog stood still, its head still inside the crisp packet.

'He thinks we can't see him if he can't see us,' Robbie whispered.

'Never mind the hedger, mac-Robbie. Look at the mac-table.'

On the table were the remains of a barbecue. Unwashed plates and glasses, half-eaten bread rolls, bits of chicken legs, the remains of a slug-infested salad and a couple of empty wine bottles. Mologan licked his lips and moved stealthily towards the table. Expertly and noislessly he dropped the discarded chicken legs and a half-chewed sausage into his bogling bag. He picked a juicy slug from the leftover salad and popped it into his mouth before tipping the rest into the bag. He scooped up the lumps of bread and picked up a grass-and-mayonnaise-covered potato. Fin pointed to the two unfinished glasses of wine. Dead midgies floated on top and a small slug had almost slithered to the top of one of the glasses.

Mologan screwed up his face and shook his head. Fin nodded his head vigorously. Mologan shrugged his shoulders. Fin crept up to Mologan. The Boggart was licking some spilled ketchup off the tabletop with his huge blue tongue.

'Get the wine too.' Fin handed Mologan the honey jar. 'It's red biddy... red wine. It's on Aggie's list.'

'Och, so it is. Ah wis jist a bittie carried awa' wi' aw this guid boglin',' Mologan whispered.

He poured the dregs of wine into Fin's jar. Then he took the chewed gum out of his mouth and stuck it carefully on a seat. 'Boglin' completed,' he smiled, and signalled for the Boggart patrol to move on. As Fin turned to see which way Mologan had gone he tripped over the hedgehog. BANG, CRASH! He bumped the table and the two empty wine bottles toppled over, rolled noisily to the edge of the table and fell to the ground. Fin froze on the spot. He looked around nervously. Robbie and Mologan were nowhere to be seen. A dog started barking and a torch flickered on in the caravan.

Suddenly an invisible Boggart arm grabbed Fin and pulled him behind a rock. As Fin, Robbie and Mologan crouched tensely in the shadows a beam of light flickered over the table, illuminating the scene for a few seconds.

'It's alright. Quiet Brizzo. Good dog. It's only a hedgehog,' said a disembodied voice from the caravan as the hedgehog, having escaped from the crisp bag, scuttled off into the bracken.

'Phew, that was close,' Fin's heart was beating very fast. Robbie stretched his legs and peered over the rock.

'The coast is clear. He's switched the torch off.'

'We'll go roun' the back o' the caravan, through the bracken,' Mologan whispered. 'Be gey quiet. The dug's still awake. An' watch where ye pit yer feet, Fin Macvisitor.'

Back at the clearing they examined their clamjamphrie.

'No a bad night's boglin',' said Mologan, gnawing on a chicken bone.

'We've got the gooseberries and the wine as well as the sting winkles,' Robbie said, placing them carefully on top of a flat rock. He consulted the list. 'Only seven items to get.'

'And the green lobster,' Fin said.

'I'd forgotten about that,' Robbie said, and sighed.

'We'll leave the lobstur till mac-last.' Mologan was picking slugs out of his bogling bag.

'I suppose we'd better get back to the tent soon,' said Fin. He was sitting on the ground, his back against a mossy rock. 'I'm exhausted.'

'Wait a mac-minute.' Mologan delved into his bogling bag. 'Wait there.' He disappeared behind a willow tree. Robbie and Fin could see the glow from his ears illuminating the leaves above his head.

'What are you doing, Mologan?' Robbie asked.

'Youse'll see.' They heard a few metallic clinks and the sound of the Boggart wheezing and blowing. Eventually Mologan appeared from behind the tree blowing noisily on shiny objects half-hidden in each hand.

'Noo,' he said. 'The first stage o' yer trainin' is macfeenished. It's time tae tak' the Boggart Oath.'

As if by magic the clouds parted and a beam of moonlight illuminated the scene.

'Stand up an' pit yer right hand oan yer neb an' yer ither hand oan yer boglin' bag.'

The boys scrambled to their feet, grabbing their plastic bags.

'Like this?' Robbie asked, covering his nose.

'Mac-fine. Noo, repeat efter me,' Mologan said solemnly. 'Ah will follow mac-dutifully the rools o' the Boggart craft an' nivver bring the ancient an' mac-venerable profession intae dis-re-mac-pute.'

The boys repeated the oath, trying not to giggle.

'Youse are noo mac-honorary Boggarts,' declared Mologan. He stepped towards them and carefully placed around their necks the commemorative Boggart medallions he had prepared for the occasion a few minutes before. The medallions were made from jagged tin can lids. Each was suspended from a length of orange baling twine which had been neatly knotted through a punched hole in the metal. The letters 'MB' were rather shakily painted in red on each one.

'Dinnae mac-touch them the noo,' Mologan warned. 'The nail paint is still a bittie mac-wet.'

'So that's what you were doing secretly behind the tree,' said Fin. 'And we thought you were going to paint your toe-nails red!'

Mologan looked down thoughtfully at his peep-toed mis-matched footwear. 'That's no a bad idea, young Mac-Robbie. It wid be a mac-change frae the mac-green.'

'I'm sure that's what Mologan the Red would have thought!' said Robbie.

Mologan nodded and laughed a deep gurgly laugh.

Fin examined his medallion. It glinted in the moon-light. He was touched by Mologan's thoughtfulness and inventiveness. 'I'll always treasure this,' Fin said. 'It's much appreciated. This is a very special occasion. We couldn't have done it without you. On behalf of my brother and...'

'Yeah, thanks Mologan,' Robbie interrupted Fin be-fore he could develop the award ceremony-type speech even further. Holding his medallion carefully, so that he wouldn't cut himself on the sharp jagged edges, he said, 'It's brilliant. Great, um, craftsmanship too.'

Mologan beamed with pride. 'It wis ma ain idea,' he said. 'A mac-memor-ayshun o' feenishin' yer mac-trainin'.'

'They're very, um, unusual. I've never seen anything like them before. What does the "MB" mean?' Fin said.

'It stands fur *Mologan's Boggarts.*'

'Mologan's Boggarts?' Fin and Robbie chorused.

'Aye. It's a braw name fur a mac-special team o' trainee Boggarts, is it no'?'

'S'pose so.' Robbie looked doubtful. 'And you're the leader? Commander Mologan, I presume?'

Mologan beamed. 'Aye, Mac-Robbie, Ah am that.' He puffed up his chest with pride.

'Aggie was right then,' Fin grinned.

Mologan and Robbie looked puzzled.

'You know. The chuckie boord. The prediction,' Fin said. '"Ye're goin' tae become a mac-chieftain",' he continued, imitating Aggie Hagg-Boggart's gravelly, croaky voice.

'Ye're right!' Mologan drew himself up to his full height. 'Except it wis *great* chieftain. She said Ah wis goin' tae become a *great chieftain*.'

'Well that's something to aim for, Mologan,' Robbie said.

CHAPTER 11

The Fernitickled Creature

Beth was listening to a tape in the caravan. The loud music woke Fin and Robbie from deep sleep. They drowsily made their way to the caravan, hungry for breakfast.

'Mum left ages ago,' said Beth, bustling about. 'You'll have to get your own breakfast.'

'Fine,' said Robbie, yawning. 'What have we got?'

'Not much,' said Fin peering into an empty cereal packet.

'There's some muesli,' Robbie said.

'I hate muesli,' Fin said.

'Just as well. Best to steer clear of muesli,' Beth said. 'It can be dangerous.'

'How?' Robbie was peering into the fridge.

'Well, someone in my class was drowned in a bowl

of muesli,' Beth grinned. 'Pulled under by a strong currant!'

'Ha-ha. Not funny!' said Fin, too hungry to appreciate Beth's sense of humour.

'I'll make an omelette,' said Robbie reaching into the cupboard for a frying pan. He took the last four eggs out of the fridge. 'Someone'll have to go and get more eggs from Iona.' He cracked the last one into a bowl.

'I'll go after breakfast,' Fin volunteered thinking it would be a good opportunity to ask her to wash his sheep-poo-soiled clothes without Mum finding out.

After they had eaten, Beth and Robbie made Fin wash up. 'After all, I cooked breakfast,' said Robbie, as he settled down to read a comic.

'And we don't want the caravan to be in a mess when Dad arrives,' said Beth as she stepped outside wrestling with her bundled-up sleeping bag and pillows. 'Any idea where the spare lilo is?'

Fin didn't want to get involved in Beth's re-organisation of their tent. While she was searching in the caravan cupboards for the lilo he secretly bundled his dirty camouflage clothes into his plastic bogling bag. He picked up two empty egg boxes and set off for the croft.

Iona was making jam. Fin could smell it as he approached the croft, wafting deliciously out of the kitchen window.

'Come away in, Finny Boy. Is everything OK? I saw your Mum leaving for the early ferry this morning.'

'Oh, yes, fine Iona, except...' He put the bag on a chair and pulled out his trousers and jacket. 'I had a wee encounter with some sheep poo and I wondered if you could, em...'

'I'll stick them in the wash now. Have you emptied the pockets?'

Fin checked the pockets and Iona bundled the clothes into the washing machine.

'I'll have them dried and ironed by tomorrow,' she said.

'You don't need to iron them,' Fin said. 'If I could get it back today I wouldn't mind if they were crumpled.'

'Oh, I see. Your Mum doesnae ken. What have you been up to, Finny Boy? Keeping secrets from your poor mother... Tch tch. How did you get so covered in sheep muck? No, don't answer that. I don't want to know.' She laughed. 'My granny would have called you a filthy wee Boggart.'

If only she knew, Fin thought.

'What kind of jam are you making?' he said, changing the subject.

'Grosset.' Iona spooned a drop of the hot green liquid onto a saucer. 'Gooseberry to you, Finny Boy. It's nearly ready.' She nodded towards the egg boxes. 'Are you needing eggs?'

'Yes, if you can spare them. Mum'll pay you later.'

'I'm a wee bit short of eggs at the moment. I had a big order from the hotel this morning and I've used up all the rest making pancakes. There'll be plenty tomorrow if you can wait.'

'That's fine. We shouldn't need them today.'

Iona began to pour the bubbling jam into jars. 'I was going to ask you a favour, Finny Boy.'

'Sure.'

'Euan and I are going to a do at the other end of the island tonight and we're hoping to stay over with my cousin at Traighgorm but we need someone to let the hens out for us in the morning. Could you do it for us?'

'No problem, Iona,' said Fin, who used to enjoy helping with some of the croft chores before Calum left home. 'I've done it before. I know what to do.'

'Thanks. Help yourself to eggs once you've collected them. There will be plenty duck eggs and there's usually a couple of goose eggs. I know your Dad's fond of them.' Iona placed small waxed paper discs on top of each jar of jam. Then she screwed the lids on tightly. 'You know,' she said, 'when I went out to pick these grossets this morning I found the strangest thing.' Iona pointed to the table. 'See that wee shell?'

Fin nodded.

'It's an arctic cowrie. Very rare. And there it was, sitting nice as nine-pence, on the kitchen garden gatepost.'

Fin felt his face redden.

'I used to collect these cowries when I was wee. There are a few down on the beach but they're difficult to find nowadays. How do you think it got onto my gatepost?'

'Maybe a seagull dropped it.'

'Aye, I suppose that's one theory, but seagulls only

take bigger juicier live shellfish. A cowrie's a bit wee and dead for a seagull to bother with.'

'Maybe the Boggart left it,' ventured Fin.

'Maybe, Finny Boy.'

Fin wondered why no one at Craigmhor called him by his real name. Finny Boy, Fin Mac-visitor!

'There's something weird about it, certainly. But wherever it came from it's kind of special. My Granny would call it a cantrip, a charm. I'll hold on to it for luck. Stick these labels on for me while I put some pancakes in a poke for you.' She spread some warm jam on a warm pancake. 'There you go. That'll keep your heart up until you get back to the caravan.'

Fin was pleased that Iona had treasured the bogling gift that he had left. He didn't feel so bad about bogling the gooseberries. She still had plenty to make jam with. He ate the warm pancake.

'Brill! You must give the recipe to Robbie,' he said, jam all over his mouth.

'Don't forget the hens tomorrow. I'll leave your clean clothes in the porch before I go.' Iona winked as she handed Fin the bag of pancakes and a pot of jam.

'Thanks. Enjoy your night out. See you tomorrow.'

Iona grinned and waved.

Fin sang loudly to himself all the way back. He stopped to pick up a heron's feather and two elastic bands. *Never passeth a good bit o' clamjamphrie without picking it up.* He was an honorary Boggart now. He had to stick to the rules.

Fin put the pancakes and the jar of jam on the table next to the medallions which Mologan had given the boys. The medallions! What were they doing there? He pocketed them quickly just as Robbie and Beth entered the caravan.

'You needn't hide them, Fin,' said Robbie. 'Beth found them when she was re-arranging the tent.'

'Robbie said you'd explain,' said Beth. 'So let's have something to drink and you can tell me all. Oh, great, pancakes. I'm starving.'

Beth poured three glasses of orange squash and put the pancakes on a plate. Robbie fetched butter and a knife and they all sat round the table. Fin and Robbie glanced at each other. Caught out.

'I was thinking,' said Robbie, 'that since Beth will now be sharing our tent it'll be difficult for us to go and, um,' he gulped, 'you know what, with em, you know who, without her noticing. What do you think?'

'Doing what?' Beth asked.

'Mmm, I'm not sure,' said Fin.

'We could do with some help,' Robbie continued, buttering a pancake.

'I could tell you a secret about butter, Beth,' said Fin.

'What's that?' said Beth.

'But I won't. You might spread it!'

'Get back to the point,' said Beth getting annoyed. 'Are you going to explain what's going on?'

'But what about, chomp, you know who, Robbie? It's really his secret.'

'I don't think he'll mind.'

'Who? *Who* will mind?'

'If we do tell you it's deadly secret,' said Fin looking Beth straight in the eye.

'I won't tell.'

'Promise?'

'Of course. Go on. I've known you were up to something since the night I saw you on the beach. Who is "you know who"?'

'Well, you know the Craigmhor Boggart?' Robbie began... And the improbable story unfolded. Beth sat speechless through most of the boys' tale.

'This is impossible to believe,' she said incredulously when they had finished. 'Are you pulling my leg? Is this some sort of big practical joke?'

'Of course not,' said Fin, pulling the medallions out of his pocket. 'How would we have got these? Mologan made them 'specially for us.'

Beth fingered the medallions carefully. 'You could have made them.'

'When would we have made them?' Fin was outraged that Beth still didn't believe them after going through the whole story in such detail.

'Oh, perhaps in the middle of the night. Maybe that's what you've been getting up to. Concocting an elaborate story and making daft Boggart medals to trick me.'

'Well, don't believe us then,' said Robbie. 'We've told you the truth. What about the mysterious stranger on the beach? Who was that if it wasn't Mologan?'

'Come with us tonight and we'll show you,' said Fin. 'Come and meet Mologan.'

'OK, I will,' said Beth. 'Just try and stop me.'

⌘

The children were pleased to see Dad.

'It's great to be back at Craigmhor at last,' he said. 'I thought the holidays would never come.'

Everyone helped to unload a pile of shopping from the car. Mum unpacked it and miraculously found places for everything inside the small caravan.

'After supper we can go for a long walk along the beach,' said Dad. 'Now tell me what you've been doing for the past week. What have you been getting up to?'

'Not much,' Fin shrugged.

'Hurumph,' said Beth, glaring at her brother.

They had just finished eating when Iona arrived.

'Hullo Bob.' She embraced Dad warmly, squeezing all the breath out of him. 'Welcome back. It's good to see you.'

'You get stronger every year Iona,' Dad wheezed.

'It's you that's getting weaker, Bobsy Boy,' Iona laughed. 'It's thon namby-pamby desk job. You've been sitting on your bottom all winter. You need some good strong Craigmhor air and plenty of long hard walks to build you up.'

'I didn't know Craigmhor had turned into some sort of health camp,' Dad said, 'but I'll make the most of your facilities while I'm here. How's Euan?'

'He sends his regards. He's finishing his chores just now. We're going up to a silver wedding party at Traichgorm tonight and we're staying over at Rhona and Tom's. That's what I came over to say. I've asked Finny Boy to let out the hens tomorrow morning. Is that OK?'

'Sure,' said Mum. 'Fin loves helping out.'

'Come over for your tea on Thursday, all of you. We can have a wee bit chat then and hear all Bob's news. Must dash. Euan'll be waiting. See you soon.' As Iona turned to go she winked at Fin and surreptitiously pointed at a plastic bag lying by the tent.

'Bye Iona. Have a good time.'

'... and thanks,' said Fin, smiling.

They sat up late that night listening to Dad's news and playing games.

'Don't bother getting undressed, Beth,' Fin said when they went to bed. We'll be going out soon. Put on something old. Dark and warm. We're going on manoeuvres.'

Soon after midnight Fin, Beth and Robbie crept out of their tent and made their way to the clearing. Even though Beth did not believe in the reality of the Craigmhor Boggart she had butterflies in her tummy and was wishing she had not bothered to get involved.

Mologan was waiting for them on his usual rock. Robbie and Fin had done their best to prepare Beth for her first meeting with Mologan. They described the Boggart, his glowing green skin and his strange cammy-mac-flag clothes, but Beth was stunned when she saw him. Her first instinct was to turn tail and run back to the camp. Her next was to laugh out loud. She did neither. She stood politely, biting her lip while the boys introduced her to Mologan and explained to him as briefly as they could why she had come with them.

'Pleased to meet you,' she said, shaking Mologan's gloved hand. She couldn't keep her eyes off his glowing green ears.

'An' you, Mac-Beth,' Mologan said genially, shaking her hand vigorously.

'Beth'll be a good help, Mologan. We'll get more bogling done if we have a bigger team.'

'Whit's thon oan yer face Mac-Beth? Yon spreckley marks,' Mologan asked, peering closely at Beth.

Beth recoiled from the Boggart's fishy breath. You've got a cheek pointing out my freckles when you've got the world's blotchiest, flakiest and most luminous skin, she thought.

'Freckles,' said Fin.

'Ah, ferniticles! Aye. Ah see noo. This is the fernitickled craitur that Aggie saw in the chuckie boord!'

'So it is, Mologan. You're right. She said a creature with fernitickles would help you. It must be Beth,' said Fin. 'Beth, you were meant to help Mologan. It was predicted.'

'Pinch me, Robbie. Am I dreaming?' Beth whispered, moving closer to her brother.

'No, you're not dreaming. He's quite real. Cool, isn't he? Good fun when you get to know him.'

'Smells a bit, though.' Beth held her nose.

'Yes, I know. But even *I've* got used to it. He doesn't smell any worse than Fin's trainers.'

'Now you come to mention it, you do have a point,' Beth laughed.

'Well, Mac-Beth, ye've got a guid bit o' trainin' tae catch up oan,' said Mologan, flattered by the unexpected, though predicted, increase in number of the bogling team. 'Welcome tae Mologan's Boggarts. Ah'll make ye a medal when ye're ready tae become a fully trained mac-honorary Boggart.'

Beth tried not to giggle. Mologan paced up and down the clearing twirling a stick.

'Ah wis hopin',' he said, 'tae feenish aw the boglin o' the mac-gredients tonight an' then have a wee confab regardin' the procurement o' the green lobstur. Have youse got yer boglin' accoutrements, mac-team?'

'Bogling bags at the ready,' said Fin, putting on a small rucksack.

'Come away, mac-Boggarts!' Mologan called as he disappeared into the darkness.

Robbie, Beth and Fin caught up with him at the tool shed.

'Tonight's mac-crucial,' Mologan explained. 'Ah cannae dae ony boglin'. Ma mac-green-ness is getting worse. Ah'm mac-stremely mac-visible. It's up tae youse.'

The boys nodded. Beth was not sure.

'Roosty caddles,' Mologan hissed. He nodded towards the tool shed. 'There's a wheen o' them in there.'

'Whereabouts exactly?' Robbie asked.

Mologan shrugged. 'Sniff them oot when ye get in there.'

'We can't do that,' Robbie said indignantly.

The Boggart snorted loudly. Beth jumped in fright.

'We haven't got a big sensitive snout like yours, Mologan,' Robbie explained.

'Can youse no' sniff things oot then?' The Boggart was mystified.

'Some things. Like bacon and dog poo and disinfectant, maybe. But rusty nails? Our noses are not that sensitive. Sorry.'

'Compared to other animals, human beings have a very poor sense of smell,' Beth added, grateful that she did, standing so close to Mologan against the wall of the tool shed.

'Wait here,' Mologan whispered. He dragged an old plastic barrel over to the wall, climbed up on it and poked his head through a small unglazed window. He sniffed deeply, snuffled a bit, sniffed again and jumped down.

'Right. Listen mac-carefully. Through the door. Twa paces. Turn right at the tool box. Dinnae fall over the tractor wheel. Step tae the mac-left at the petrol can. Feel yer way alang the workbench an' just behin' the roll of chicken wire there's a box o' roosty caddles.'

'You can tell all that by sniffing, Mologan?' Fin asked, impressed.

'Aye, an' mac-centuries of practice, Fin Mac-visitor.'

'Em, I'll wait here,' said Beth.

'OK-mac-dokay,' said Robbie. 'Come on, Fin.'

Outside the tool shed Mologan and Beth waited, listening. The door squeaked open. 'Rustle. Clunk. Ouch. Shoosh.' Silence. 'Rasp. Clink. Shhh!' Silence again. Metallic sounds. 'Fi – in!' A longer silence. A squeak and a very soft bang. 'Here we are,' Fin whispered. 'We got them.' He held several small rusty nails in his hand.

'Well, that was easy. We were as quiet as Boggarts,' Robbie said.

Mologan snorted. 'Quiet? Hurumph.' He sprayed snot over Beth. 'What did you leave?' he demanded.

'A mint humbug,' said Robbie.

Gran had given Dad some sweets for the children including mint humbugs, which none of them liked. Robbie had put some in his pocket, planning to 'leave' them when they were bogling.

'Guid. Onwards an' mac-upwards!' said Mologan. 'Whit's next?'

Mologan's Boggarts crept towards the croft.

They sheltered behind an old rusty tractor which looked as if it hadn't been moved for at least twenty years. Mologan pulled the grubby and crumpled list from his sporran and they consulted it by torchlight.

'What's a greenichy kail wurum?' Beth asked.

'Youse ken. Wan o' thon greenichy mac-beasties whit bide oan the kail. An' they make holes in it,' Mologan said

'Greenfly?' Robbie ventured.

'Naw, it's kinna mac-wriggly an' greenichy!'

'A caterpillar?' Beth asked.

'Aye, Mac-Beth.'

'What else do we have to get?' Robbie asked.

Fin peered at the list.

'Ten puggie nits?'

'Yon wee broon roon things that hing oan the bird table in a wee rid mac-fushin' net,' Mologan explained.

'Peanuts?' Fin said.

Mologan nodded.

'That's easy. What's next?' Beth took the list out of Fin's hand. 'Herr o' a birsie dug?'

Mologan pointed to the untidy tuft of hair sprouting from the top of his head.

'Ah, wiry hair. Hair from a wiry dog!' Robbie guessed.

'There's a wiry dog at the holiday cottage,' Beth said. 'An Irish wolfhound. I met it yesterday taking its owners for a walk. It's called Phoebe.'

'Phoebe?' Fin laughed. 'What kind of name is that for a wolf-hound?'

'I think it's a nice name. What's wrong with it?'

'Uch, Beth, a big fierce dog like that should have a real name. Something strong and wild. A noble and brave name. Something more suitable than namby-pamby Phoebe!'

'What should it be called, then, Fin?'

'Never mind what the dog should be called. Is it possible to get some of its hair?' Robbie snapped.

Beth made a face at him and stuck out her tongue.

'Is the dug mac-fierce?' Mologan asked.

Beth shrugged. 'It seemed friendly enough,' she said 'when it was on a lead and with its owners.'

'I suggest we concentrate on these three things first and see how we get on,' said Robbie.

Mologan cleared his throat. 'Who's the mac-captain o' this patrol? Who maks the decisions 'roon here?'

'OK, Mologan. You decide,' Robbie said.

Mologan cleared his throat. 'We'll mac-concentrate oan whit ye said.'

Fin and Beth grinned. Robbie shrugged, exasperated.

They crept round to the back of the kitchen garden.

'Noo, youse mac-sperienced Boggarts loup yon wall, mac-stremely quietly. Fin Mac-visitor, you bogle the three greenichy kail wurums frae thon cabbage patch, an' Mac-Robbie, we need ten puggie nits. There's aye a puckle oan the bird table.'

Very slowly and silently the boys slid over the wall. In the cover of the shadow of the house they crept along the edge of the raised vegetable beds. Fin knelt down by the cabbage patch, hoping that Iona hadn't sprayed the cabbages with some insecticide that would kill the caterpillars. He peered under the leaves, shading the light of his torch with his hand. There were loads of caterpillars. A veritable party of kail wurums feasting on the underside of the leaves. It took a matter of seconds to pick some off the cabbages and stuff them into a jar.

Meanwhile, Robbie, breathing heavily, reached the bird table. A small red net of peanuts was suspended from a hook. He reached up and tried to poke some nuts out of the bag without success. He squeezed and stretched and prodded to no avail. Panicking slightly, he tried to stretch the bag to make the holes bigger. He pulled at the tough red net as hard as he could.

'Rrrip!' The bag suddenly and unexpectedly tore apart and peanuts rained out all over Robbie and onto the ground. Robbie glanced over to the wall where Mologan's ears could clearly be seen pulsating with annoyance.

'Come on,' Fin hissed in Robbie's ear. 'Pick some off the ground quickly and let's get out of here.'

They each grabbed a handful of peanuts and soil and ran, in the Boggart's crouching position, back to the wall.

'Wait,' said Robbie. 'I haven't left anything.' He ran back to the bird table and left a humbug on top.

Beth and Fin helped the breathless Robbie over the wall.

'Phew, that was close. Do you suppose anyone heard us?' Robbie glanced towards the dark windows of the croft house.

'Doubt it,' said Beth.

'Good. Are our bogling skills improving, Mologan?'

The Boggart snorted and sighed. 'No' mac-zactly.'

'What Mologan is trying to say politely,' said Beth, grinning, 'is that no one heard you because they're not there. The house is empty. Iona and Euan are away for the night.'

'Pants!' said Fin. 'All that effort for nothing.'

'Guid mac-practice, though,' said Mologan. 'Noo, where's this birsie dug?'

CHAPTER 12

A Birsie Dug and Eleven Yellow Fingers

Mologan's Boggarts crept along the gravel path beside the holiday cottage.

'Scrunch, scrunch.' It was difficult to move quietly on a gravel path.

Mologan put a gloved finger to his lips. 'Shhh, dinnae disturb the dug.'

They edged forward inch by inch, pressed against the garden wall. They moved slowly, silently. Mologan stopped suddenly behind the garden shed.

'Mac-listen.'

They stood still as statues, listening. A low, rasping, wheezing sound could be heard.

Fin shivered. 'What's that?' he whispered.

'Snorin',' Mologan said. 'Ah'll wait here. If the dug sniffs me or sees the glow o' ma lugs it'll bark.'

Fin, Beth and Robbie crept along the shadow of the wall until they were level with the door of the shed. Peeping over the top of the wall they could see the chained-up wolfhound lying in the doorway fast asleep.

'What now?' Fin whispered.

The dog sniffed in his sleep. He sniffed again, made a snuffly noise then suddenly opened one eye. Mologan's Boggarts ducked behind the wall. They could hear the dog moving. It stood up and walked towards the wall. It sniffed loudly, then without warning its big head appeared over the wall, staring at them curiously. It opened its mouth, ready to bark.

'Good girl,' Beth said gently, holding her hand up for the dog to sniff. 'Good dog, Phoebe.'

Phoebe sniffed Beth's hand, then licked it. Beth pulled a chocolate digestive biscuit from her jacket pocket and offered it to the dog. Phoebe gobbled it up, licked her lips and panted expectantly.

'I've only got two biscuits left,' Beth whispered. 'Let's get the hair now.'

'How?' said Fin.

Silence. They hadn't worked this out. Robbie stood up. The wolfhound licked the top pocket of his jacket excitedly.

'She smells the humbugs. Shall I give her one?'

'Don't be daft, Robbie. You'd choke the poor thing,' Beth said. She stroked the dog's head. Phoebe continued to pant and sniff at Robbie's pocket, slavering all over his jacket.

'Do something, quick. This is disgusting.'

'Look.' Beth was rubbing the dogs head. 'Her hair is rubbing off. She's moulting.'

Suddenly a light switched on in the holiday cottage. The children ducked down behind the wall. The dog didn't seem to notice and tried to lean further over the wall, whining softly. The trainee Boggarts didn't move a muscle. Phoebe dribbled onto Robbie's head. He felt slightly sick but kept still, despite the urge to wipe his head. They heard a toilet flush. The light clicked off. Phoebe whined.

'Take this.' Robbie handed Beth a comb.

'A comb? How come you've got a comb?' Fin said, shocked. 'I never thought you were the comb-carrying type, Robbie.'

'Thought you were more of a honey-comb carrying type,' said Beth. 'You're not usually interested in anything you can't eat.'

'Trouble with a honey-comb is that it makes your hair all sticky,' Fin laughed.

Phoebe growled.

'If she was my dog I'd call her something scary like Growler,' said Fin.

'But she's not scary.' Beth fed Phoebe another biscuit. 'Now give me the comb. There's only one biscuit left.'

Beth gently combed the dog's moulting hair and collected a large handful. The dog purred contentedly like a cat, enjoying the experience. When she had enough hair she gave the last biscuit to the dog.

'Let's go,' she whispered.

The children ran back along the shadow of the wall to where Mologan was waiting. Phoebe, shocked by their sudden departure, scrabbled at the wall trying to follow them, but was held back by her short chain. Unable to move any further, she whined, then began to bark. She barked and barked.

'Let's mac-move,' Mologan hissed.

A light clicked on in the cottage. Then another light.

Mologan and his Boggarts scuttled back along the gravel path, slithered down a small slope and lay breathless in a patch of bog cotton.

'What did youse leave the poor dug?' Mologan asked.

'Oh, Mologan,' Beth was still breathless, 'You *are* a stickler for the rules.'

'Aye. Jist so, Mac-Beth.'

'I suppose we left some chocolate biscuits.'

'Whaur, mac-zactly?'

'In the dog's tummy,' said Beth.

Mologan scratched his head, puzzled.

'And where did you go when we were risking life and limb, bogling the hair from that horrible savage slavery animal?' Robbie asked Mologan.

'Uch, Ah wis checkin' the bins an' Ah wis puttin' the rid nail mac-paint back.'

'Where?' Beth asked.

'In the coal shed.' Mologan smiled a wide smile which exposed his fangs. 'Rool nummer five, return wan percent o' all clamjamphrie...'

'...but tae a different mac-place,' Fin laughed.

Beth tutted.

The bogling team waited silently until the dog had stopped barking and the lights had gone off again in the holiday cottage.

'Who's got the mac-list?' Mologan asked.

They all looked at each other expectantly.

'Someone must have it,' Beth said.

Robbie, Fin and Mologan shrugged.

'You had it last, Beth. I remember you snatching it out of my hand,' said Fin.

'I did *not* snatch it,' Beth said indignantly. 'Anyway I gave it back to Mologan.'

'We've lost the list!' Mologan screwed up his face and dramatically buried his head in his hands. 'We're really mac-done-for noo. Ah'll never get aw the mac-gredients fur the mac-mixture withoot the list. Ah'll aye be greenichie. An when youse mac-visitors go hame Ah'll mac-starve tae death.' He moaned and snorted tearfully.

'You are *such* a drama queen, Mologan. Don't make a fuss,' Robbie said. 'The list can't be far away. We can retrace our steps. We've probably dropped it somewhere. I'll go and have a look.'

Beth held him back. 'Wait, let's check our pockets first. One of us might have it.'

'Naw, it's mac-definitely lost,' Mologan moaned pessimistically. 'Ma Boggart intuition tells me Ah'm doomed.'

Fin, Beth and Robbie checked all their pockets and couldn't find the list.

'Try your sporran, Mologan,' Beth suggested.

'It's hardly mac-worth it,' Mologan huffily opened his sporran and peered inside. 'Naw, mac-empty,' he whispered. A tear rolled down his cheek and his nose started to run. He sniffed and made to wipe the green snot with the back of his hand.

'Mologan!' Beth said, disgusted, 'haven't you got a tissue or something?'

The Boggart snorted, reached down and pulled out something grey and crumpled which had been tucked in his sock. 'Aye, Mac-Beth, Ah've somethin' here,' he said and blew his nose.

'Wait. Mologan!' Robbie grasped the Boggart's arm. But it was too late. 'Yuch, Mologan, *that* wasn't a tissue, it was the list! You've blown your nose on the list!'

Mologan held up the wet, crumpled and green-streaked list. He chortled. 'Uch, it's here efter aw. It's no mac-lost.' He spread the list on a flat stone, wiped the snot off with the hem of his kilt and tried to un-crumple the parchment.

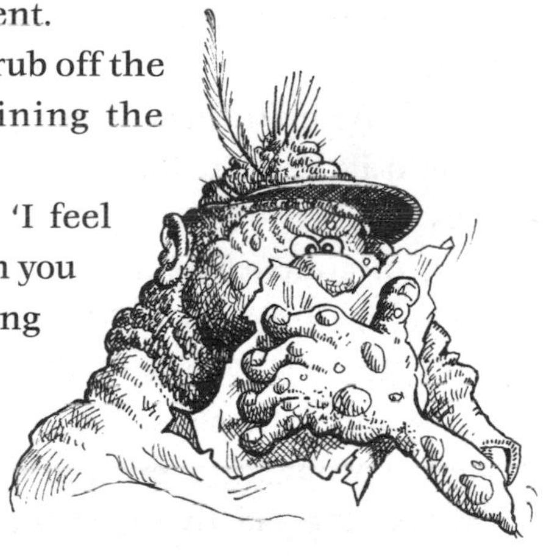

'Careful you don't rub off the ink,' said Fin, examining the list.

Beth looked away. 'I feel sick,' she said. 'How can you touch that? Don't bring it anywhere near me.'

'Nor me.' Robbie screwed up his face in disgust.

Mologan and Fin looked puzzled.

Fin shone his torch on the list. 'It hasn't smudged too much. It's still readable.'

'Good. You and Mologan can read it,' said Robbie. 'What else do we have to bogle?'

Fin and Mologan deciphered the blurred, sticky parchment.

'Only four more ingredients as far as I can see,' Fin said. 'Five yella fingers, one goose yowk, a gizzard and a wee shoo orange goo. I can get the goose yolk. I'm letting out the hens and ducks and geese tomorrow and Iona said I can help myself to eggs. She particularly said to take some goose eggs.'

'That's not exactly true bogling,' Robbie pointed out. They all looked at Mologan for confirmation.

The Boggart rubbed his chin. 'Weel, seein' as we're a bittie short o' mac-time... an' ye'll be boglin' the egg mac-technically, frae the goose... an if ye dinnae get the permission o' the beastie tae tak' the egg... an' if ye leave somethin'... Ah think it wid be hunky mac-dory.'

'Good,' Beth grinned. 'Now what's five yella fingers?'

'Could be thon yella mac-nanna things.' Mologan suggested.

'Yes, of course. Bananas!' said Robbie. 'We've got some in the caravan. Loads! That's easy. But what about the orange goo? What's that?'

Everyone shrugged, puzzled. Robbie, Fin and Beth looked at Mologan expecting him to know.

'Ah'll have tae think aboot that yane,' Mologan

scratched his head. 'Right mac-itchy this bala-mac-clava. Mibby it's a kinna mac-fungusy stuff.'

The children couldn't offer a better explanation.

'We'll leave that till ramorra,' Mologan suggested. 'Ah'll consult wan o' ma books mac-later. We should concentrate oan the mac-nannas the noo.' He stood up. 'Follow me alang the ledge. Mac-quiet noo, there's new mac-visitors at the big carry-mac-van. Forward mac-Boggarts!' and Mologan was off like greased lightning heading for the camp-site.

They bumped into Mologan behind a canvas wind-break next to the big caravan. It was a very neat and well organised encampment. Peter and Barbara had constructed a fence of stripey windbreaks around the caravan enclosing all their belongings. There was a barbecue in one corner next to a clean, scrubbed table with its central umbrella neatly furled and tied in place. Folding chairs were tidily stacked and children's toys were packed away in a fish box and stowed under the caravan. Four pairs of wellies were suspended up-side down on wooden poles which had been hammered into the ground in a neat row. On a carefully positioned washing line hung a pair of child's socks, four spotless face flannels and a pair of yellow rubber gloves.

'Look.' Mologan pointed to the washing line. 'five yella fingers!'

'So it is,' said Fin. 'Do you suppose that's what Aggie meant?'

'Dunno,' Mologan whispered. 'Might be.' He paused thoughtfully. 'Or it might be the mac-nannas.'

'I know,' said Beth. 'We'll get both. I've an idea. You lot wait here. I'll be back in five minutes. You won't do anything till I get back, will you?' Without waiting for a reply she slipped round the back of the caravan and disappeared.

Fin, Robbie and Mologan crouched behind the windbreak waiting for Beth to return. They sucked mint humbugs. Robbie and Fin thought they didn't taste too bad when they pretended they were SAS rations. Mologan slurped his happily and amused himself by dropping piles of sheep poo over the windbreak into the spotless enclosure.

Beth reached their own caravan out of breath. She stood behind the tent for a couple of minutes, recovering. Then, very quietly, she opened the caravan door and crept inside. Mum and Dad were sleeping peacefully. She could hear their breathing. As silently as she could she slid open the cupboard door under the sink. It was a bit stiff so she had to force it slightly. It slid open suddenly with a thump. Dad groaned and turned over. Beth froze, but the sleepy breathing resumed.

Finding it difficult to see what she was searching for in the dark Beth's hands groped around in the cupboard for a few moments before she found what she was looking for. She shoved the pink rubber glove into her pocket.

Next, she crept over to the table and gently lifted a bunch of bananas from the fruit bowl.

Dad grunted. 'Who's that?' he mumbled sleepily.

'Just me, Dad,' Beth whispered, not wanting to wake Mum. 'It's OK, I'm just getting something to eat.'

Dad poked his head out of his sleeping bag. 'But it's the middle of the night!'

'Night starvation,' Beth said. 'Night, night. Kiss, kiss,' She blew a kiss and quickly slipped out of the door, closing it softly behind her.

Beth returned to the rest of the bogling team, grinning.

'Look,' she said, pulling out the pink rubber glove. 'What do you think?'

'But we need a yellow one,' Fin said.

'Exactly,' Beth looked smug. 'What did you plan to leave in it's place?'

Mologan, Fin and Robbie looked blank.

'Typical!' Beth said. 'You never think ahead. Just as well there's a woman on this bogling team.'

Mologan bristled indignantly.

'You can't take poor Barbara's rubber glove off her washing line and leave her without. She'd go mental. You know how obsessive she is about cleaning, even on holiday. I thought we could leave this one in its place.'

'Where did you find it?' Fin asked.

'Remember Auntie Morag came up to Craigmhor a couple of years ago and someone gave us some fish they had caught, and she said she couldn't possibly gut them with her bare hands? She bought these rubber gloves and they've been under the sink ever since.

Mum'll never use them. She's been threatening to throw them out.'

'Let's get boglin',' said Mologan. 'Guid work, young Mac-Beth! Volunteer Boggart required tae bogle the yella fingers.'

'I'll go,' Robbie volunteered. 'What's the best way in?'

'Crawl under the windbreak,' said Beth, pulling up the striped canvas and creating a narrow gap. 'Here's the pink rubber glove. It's the right hand. Bogle the right-hand yellow glove.'

'I'm not daft,' Robbie growled, as he slithered on his tummy under the canvas, carefully avoiding the sheep poo which Mologan had dropped onto the grass.

Mologan, Fin and Beth held their breath as Robbie tip-toed past the caravan. He reached the washing line and made a thumbs-up sign. He stretched up to unpeg a rubber glove but it was out of reach. The washing line, suspended between the caravan roof and a nearby tree, was high off the ground and seemed to have been made for a giant to hang washing on.

Robbie jumped up, trying to reach the rubber glove. He just managed to touch it and it swung limply on the line.

'Jump higher,' Beth whispered encouragingly, although Robbie didn't hear her. He leapt up into the air stretching as far as he could and caught the middle finger of the glove between his thumb and forefinger. As he pulled the glove back down, the washing line stretched. 'Swack!' The clothes peg sprang off, catapulted towards the caravan, and landed on the roof with a metallic clatter. The washing line recoiled with a loud 'thwang!' and continued to reverberate silently for a few seconds. Robbie stood frozen, his hand still in the air holding the floppy yellow glove.

There was a creaking sound. Someone turned over in bed in the caravan. He held his breath. He ducked down behind the row of wellie boots and crouched silently, listening for any sound or sign of movement in the caravan.

'Psst, psst.' A hissing sound came from Robbie's left. He jumped. Mologan's green face peered over the wind-break.

'Mac-Beth says it's the wrong mac-glove!' Mologan hissed.

Robbie's heart missed a beat. Oh, no, he thought. How stupid.

Mologan was suddenly beside him. 'Dinnae mac-worry. Haud oan.'

'Mologan, don't be daft. You'll be seen,' Robbie whispered.

The Boggart recklessly crept over to the caravan and remarkably noiselessly emptied all the toys out of the fish box.

'Staun oan this Mac-Robbie.' He positioned the fish box under the washing line.

Quickly, Robbie jumped up on the box and un-pegged the right glove. He substituted it with the pink one and replaced the left-hand yellow glove.

Mologan was lifting the windbreak to create a gap for their escape. He was smiling broadly.

'Leave these,' he hissed, thrusting some cold hard round objects into Robbie's hand.

Robbie looked. 'Yuch, snails!' He had a strong desire to throw them away immediately. He cringed, looking at the Boggart for instructions as to what to do next.

'Oan tap o' the mac-wellies,' Mologan nodded towards the row of upturned boots.

Robbie carefully placed a fat shiny snail on the sole of each wellie.

Mologan was still beaming happily when they reached the clearing.

'That wis the greatest ever bogle mac-perpetrated by Mologan's Boggarts,' he said proudly. 'Ah fair enjoyed that bogle. A wee mac-classic! Weel done, youse.'

'And look, Mologan,' Beth pulled a bunch of bananas from under her jacket.

'Even mac-better, Mac-Beth – mair yella fingers, jist in case. Ah'll pit them in ma boglin' bag.'

Beth handed the bananas to Mologan.

'There's six mac-nanas here,' he beamed. Ah'll huv the mac-extra wan fur ma mac-supper.' He poked Beth with the spare banana. 'An' whit did ye leave fur the mac-glove an' the mac-nanas?'

'I left a kiss.'

'Ehhh, yuch,' Fin said.

'Too soppy for words,' said Robbie.

Mologan screwed up his face in disgust.

'Well it's better than a fart,' Beth giggled.

'Dunno aboot that, Mac-Beth.' Mologan looked thoughtful. He snorted then stuffed the whole banana into his mouth horizontally, without peeling it.

'Mologan, what's yellow and smells of bananas?' Fin asked.

Mologan scratched his head and shrugged.

'Monkey sick!'

Mologan shrugged again.

'That's a sick joke, Fin,' Robbie said. 'Anyway Mologan'll not get it. He doesn't know what a monkey is. Do you Mologan?'

The Boggart didn't speak. His mouth was stuffed with half-masticated banana.

Beth was feeling tired and was longing to get to bed. 'What about this green lobster, Mologan?' she said, changing the subject.

'Shoosh,' Mologan hissed, spitting bits of half-chewed banana. 'This is a top secret, chomp, mac-mission.'

'Why?' Beth asked.

'Weel, it's mac-stremely dangerous fur a stert, an' um, it's mac-stremely hush-hush.'

'You'd better explain, Mologan. Have you got a plan?' Robbie asked.

Mologan moved closer to the children. 'Youse ken that Roary Borealis has the green lobstur?'

They nodded.

'An' he's the meanest, maist mac-nasty, evil an' bad temper't Boggart this side o' Ben Mhor?'

They nodded again.

'An' that he bides oan Eilean Bodach in a cave ablow the big standin' stane?'

'We know all this, Mologan,' Robbie whispered. 'How do you plan to bogle back the lobster if this Boggart is as dangerous as you say?'

'Mac-cunnin', an' the help o' a weel mac-train't boglin' team.'

'We'll have to be very careful. He'll be hopping mad when we bogle the lobster back,' Beth said.

'He'll be roarin' mad,' said Mologan. That's why he's called Roary Borealis. His roar is as mac-powerful as the North Wind. He's been known tae knock ower a Boggart wi' his roar, an' flatten him forbye.'

'So how are we going to bogle the lobster from under his mac-nose?' Robbie asked, feeling dubious about the mission and rather worried about their safety. 'It sounds too dangerous to me.'

'Uch, dinnae mac-worry. Wait till youse hear ma sleekit mac-plan.'

CHAPTER 13

Orange Goo and a Sticky Situation

'It's strange that my fishing box has suddenly disappeared,' said Dad, tying his boot-laces.

'Bob, you've gone over this several times.' Mum stretched over him to reach her hairbrush. 'It's only a cheap plastic box full of smelly old lines and hooks. Hurry and get ready. Iona and Euan are expecting us soon.'

'But Lizzie, you don't understand,' Dad continued. 'I left it in the canoe and it disappeared.'

'The canoe was wrapped in the tarpaulin. Who on earth round here would go to all the trouble to unwrap it and steal a grubby fishing box? It was probably just...' – she pursed her lips to apply some lipstick – 'the boys playing games. They've been acting kind of funny all this holiday, as if they've got secrets.'

Beth looked up from her book. 'The same thing happened with your specs, Mum. They disappeared mysteriously then appeared again a few days later.'

'What was that about your specs, Lizzie?' Dad was peering into a cupboard. 'Where will I find the...?'

'Come on. Are you ready Beth? Where are the boys?' Mum bustled around the caravan. 'ROBBIE! FIN!'

The boys were leaving Mologan's supper at the secret door. Strawberry yogurt, an orange, four pink coconut marshmallow biscuits, a piece of cheese and two slices of bread and butter. Fin also left the goose egg that he had got that morning when he had let the hens out and collected Iona's eggs. He had wrapped it carefully in loo roll to protect it and at the last minute had written on it, 'INGREDIENTS FOR POTION: DO NOT EAT', in case Mologan might be confused.

Dad found the bottles of wine he had been searching for and slung his jumper over his shoulder.

'Coming, Beth?'

'Yes, I'll tell you about Mum's specs on the way.'

Wonderful food smells greeted them at the croft.

'Come away in,' Iona called from the steamy kitchen.

Euan was sitting on his usual chair by the Rayburn stove reading a farming newspaper, his worn and greasy old cap still on his head and Laddie curled up by his feet. He rose to greet them, smiling warmly.

Shaking Dad's hand he said, 'It's good to see you back, Bob. Pity the weather's not been so good so far. It's been a wee bit choppy out in the bay for that canoe of yours these past few days. The forecast's not promising for the rest of the week. There's low pressure coming in from the west. There's bound to be some heavy rain.'

'We can always rely on you for an accurate forecast,' Dad said. 'I suppose it's all your experience, the crofter's instinct.'

'Och, no,' Euan laughed. 'It's the satellite TV. Have you seen my new digital system?'

'You can get TV here now, Euan?' Dad knew that there was no normal terrestrial signal available at Craigmhor.

'Aye, a hundred and seventy three channels. Come ben, and I'll show you.' Euan and Dad wandered out of the kitchen. 'You'll have a wee dram, Bob? I've got a nice wee twelve-year-old "Traichgorm" for you to try.'

'Aye, that would go down a treat, Euan. How long have you had the digital TV then...'

The living room door closed.

'Never mind them,' Iona said, pouring glasses of Irn Bru. 'Euan watches all the weather forecasts at this time of night – all hundred and seventy three of them! We'll not see them for at least half an hour. Sit yourselves down and give me your crack while I peel the tatties.'

They all sat around the big kitchen table in the warm, cluttered kitchen.

'A wee glass of wine, Lizzie?' Iona offered.

'Yes, please,' said Mum. 'I'll get it. One for you Iona?'

'Aye, thanks, pet,' said Iona, emptying an enormous amount of potatoes into the sink.

'Can I help? Robbie asked.

'You can put Laddie outside, Robbie Boy. He shouldn't be in the kitchen. Euan and Calum are too soft with him.'

'Come on, Laddie.' Robbie rubbed the dog's head. Laddie whined, not wanting to leave the warm kitchen.

'If you don't mind getting your hands dirty, give him these.' Iona handed Robbie two squelchy plastic bags. 'His food bowl is in the scullery.'

'What is this?' Robbie asked peering at the bloody contents of the bags.

'Giblets,' Iona said, attacking a potato with a huge knife.

'Oh, are we having chicken?' Fin asked.

'Aye, Finny Boy. They're in the oven now.'

'Some of your own chickens? I noticed you had lots of cockerels when I let them out this morning.'

'Uch, no,' Iona laughed. 'I got them in the butcher's in Traighgorm this morning. I can't be doing with all that plucking nonsense.'

'Don't you use the giblets for gravy?' Robbie was curious. 'I read in that cookbook you lent me that that's what chefs did.'

'Get away with you, Robbie Boy. That's far too messy and time consuming. I use these gravy granule things. Anyway, it's a chicken casserole, so Laddie can have the giblets. He loves them.'

'What exactly are giblets anyway?' Robbie asked.

'The innards and gizzards and nasty unpalatable bits,' Iona laughed.

Robbie winked at Fin. Fin didn't know why. Laddie was sniffing excitedly at the bags in Robbie's hand.

'This is a horrible conversation,' said Mum. 'It doesn't matter what they are. Go and feed them to that poor dog before he starves.'

'I feel sick just thinking about giblets,' Beth said.

Robbie led Laddie out to the scullery. He emptied the contents of one of the plastic bags into the plastic ice cream container which Iona had recycled as the dog's feeding bowl. He wrapped the other bag of giblets in a plastic carrier bag which was lying on top of the freezer and tied it very tightly to prevent it leaking. 'Aggie can poke about in this and decide which bit is the gizzard,' he thought.

He couldn't believe his luck. Aggie needed a gizzard for Mologan's potion. The trainee Boggarts hadn't even worked out how they were going to bogle such a strange item, in fact they weren't quite sure exactly what gizzards were, and by chance he had the opportunity to bogle one so easily. 'I hope this is what she means,' he thought. 'Perhaps a gizzard is something different in Boggart language. I'll ask Mologan.' Robbie slipped outside and left the bag beside the dustbin so that he could pick it up later. Returning to the scullery, he washed his hands. He patted Laddie. 'I'll give you a treat tomorrow, boy,' and returned to the kitchen.

'Thanks Pet,' said Iona, placing the huge pot of potatoes on the stove. She sipped her wine. 'Remember I told you that I'd found a wee cowrie shell in the garden, Fin?' She sprinkled salt into the pot.

'Yes,' said Fin. 'A rare arctic cowrie.'

'That's right. Well, I went to give some scraps to the hens this afternoon and what do you think was sitting on the fence post next to the hen-house?'

Fin shrugged and his face reddened.

'Just another wee cowrie, Finny Boy. Strange, don't you think? Did you see it when you were feeding the hens this morning?'

'Kinda spooky,' said Beth, glancing at Fin.

'Aye, I've never seen the like of it. I can't think where they're coming from unless that Boggart's up to his tricks.'

Fin felt his face blush even more.

'I'm going to the loo,' he said, getting up.

As Fin washed his hands he scanned the shelf above the wash-basin, reading the labels of all the jars and bottles. 'Coconut oil shampoo for dry unmanageable hair, luxury bubble bath, silky smooth hair conditioner, antiseptic cream for cuts and abrasions, ultra-strong gel for complete hold on oily hair.'

Fin's eyes lingered on the jar of bright orange hair gel. He dried his hands and picked up the jar, examining it carefully. 'Mmm,' he thought, 'This might do for Aggie's potion. It's orange and it's definitely gooey. This might be the nearest we'll get to finding the last item.'

A sudden pang of guilt overcame him. 'No,' he thought, 'it's Calum's hair gel. I can't take it. This is definitely stealing. Bogling dog hair and caterpillars is different. That's not the same as taking something which really belongs to anyone. Stealing from a friend is even worse.'

He put the jar back on the shelf. He paused at the door. 'Perhaps Calum wouldn't mind if I bogled a very small amount. I'm sure he'd give me some if he was here to ask..' Fin bit his lip. 'Maybe, if I leave something...' He shoved his hands into his pockets, drawing out a handful of contents. 'Ah, I'll pay for it! He picked out a fifty pence piece and placed it on the shelf and opened the jar. He scooped up a small quantity of the gooey orange gel with his fingers. Suddenly, his hand still in the jar he stopped dead. He had nothing to put the stuff in. He frantically looked around the bathroom. Nothing. 'Curses. What'll I do now?'

Fin stood in the bathroom, thinking, his hand still in the jar of sticky orange gel, like a bear caught stealing honey. Remembering he had an empty film container in his jacket pocket he quietly opened the door and crept out into the hall where they had dumped their jackets on arrival. He had just pulled the container out of his jacket pocket when the living room door opened and Euan and Dad came into the hall. He shoved the container into his trouser pocket.

'Hullo, Fin. What are you up to?' said Dad.

Fin kept the hand, still stuck in the jar, behind his back. 'Oh, nothing,' he said nonchalantly, then, seeing Dad's puzzled expression said, 'I was getting a, um, tissue from my pocket.'

'Excuse me.' Dad smiled and squeezed past Fin. Handing Fin his whisky glass he said, 'Hold this. I won't be a minute,' and went into the loo. The door closed behind him.

Euan smiled.

Fin smiled awkwardly. He now had no free hands.

'And how are you enjoying your holidays?' said Euan genially. 'I've hardly seen you around the croft this year. Have you been down on the beach?'

'Um, yes, quite a lot,' said Fin, fidgeting with embarrassment. 'We've been playing in the woods mostly, and having picnics and stuff.' Fin felt a guilty sweat break out all over his body. There was a silence, as Euan sipped his whisky.

'How are the sheep, Euan?' Fin asked. 'Lambing go well this year?'

'Aye, not bad. Eighty-nine lambs. We didn't lose many but one or two of then developed a wee bit of lameness. I think the weather was to blame. It was very wet.'

Fin snuffled. His nose felt itchy but he couldn't scratch it. He screwed up his face, wrinkling his nose, trying to alleviate the itch.

'Did you not find your hanky?' Euan asked, thinking Fin was about to sneeze.

'Em, no.' Fin scanned the hall for some uncluttered surface which he could sit the whisky glass. The loo flushed. 'I'll get some toilet tissue instead.' He nodded towards the bathroom door as Dad emerged.

Fin pretended to sneeze as he closed the door behind him.

'I hope you're not catching a cold,' called Euan in a concerned tone.

Safe inside the bathroom, guilty thoughts raced around Fin's head. He leaned against the closed door. This bogling business wasn't as easy as he'd thought. Bogling the hair gel... it made him feel uncomfortable. That kind of bogling was very close to stealing. He had already lied to Dad and Euan to cover up what he was doing. Fin told himself that it was only a white lie, not a real nasty big fat malicious lie, but it had still made him feel extremely guilty. Standing there in the hall with Calum's hair gel hidden behind his back – Calum's stolen hair gel – and Euan being so nice and kind and concerned... Fin cringed with embarrassment. How had he ever got into this? Bogling from his friends – how could he ever make it up to them?

Fin made up his mind to put the hair gel back. He wouldn't bogle it. It would be on his conscience every time he saw Calum or Euan. As he scraped the gel carefully back into the jar Fin thought of a plan. He could buy some hair gel in Clachnacala and get Robbie or Beth, or better still, Mologan to bogle it from him. Maybe it wasn't bogling in the true Boggart sense but technically the orange goo would be bogled. He washed his hands, smiling to himself, pleased that he had resolved the problem without letting Mologan down. Fin checked the price-label on the jar of gel. It said, 'Clachnacala Village Store: £1.25'. Great, he could buy some in the village. He'd get Dad to take him into Clachnacala tomorrow.

Fin felt relieved. He couldn't help smiling to himself as Iona served up his favourite starter.

Another ingredient almost bogled, and prawn cocktail for supper! he thought.

They tucked into a sizzling chicken casserole with a mountain of steamy mashed potatoes followed by home-made apple pie with runny custard and ice cream.

'You'd think I'd been starving you,' said Mum as all three children and Dad tucked into second helpings of pudding.

'Uch, it's the fresh Craigmhor air,' said Iona. 'Anyone for any more? There's another apple pie in the oven. Come on Bobsy Boy, you could manage a wee slice, couldn't you pet?'

⌘

There was a note on Robbie's pillow.

SHORT MEETIN AT MIDNIT
TAE DISKUSS MAC STRATYJEES
USHUL PLASE
URE CHEEFTUN

Beth deciphered Mologan's message. '"Short meeting at midnight to discuss mac-strategies. Usual place. Signed, your chieftain." What a cheek,' she said, 'He's getting a bit above himself. "Your chieftain", indeed!'

'Well, Aggie Hagg-Boggart predicted that he'd become a great chieftain. Mologan's only fulfilling his destiny,' Robbie said.

Fin laughed, 'It's a bit pompous, though. He'll be calling himself Adolf Mac-Boggart next.'

'Or Chairman Mao-logan,' Robbie added. 'I think all this bogling training has gone to his head.'

'He's always had a big head,' said Fin. 'Have you ever noticed how enormous it is?'

Beth nodded. 'And his mouth... he could swallow a sheep sideways!'

'I can just imagine Mologan mentioned in history books,' Fin laughed. 'Mologan, famous Boggart Chieftain of the Western Isles, founder of the fearless guerrilla bogling squad, Mologan's Boggarts, and a picture of him resplendent in his kilt with his balaclava helmet and peep-toed wellies.'

'We shouldn't make fun of Mologan,' said Beth, holding her tummy, which was sore with laughing. 'It's rather cruel. He's so sweet, with his gardening gloves and his snazzy tea-towel neckerchief and his big snotty nose.'

'Be – eth!' Fin reprimanded, then burst into another fit of giggling.

'Well, are we going to meet him?' Robbie checked his watch. 'It's nearly midnight.'

'S'pose so,' Beth groaned. 'I'm exhausted. We'll have to make sure it's a short meeting.'

'I've something to suggest regarding the bogling of the rest of the ingredients,' Fin said.

'And I've got some of the rest of the ingredients,' said Robbie proudly holding up the plastic bag of nasty chicken guts.

Mologan was waiting for them. He had stuck a large feather into his balaclava and was striding up and down the small clearing, theatrically twirling his stick and singing softly to himself. He smiled broadly as the children approached.

'Welcome mac-Boggarts,' he said. 'Did youse bring ony mair scran?'

'You're always thinking of your tummy, Mologan,' Beth said.

Mologan patted his round stomach.

'Sorry, I didn't think you'd be hungry,' Robbie said. 'Did you get the supper we left earlier?'

'Ah liked thon squidgy mac-bannocks.' Mologan licked his lips.

'The pink coconut marshmallow biscuits?'

Mologan nodded.

'I'll leave some more of them tomorrow, but look at this, Mologan.' Robbie handed the plastic bag to the Boggart. 'Gizzard... and other assorted em, squelchy things. I thought that Aggie could sort it out herself. Is it the right thing? Part of a chicken's intestines?'

Mologan took the bag from Robbie and sniffed it. He patted Robbie on the back. 'Weel done Mac-Robbie. It's the very mac-thing. Gizzards, right enough! Is there onythin' else oan the mac-list tae be bogl't?' He searched his sporran for the grotty parchment.

'Actually, Mologan...' Fin began. 'There is a bit of a problem.' He fidgeted, and picked distractedly at a piece of lichen which was growing on the tree branch which he had climbed on to.

Mologan, Beth and Robbie looked at Fin quizzically.

'It's this bogling,' he began, still picking at the lichen, 'I don't mind bogling sting winkles or greenichy kail worms or some red wine that someone won't want because slugs have crawled into it, but...' he paused and swallowed hard. It was difficult to explain how he felt. He didn't want to hurt Mologan's feelings. After all, bogling was the Boggart's profession and his life's work. 'But, I tried to bogle some orange goo earlier tonight. It was really Calum's hair gel. I almost had it bogled. I was about to put it into a container... but I couldn't. I felt that I was stealing. Sorry, Mologan. I couldn't take the orange goo.'

Mologan snorted. 'Uch, boglin's no the mac-same as stealin', Fin Mac-visitor. Ah tell't ye when ye were doin' yer mac-trainin' that ye always leave somethin' when ye bogle. It's mac-different.'

'It's maybe OK for a Boggart,' said Fin, 'but we humans can't do some kinds of bogling, 'specially not from friends. It doesn't seem right to take something that belongs to someone else without asking.'

'Are ye sayin' that it's wrang tae bogle, Fin Mac-visitor?'

'Well, sort of. I think some kinds of bogling are OK and some aren't.'

'But it's ma profession, ma mac-instinct tae bogle.' Mologan was exasperated and confused. 'An' Ah always leave somethin'!'

'But that doesn't make it right, Mologan,' Beth said, continuing Fin's point. 'You might leave something that the bogled person doesn't want.'

'Like mac-what?'

'Well, a slug or a bit of slime,' Beth suggested.

'Dae ye think that's no' enough?' Mologan was puzzled.

'That's not the point,' Fin said. 'Why would a human need a worm or a bogie on their pillow?'

The Boggart rubbed his big nose thoughtfully.

'Ah didnae ken that folk didnae like what Ah macleft,' he said, hurt. 'Whit dae youse think Ah should leave?'

'If you didn't bogle directly from people you wouldn't have to leave anything, I suppose,' Beth reasoned.

Mologan gulped. A tear trickled down his face. 'Apart from the fact that it's ma profession tae bogle an' that's whit Boggarts dae,' he sniffed, 'how are we tae get the ingredients for Aggie's mac-mixture if youse decide no' tae bogle ony mair?'

'You might have to finish bogling the ingredients yourself, Mologan,' Fin said.

Mologan snorted and wiped his running nose with his sleeve. 'Youse ken Ah cannae, sniff, on account o'... the green-ness!'

'You did a bit of bogling last night, Mologan,' Robbie said. 'When I was trying to bogle the rubber gloves you came and helped me.'

The Boggart scratched his tuft of wiry hair. 'Aye, so Ah mac-did, but only because Ah ken't it was macsafe.'

'Look, said Fin, 'I'm sorry I started all this. I don't want to stop Mologan getting all the mac-gredients. I have a suggestion.'

Beth, Robbie and Mologan looked at Fin with anticipation.

'Well, now Robbie's got the gizzard, apart from the lobster we've only got to get the orange goo. I thought that I'd buy some in Clachnacala, and Mologan, or another trainee Boggart, could bogle it from me.'

Mologan looked doubtful. 'That's stretchin' the rools a wee bittie, Fin Mac-visitor. An' onyways, whit would we leave ye since youse mac-humans dinnae like ma normal mac-gifts?'

'But I'm a Mologan's Boggart,' Fin patted Mologan's hump cheerily, 'I'd be quite happy with a dead spider or a couple of maggots.'

'Have a look at the list, Mologan,' Beth said, still avoiding touching it herself. 'Check we've got everything else Aggie needs.'

Mologan peered at the filthy and almost indecipherable parchment. He read slowly, 'Ten puggie nits, nine sting winkles, hair o' a birsie dug.'

'Got all these,' Robbie said.

'Three greenichy kail wurums, five yella fingers, fower roosty caddles,' Mologan continued. 'Aye, rid biddie, wan goose yowk, seeven grossets an' a gizzard or a wee shoo orange goo. There!'

'Does it say "or a wee shoo orange goo", Mologan?' Robbie took the parchment from Mologan's hand, forgetting that it was covered in dried snot and slug slime and other unmentionable things. 'Yes, look Beth.'

Beth recoiled.

'It says gizzard *or* orange goo, so we only have to get one or the other. We needn't bother with the hair gel.' Robbie handed the parchment back to Mologan. 'That means we've got everything on the list.'

Fin cheered up. He slid down off the branch and stamped his feet to get the circulation back.

'Except the mac-lobstur,' said Mologan, stuffing the parchment into his sporran. 'Will youse help tae bogle Horace back for Aggie? Ah've worked oot a special mac-plan an' it needs the whole mac-team tae succeed.'

'Well, technically we'll be taking back something that's been stolen from Aggie. I don't have a problem helping to bogle back the lobster,' said Beth. 'What do you think, Robbie?'

'I suppose we ought to help Mologan finish the job, we're so nearly there now. I don't mind going.'

Fin shrugged. 'OK. We'll not exactly be stealing from Roary Borealis. I'll come.'

Mologan sighed sadly.

'I thought you'd be pleased, Mologan,' Fin said.

'Ye ken whit ye wis sayin', Fin Mac-visitor, aboot stealin' an' boglin'? It makes me unco sad,' the Boggart sniffed.

'Why, Mologan?'

'Uch, Ah thought Ah wis daein' a grand job an' providin' a mac-valuable service tae the community.'

The children exchanged glances, each feeling rather sorry that Fin had ever mentioned his doubts about bogling to Mologan in the first place.

Mologan continued, 'Are youse sayin' that fowk dinnae like bein' bogled?'

'Well, I suppose so.' Fin kicked at the grass distractedly. 'Mum was very annoyed when you bogled her specs.'

'Mmm,' Mologan scratched his ear. 'An that they dinnae mac-like aw the stuff Ah leave in return?'

'Um... no, not really.'

'Ah'm mac-devastated.' Mologan sat down with a soft squelch on a mossy rock and put his head in his hands.

The children didn't know what to say. Each one of them felt uneasy and very guilty that they had unwittingly undermined the Boggart's confidence in his ancient profession and destroyed his purpose in life. Mologan grunted loudly and tearfully.

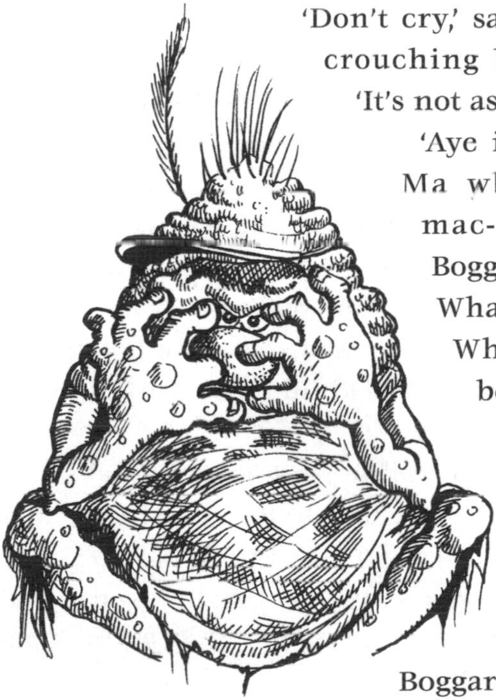

'Don't cry,' said Robbie, softly, crouching beside Mologan. 'It's not as bad as it seems.'

'Aye it is, Mac-Robbie. Ma whole life's been mac-wasted,' the Boggart snorted sadly. What'll Ah dae noo? What's the point o' bein' a Boggart?'

'But you do all sorts of other good things, Mologan,' said Robbie, gently patting the Boggart's hump.

'Like what, fur mac-zample?'

'Well, um, er.' He looked desperately at Beth and Fin for help.

'Like collecting clamjamphrie,' Fin volunteered.

'Yes, just think what a mess this croft would be in if you didn't pick up all the rubbish,' Robbie added.

'And the beach,' Beth continued, 'Look how clean and tidy it is. You're so eco-friendly, Mologan, you don't take anything unsustainable from the environment. You don't destroy or damage anything, in fact you add to it!'

Mologan scratched his head. 'Un-mac-sustainable?' he mouthed quietly to himself, puzzled.

The boys nodded their heads rather theatrically in agreement, smiling encouragingly at Mologan. The Boggart perked up, straightened his shoulders and wiped green snot from his large damp nose with the back of his hand.

Warming to the positive theme, Robbie carried on. 'You recycle things all the time. Food from the bins, things people throw away, any old junk. And you eat all the nasty pests. The snails from the kitchen garden, slugs from the tattie field, and the caterpillars off the cabbages.'

'And maggots and warble flies, and the ticks you pick off the sheep,' Beth added, 'that must be a real relief to them'

Mologan was cheering up. 'A Boggart must dae nae harm tae man nor beastie. It's part o' the boglin' mac-rools,' he said proudly.

'And,' Fin said excitedly, poking Mologan's chest, 'You protect the croft. You've taken care of Craigmhor for centuries.'

Robbie and Beth looked at him curiously.

'You know, looking after all the plants and animals. And nobody would dare to come here and break in or steal things at night when there's a big, scary Boggart creeping about, rattling windows and being um...'

'...fierce and assertive.' said Robbie, thinking quickly.

'Fierce and mac-certive?' Mologan drew himself up to his full height.

'And mac-scary' said Fin.

'Mac-fierce, like an ancient warrior?'

'Yes, a kind of eco-warrior,' said Beth, grinning. She winked at Fin and Robbie.

Mologan stood up and straightened his kilt. 'What's an eco-mac-warrior?'

'It's a sort of mac-champion of the environment. They look after the planet and stuff,' Fin said, creatively.

'A mac-champion? A mac-champion o' the planet?' Mologan always liked the idea of being a champion... of anything!

'Oh, yes,' Fin continued, 'it's an important job. If there are lots of eco-warriors taking care of lots of wee places like Craigmhor and making sure they're tidy and unpolluted, and the wildlife is protected, then the planet is in good hands.'

Mologan looked up through the trees. Stars twinkled in the clear sky.

'Aye, it's mac-portant... the planet,' he mumbled thoughtfully to himself. Mologan's Boggarts stood in silence for a few minutes contemplating the beauty of the universe.

'Jist wan question though, young Mac-visitor. What does an eco-mac-warrior wear? Does he have mac-special clothes or a shiny mac-helmet?'

'In your case, Mologan, a knobbly green woollen balaclava helmet!' Fin laughed.

CHAPTER 14

Roary Borealis

The tide was out when four shadowy figures crossed the tidal sound to Eilean Bodach. They climbed silently through the thick heather and bog myrtle to the cairn at the the highest point of the island, resting there while Mologan reminded them of his 'sleekit' plan to bogle Aggie Hagg-Boggart's prize lobster back from Roary Borealis.

'Noo, we mustn't make a move until Roary has gone oot boglin', an' wance we're in the cave we'll hae tae grab Horace an' get oot as fast as we can.'

Mologan's Boggarts nodded.

'An' remember,' Mologan continued, 'Roary has won aw the smellin' contests at the Boglin' Compie-mac-tishun these past three-hunner years. He's got a gruntle like a grumphie, that Boggart. He could probably smell us already if we werenae downwind o' his cave.'

Beth didn't know what a gruntle or a grumphie were, but this information didn't fill her with confidence in the mission.

'An',' Mologan added, 'although he cannae stand the daylight he can see like a houlet in the daurk, so we'll have tae be very mac-carefu'. Ony questions, mac-Boggarts?'

'What's a houlet?' Fin whispered.

Mologan tutted, shocked at Fin's ignorance. 'Wan o' yon burds that flies at night an' eats mice an' stuff,' he hissed.

'Oh, an owl?'

'Aye.' Mologan scowled at Fin and shook his head. 'Are youse mac-ready noo?'

The children nodded silently. Beth, Robbie and Fin were secretly wishing that they hadn't got involved in this and they were safely tucked up in bed, asleep, and having a normal holiday.

'Let's go then, mac-Boggarts!' Mologan whispered, sliding down the hill on his bottom. The children reluctantly followed, trying to put into practice all the Boggart skills they had learned. They would need them tonight.

They lay on their tummies on top of the cliff overlooking Red Bay. Checking that they were downwind of the evil Boggart's cave, Mologan took off one of his gardening gloves, licked a long luminous finger and held it aloft like a beacon. He took a few deep sniffs and stuck out his blue tongue.

'Guid, we're jist mac-fine,' he whispered. 'See yon standin' stane?'

The children nodded.

'Keep an eye oan that. It's Roary's front mac-door.'

They lay in the jaggy, springy heather for some time. It grew darker. A spider crawled over Fin's hair. Mologan noticed it, carefully picked it off and slipped it into his sporran, adding to the collection of grubs, slugs and caterpillars he had collected during the walk to the island.

'Look,' Mologan whispered suddenly.

They all squinted into the darkness. A bulky, hunched figure had emerged beside the standing stone and was silently moving towards the other side of the bay. The silhouetted Boggart disappeared behind some jagged rocks.

'He's leavin',' Mologan hissed. 'Boggarts, advance!' He led them down the steep path onto the machair.

Mologan was sniffing the air constantly, and beckoning them reassuringly with a gloved hand. His luminous ears glowed dangerously in the dark. Every time Beth caught sight of Mologan's glowing ears she couldn't help smiling. They looked so ridiculous. She smiled even though her tummy seemed to be full of butterflies and her heart was pounding.

Mologan's Boggarts reached the standing stone. Mologan looked around, his eyes darting from rock to rock. He sniffed deeply and disappeared behind the huge granite slab. Robbie, Beth and Fin followed him and found themselves in the entrance to a dark, steep tunnel. Rough steps were hewn in the rock and the walls were damp and slimy. Robbie flicked on his torch, illuminating the high vaulted tunnel. Stalactites dripped water onto their heads, strange white toadstools grew in cracks and crevices and pale creepy-crawlies like giant centipedes scuttled out of their way as they progressed downwards, deeper and deeper into the earth. As the steps became damper and slimier, Mologan moved more slowly for the benefit of his trainees, who were not yet adept at moving quickly along dark, slippery tunnels.

Suddenly the children became aware of a strange, pungent smell. It was rather like the smell in Mologan's cave, which they had become quite used to, but this smell was richer, more acrid, more like smelly feet and rotting fish. As they continued along the passage the smell became stronger, like putrid boiled cabbage, rotting seaweed and fishy dog poo all mixed together. Beth gagged. She pulled her polo-neck over her mouth and nose to filter the smell.

Robbie held his nose. 'It's like the smell of rotting meat,' he whispered, as they stopped at a junction.

Mologan sniffed, and pointed to the left. Beth gagged again.

'Shoosh,' Mologan hissed.

They passed a few caves which were piled with heaps of decaying and rusty clamjamphrie, then, turning a sharp corner, they entered a huge dimly-lit cavern.

The children shone their torches around, forgetting the dreadful stench in the horror of what they now saw. The cave walls were hung with gory trophies of Roary Borealis's nasty form of bogling. Their torch beams illuminated piles of discarded bones scattered around the cave floor. Skulls and horns of dead animals were lined up on rock shelves and suspended from the cave walls. Some skulls, which still had rotting fur and flesh on them, were impaled onto the jagged tops of stalagmites. They could make out a sheep's head, a small furry head that looked like an otter, a seal's skull and a decomposing rabbit's head with maggots squirming out of the eye-sockets.

Beth was sure she was going to throw up. Robbie, Fin and Mologan stared silently at this scene of carnage and cruelty, horrified by what they had discovered.

The cavern floor was greasy and slippery and strewn with a squalid array of animal teeth, half-gnawed bones and rancid bits of entrails. They had to walk carefully to avoid slipping and falling onto the filthy, bloodstained surface.

'That Boggart should be called Gory Borealis,' Fin said, trying to lighten the situation.

They shone their torches in a different direction. A mountain of shells was piled up in a corner, mixed up with gnawed bones and fish-heads. The usual Boggart clamjamphrie lay strewn around: fishing buoys, nets, fish boxes, driftwood, plastic bottles.

Mologan was rummaging about in a pile of junk. 'Look at this,' he said, holding up a rotten lump of seaweed-covered, worm-eaten wood. 'Nae class!' He picked up a red plastic box from the top of the heap. 'Whit's this?' he said, prising off the lid.

'It's our fishing box,' exclaimed Fin. He took it from Mologan and examined it. 'It's the one that went missing from the canoe!'

'Your mac-box?' Mologan seemed puzzled. He scratched his ear. 'Are ye mac-sure?'

'Of course, it's Dad's old sandwich box. I'd recognise it anywhere. Look, all our fishing stuff's inside.'

Mologan's eyes narrowed and he grimaced, showing his fangs. 'Of all the mac-cheatin' mac-sneaky...' he growled. 'That nasty mac-scoundrel has bin boglin' ma patch. Ah've got the ancient boglin' rights tae...'

Beth squeezed Mologan's arm. 'Mologan, stop, please. This is so horrible. I can't bear to be here another minute more than necessary. Can we please find the lobster and go?'

Just then, Robbie whispered loudly, 'Over here. I've found the lobsters.'

Robbie was kneeling beside a large rock pool. He shone his torch across the dark water. In the centre of the pool a pinnacle of dark, slimy rock stuck out of the water. On top of this thin, jagged island sat a peculiar golden object cast in the shape of a lobster-creel balanced on the upturned claws of an upright, outsized golden lobster. Glinting in the light of Robbie's torch beam it reflected the light back into his eyes.

'Wow', he said, shielding his eyes from the glare, 'What's that?'

Mologan peered across the water. 'It's the Golden Creel trophy. Roary Borealis's pride and joy. He wins it every time fur his green lobsturs at the Boglin' Compie-mac-tishun,' he said in a hushed, awestruck voice.

'Never mind that, look in the pool, Mologan,' Robbie said.

There were five green lobsters in the pool basking under the surface of the water, gently blowing bubbles.

'They're beautiful,' said Fin, admiring their mottled, emerald green shells speckled with turquoise blue spots. 'Which one do you think is Horace?'

The lobsters seemed to wake up. They wiggled their antennae around in an agitated manner and blew bigger, noisier bubbles. They snapped their claws, staring maliciously at Mologan and the children.

Beth zipped her cagoule right up over her nose. 'Please hurry,' she said. 'I feel very sick.'

'Ah dinnae ken which wan is Horace,' said Mologan. 'Which wan dae youse think is the maist braw?'

'Mmm,' said Fin thoughtfully, 'I think that small one on the right is quite good looking.'

'Aye, but Aggie's Horace is a fair size. Mibby that wan in the mac-middle?'

'Hurry up. Please hurry.' Beth pleaded.

'But how can we tell which is Horace? It would be a complete waste of time if we took the wrong lobster back to Aggie,' Robbie said.

'Call his name then. Try calling his name,' Beth snapped impatiently.

Mologan crouched down beside the pool and called in a soft gurgly voice, 'Horace, Horace.' He leered into the water. 'Horace, it's yer uncle Mologan come tae take ye hame.'

The biggest lobster pushed its way to the edge of the pool and looked at Mologan, head tilted to one side.

'Are you Horace, then?' Mologan whispered.

The lobster raised its claws out of the water and snapped them noisily.

'That's him. Grab him, Fin,' Robbie said excitedly.

'Are you sure it's him?' said Fin, rolling up his sleeve.

The lobster came closer, blowing bubbles.

'Aye, look, he's mac-smilin'. He knows his Uncle Mologan,' Mologan grinned.

None of the children could see anything which resembled a smile on the lobster's strange face. If he did have any expression at all it was angry and aggressive.

Fin knelt down at the edge of the pool and plunged his hand into the water. Immediately he recoiled. 'Ouch, he nipped me!' Fin sucked his finger.

'Grab its back, like this,' Robbie demonstrated by lifting the lobster out of the water. It wriggled and snapped ferociously. The other lobsters thrashed about in the pool angrily, splashing and gurgling. Horace writhed and wriggled in Robbie's hand, trying to bend backwards and nip him with his monstrous green claws.

'We need to tie his claws,' said Beth, forgetting how she was feeling for a moment. She looked around for something suitable.

Fin delved into his pocket and soon found a couple of elastic bands. 'I knew they'd come in handy,' he said, as he deftly snapped them onto Horace's claws with help from Beth. Robbie popped the irate creature into Mologan's bogling bag.

Fin picked up the plastic fishing box and stuffed it into his rucksack. Bending to pick up the rucksack he slipped on a piece of decomposing fish gut. Struggling to keep his balance he landed on his bottom on the grimy floor and his foot slid into the rock pool. The four remaining lobsters splashed towards him agressively snapping their claws. Fin pulled his foot out of the water just in time to escape being nipped by the belligerent green creatures. The smallest lobster made a last lunge at Fin's trailing boot lace and grabbed it tightly. The lobster was dragged out of the dark water as Fin backed off. He stood up and began to move away but the creature hung on tenaciously.

'Get off!' Fin shook his foot crossly and continued to move backwards. The lobster clung on tightly. 'Let go. We don't want to take you back with us as well. Help, someone! Get this creature to let go.' He hopped up and down with the lobster dangling from his boot.

Beth and Robbie couldn't help laughing but Mologan stepped forward and tapped the lobster sharply on its upturned tail with a flick of his finger nail. The creature was so surprised that it turned round and let go of the lace. The lobster stared at Mologan and the children for a second, glowered nastily then scuttled back to the safety of the pool.

'Let's get out of here now,' said Robbie, leading the bogling team towards the passage.

Robbie, Fin, Beth and Mologan had not gone far and were turning into the entrance of the long steep tunnel that led to the door under the standing stone when they heard the ominous sound of loud, echoing footsteps. They switched off their torches and froze. Hearts thumping, they pressed themselves against the damp, fungus-encrusted, drippy wall. They heard a deep booming voice reverberating down the tunnel. The rocks they were leaning against vibrated with the sound. Roary Borealis was stomping down the passage towards them. He was singing, in a deafening roar, a rather nasty, rowdy bogling song. Snatches of the words rung in their ears.

...seals an' dolphins, otters' wains,
Bring them hame an' suck their brains...

The ear-splitting singing was becoming louder. The bogling team stuffed their fingers into their ears, turned and stumbled back along the tunnel. Roary Borealis suddenly stopped singing and sniffed the air with his huge pig-like snout.

'WHA'S THERE?' he roared.

The roar created a strong gust of air which hit the intruders like a massive smelly whirlwind, almost knocking them over. Before they had a chance to recover, Roary Borealis was towering over them, filling the passageway with his enormous bulky body, his small eyes glinting maliciously in the dark. The massive Boggart breathed in and appeared to swell to an even greater size.

'BRIGANDS AN' MAC-PIRATES!' he bellowed, his foul breath flattening the children against the wall and almost deafening them in the process. Roary Borealis roared again, like a gigantic lion, and dropped his blood-stained bogling bag on the ground. The bag squirmed around as if there were something live inside. The Boggart brandished his knobbly, thorny stick and kicked the bag aside.

In the darkness the children couldn't see what Roary Borealis looked like. He was a monstrous, burly, stick-brandishing silhouette, oozing a disgusting and sickening smell. He moved towards them, poking them with his stick. They had no option but to retrace their steps back to the cavern. The Boggart roared a few times to push them down the tunnel.

When they reached the cavern, Roary Borealis herded the children into a corner and onto the mound of discarded shells. Their hearts throbbing with fear, they scrambled up the slope of loose and shifting shells and fish bones, trying to move away as far as they could from the angry Boggart. The mound kept slipping and moving beneath their feet, preventing them from making progress and forcing them at last to sit down, wrist-deep in crab claws, fish heads and gnawed bones. Roary Borealis stared at them closely, making their flesh creep, his foul, stinking breath enveloping them in a sickening fog. He laughed, showing a gigantic mouthful of broken yellow fangs, then suddenly backed off and began to pace around the cave, sniffing and snorting. It was only then that the trembling, terrified trainee Boggarts noticed that Mologan was not with them.

Roary Borealis picked up an untidy, knotted length of baling twine. He licked his thin blue lips and screwed up his eyes menacingly. His enormous chin jutted upwards, almost touching his snout. Yellow saliva dribbled from his fangs and trickled down his massive jowls. His loud snorts echoed around the cave. Making his way towards Fin, Beth and Robbie, he roared again, flattening them against the shell mound. He began to wind the baling twine around all three of them. The children struggled but the Boggart was too strong for them to resist. The smell from his oxters was unbelievable. They had never smelled anything so bad. Robbie thought he was going to pass out, asphyxiated.

Roary Borealis tied strong complicated knots in the baling twine, all the time whispering hoarsely to himself, 'What'll Ah dae wi' ye noo? What'll Ah dae wi' ye noo? Cut youse up intae wee sma' pieces. Sma' wee tasty pieces. Feed youse tae ma lobsturs. Dinner fur ma

lobsturs.' Having used up all the baling twine he stood back and stared at the children. He laughed evilly.

'NOO, WHAT ARE YOUSE MAC-VISITOR WAINS BOGLIN' FRAE ROARY BOREALIS'S CAVE?'

Unable to cover their ears the children winced in pain. They said nothing.

'AH KEN,' he bellowed, 'YOUSE ARE EFTER MA MAC-TROPHY. YOUSE ARE BOGLIN' THE GOLDEN CREEL!' Roary Borealis turned and strode towards the rock pool. The children heard him sigh a thunderous sigh of relief when he saw the trophy was still safe.

The monstrous Boggart bent down beside the rock pool and said in a surprisingly soft voice, 'An' how are my wee lobstery-wobsterys then? Were youse mac-frightened by these nasty mac-pirates?'

The lobsters gurgled and snapped in the water.

'Roary Borealis thought they had bogle't oor Golden Creel, but youse widnae let them near it, wid youse?' The Boggart stroked one of the lobsters' heads fondly and smiled a sickening, dribbly smile.

Fin caught Beth's eye and they smiled despite their dreadful situation. Perhaps Roary Borealis had a soft side to his personality. Robbie was trying to undo a knot behind his back. Fin and Beth squeezed up closer to slacken the twine.

Relieved that his golden trophy was still safely on its pinnacle in the middle of the pool, Roary Borealis continued to talk contentedly to his pet lobsters.

'Thon brigands couldnae get past youse tae bogle the trophy, ye snappy wee divils. Whaur's big Horace?'

He splashed his huge thick fingers delicately at the edge of the pool. 'Come oan, Horace Boy, come an' see Daddy.' The Boggart glowered into the water. 'Whaur are ye, Horace?'

Silence.

'Wan, twa, three, fower.' Roary Borealis counted the lobsters, pointing at each one in turn. 'FOWER!' he roared, 'WHAUR'S HORACE?'

Clumsily getting to his feet the Boggart turned angrily towards the children.

'WHAUR'S HORACE?'

Beth, Robbie and Fin recoiled from the ear-splitting roar. As the Boggart's question reverberated in the echoing cavern there was a loud metallic crashing sound behind him. He swung round. Another crash, like bottles smashing. Roary Borealis lumbered into the passage to investigate.

Silence.

'AARGH!' A huge roar. BANG, CRASH... Another deafening roar.

Suddenly Mologan appeared in the cavern. The children sighed with relief as the luminous green eco-warrior Boggart Chieftain moved swiftly towards them. He looked mournfully at the knotted twine.

'There's a knife in my pocket, Mologan,' said Robbie. 'Boy, we're glad to see you.'

Mologan dumped his bogling bag on the ground and slipped off his gardening gloves. He managed with difficulty to push his enormous hand into Robbie's jacket pocket, which ripped completely on one side as the Boggart pulled out the pen-knife. Mologan quickly cut through the baling twine.

'Where's Roary?' Fin asked, as they struggled to free themselves from the tangle of twine.

'Ah mac-wrapped him in a fushin' net,' said Mologan, grinning. 'We'll have tae mac-hurry.'

As the children freed themselves from the last fragments of the twine, another loud roar came from the tunnel. Suddenly Roary Borealis appeared in the cavern, draped in a tangled and torn fishing net, trailing a confused mass of fishing buoys and an old anchor. They were cornered. The irate Boggart was blocking their only means of escape.

CHAPTER 15

The Conger Eel with the Bonny Name

Beth's heart sank. She stepped back and leaned against a stalactite. She felt the torch in her pocket clunk against the rock. A thought flashed through her head. Mologan's briefing before the mission: 'He cannae staun' daylight.' Quickly she pulled out the torch and shone the beam directly into Roary Borealis's eyes.

The Boggart roared in annoyance, trying to lift his massive hands to cover his eyes, but he was hampered by the tangled net. Closing his eyes he fell to his knees, bellowing and howling angrily.

Fin and Robbie clicked on their torches and illuminated the Boggart.

'NAW, BAUD LIGHT, BAUD LIGHT,' Roary Borealis cried, trying to put his hands over his monstrous head which now rested on the cave floor, his great bulk blocking the entrance to the tunnel.

'Skedaddle!' Mologan called. He was already running towards a small passageway behind the lobster pool. Beth, Robbie and Fin were behind him in a flash, jogging along a narrow tunnel with a sandy floor. The walls were covered in shiny white molluscs.

'Ah think we're under the sea,' Mologan panted, as they stopped at a junction.

'Which way?' Robbie asked, breathlessly.

'East,' said Beth, 'Towards the land.'

Fin quickly pulled out his pocket compass, scattering coins on the ground. 'That way.' He pointed to the tunnel on the right. He bent to pick up the coins which had fallen out of his pocket.

A low, echoing roar reverberated up the tunnel.

'Nae time fur that.' Mologan pulled Fin to his feet by his rucksack straps. 'Come oan!'

The tunnel was now damp and rocky underfoot. Water dripped from the walls and patches of slime made running too dangerous. They slowed down. The passage became smaller and narrower. They could feel and smell the breath of the furious Boggart pursuing them like a stinking tornado.

'Mac-faster!' shouted Mologan, who was bringing up the rear as they slithered and slipped in the darkness.

Mologan tripped over a low step, stubbing his toe. The sole of his peep-toed trainer caught under a rock and pulled off. Barely pausing, he cursed loudly and ran on in one wellie and a wet sock.

Roary Borealis, catching up fast, tripped over the discarded trainer and fell flat on his gruntle face. This made him even madder and angrier and he puffed himself up to bellow. Just at this point the tunnel became narrower. With a squelchy scrunch the Boggart became wedged between two enormous rocks and couldn't budge. The more he breathed in to roar, the more tightly he was jammed.

Breathlessly, Mologan's Boggarts ran along the tunnel, putting more distance between themselves and Roary Borealis.

'Keep mac-movin', Mologan encouraged. 'We're no oot yet.'

The tunnel suddenly changed direction and they were moving downhill, slipping and sliding on a wet muddy floor.

'I'll have to stop,' said Fin. 'I've got a stitch.'

Mologan grasped his arm. 'Nae time. Come oan.'

But Beth had also stopped. 'Just stop for a second, Mologan,' she wheezed. 'Let's get our breath back.'

'This torch battery is getting low,' called Robbie, who was in front of the others. 'I can't see clearly what's ahead.'

Mologan squeezed passed them in the narrow passage treading clumsily on their feet and pressing them against the jaggy rock wall. 'Ah'll lead then. Youse can follow ma ears. Are youse mac-ready noo?'

'Shoosh,' said Beth. 'What's that noise?'

They all listened intently.

'Is it Roary? Has he managed to squeeze through the tight gap?' Fin whispered.

'No, it's in front of us,' Robbie said.

Mologan sniffed the air deeply and wiggled his green ears.

They heard a distinct splashing and gurgling sound.

Beth shone her torch ahead of them, illuminating the tunnel and throwing a huge shadow of Mologan onto the low ceiling. They all followed Mologan, creeping slowly and silently along the passage. Suddenly Mologan stopped and they all bumped into each other's backs.

'Ouch!'

'Ow!'

'Mologan!'

'Shoosh! Gie's the mac-torch.'

Beth passed the torch to Robbie who handed it to Mologan.

'Mouldy-mac-maggots! Jist as weel we stopped runnin'. Look.' Mologan pointed the torch beam ahead. The floor of the tunnel came to an abrupt end only a metre away and a murky pool of water blocked their way.

'Gosh, lucky we didn't fall into that,' Beth exclaimed.

They all stood at the edge of the black water.

'How deep is it?' Fin asked. 'Poke your stick into it, Mologan.'

As he spoke the water rippled. A second later the surface broke and a huge brown snake-like head with a gaping jaw and razor-sharp teeth rose out of the water, eyes glinting in the torch light.

Mologan, Fin, Beth and Robbie stepped backwards, gasping in fright.

The creature reared its head further out of the water, gurgling loudly and snapping its ferocious jaws.

'What's that, Mologan?' Robbie croaked, his throat tight with apprehension.

'It's the biggest conger eel Ah've ever mac-seen.' Mologan moved nearer and stared at the creature. 'Ah did hear that Roary Borealis was gey fond o' these craiturs an' had bin feedin' wan up fur the "fiercest beastie" compie-mac-tishun. Ah think he called it a right bonny name like Debbie or Elvera or somethin'. Mibby this is it.'

The eel swam to the edge of the pool. Thrashing its tail it stared back at him. Its brown mottled body was as thick as a drainpipe and the creature appeared to be about three metres long. It raised up its head like a dragon and made a lunge at the bogling team.

'Wow, it's ferocious,' said Fin unnecessarily.

'An' gey cunnin',' Mologan whispered. 'Keep yer een oan it.'

'I read somewhere about a conger eel that lived under a pier and it grew to about three metres long and lived for about a hundred years,' said Robbie. 'Fishermen tried to catch it and never succeeded. They said it was too clever, and its jaws were so powerful it even bit through an iron chain.'

'Thanks for that helpful information, Robbie,' Beth retorted.

The conger eel slipped slowly and quietly beneath the surface, leaving only faint ripples.

'Is there any way across or do we have to turn back?' Fin asked, staring nervously into the darkness behind him.

'Haud yer mac-panic. Dinnae git yer plaid in a fankle. Let's look see.' Mologan peered across the pool.

They could hear loud, heavy breathing behind them, punctuated by the grunts, groans and curses of the trapped Boggart.

'I can see the other side. It's only about two metres across,' said Beth, shining her torch over the dark water.

'Only two metres?' Robbie sighed. 'Can't we squeeze around the edge?'

'No, the water stretches right across, right up to the walls.' Fin's torch beam investigated the edges of the pool.

They heard a loud rumble behind them like a rock-fall and some loud cursing.

'Can we jump?' Robbie asked desperately.

'Dinnae be mac-daft,' Mologan growled. He peered into the water. 'Look, jist there.' He pointed with his stick. 'Stanes. Mac-steppin' stanes.'

They could make out three black slimy stones with flat tops sticking out of the water only millimetres above the surface. They moved closer to examine them.

Suddenly the conger eel surfaced noisily. They jumped back in fright.

Shocked, Robbie dropped his torch onto the ground and it rolled into the water before he could retrieve it. The eel made a quick lunge for it and grabbed it in its great jaws. It crunched up the torch in a frenzy of munching and gnawing, chewing easily through the mangled metal and swallowing the batteries whole.

'That was a heavy-duty torch,' Robbie said, stunned. 'And it's swallowed the batteries!'

'Perhaps it's an electric eel,' Beth said.

'Won't do her any good then,' Fin laughed. 'The batteries were flat.'

They heard another rumble of falling rocks behind them and a great blast of stinking air roared down the tunnel.

'I think Roary's moving again.' Robbie gasped. 'Let's get going. We'll have to cross the stepping stones.'

'If we fall in the pool this eel will strip our bones as quick as a piranha.' Fin shivered.

Mologan was already poised on the nearest stone, his arms outstretched to help him balance. He stepped cautiously onto the second stone, slipped and just managed to steady himself as the conger eel appeared and snapped at his foot. He pushed the eel's head back with his bogling stick. This antagonised the creature and it raised itself out of the water, grabbed the stick and bit a large chunk off the end. It then thrashed around angrily chewing it into match-wood. Mologan jumped to the safety of the far side of the pool.

'Quick, whiles the beastie is distracted,' he called to Beth, stretching out what was left of his bogling stick for her to grasp.

Beth was balanced precariously on the second stone when the eel approached again, eyeing her feet hungrily. Her heart was thumping and she felt as if she were suddenly frozen to the spot.

'Jump, Mac-Beth!' Mologan urged. 'Jump! Ah'll catch ye.'

Beth did not dare to move. The evil-looking conger bared its razor-sharp teeth and looked her in the eye.

'Distract it, someone. Feed it something else before it eats my legs,' Beth croaked. 'Quick. Throw something in the water.'

Fin was just about to throw his torch into the pool but hesitated, realising that it was too important to lose when Robbie called, 'Mologan, the creepie-crawlies and slugs.'

Mologan looked quizzically at Robbie. The eel snapped its jaw very close to Beth's right leg. She pulled it out of the way quickly, steadying herself with the chewed end of Mologan's stick. But her left foot was sliding backwards into the dark water.

'You know. In your sporran!' Robbie shouted.

Quick as a flash, Mologan understood, and thrust his hand into his battered sporran, grabbing a fistful of the wriggling grubs and insects he had been collecting on their journey to the island. He tossed them into the air and they landed with a series of small splashes all over the surface of the pool.

Immediately distracted, the conger eel turned towards its free meal and began to devour the slugs and grubs in a frenzy of snapping and splashing.

Beth's foot slipped into the water but Mologan tugged the bogling stick with such a force that she managed to regain her balance and propel herself forward, barely touching the third stone and landing safely on all fours at Mologan's feet.

'Right, Mac-Robbie,' Mologan called, pulling another handful of creepy-crawlies from his sporran. 'Jump, noo!' He threw them as far across the pool as he could. The eel began another frenzy of excited gobbling.

Suddenly there was a loud rumbling noise behind them and a gust of foul smelling air blew along the tunnel. Robbie took a deep breath and stepped carefully across the stepping stones, grasping Mologan's outstretched hand gratefully as he reached the other side.

They could now hear Roary Borealis thundering down the tunnel towards them, cursing and roaring.

'Quick, Fin,' Beth shouted.

Mologan cast another maggoty snack into the pool.

A tornado of fetid breath blasted towards them, knocking Fin over as he approached the water. He fell to his knees at the edge of the pool, his hands slipping into the water. The eel turned towards him, sensing the sudden availability of a bigger meal. Fin jerked his hands out of the water and struggled to his feet. The sound of gigantic footsteps boomed ever nearer. Another ear-splitting roar and a rancid gale blew down the tunnel, lifting Fin off his feet and propelling him over the pool. His right foot landed momentarily on the third stepping stone and three pairs of helping hands pulled him to safety.

As Mologan's Boggarts helped the breathless Fin to his feet they looked back. The dark pool was alive with the thrashing and splashing of the enraged conger eel while the monstrous shape of Roary Borealis stared at them angrily from the other side.

'Mac-run!' Mologan hissed, already moving along the tunnel. The children followed close behind him, their eyes now accustomed to the gloom and to following the dim glow of the Boggart's ears.

On the wrong side of the pool Roary Borealis stared into the water.

'Whit are ye daein' here, in this cave, Mhairi-Anna?' he whispered hoarsely to the conger eel. 'This is no' yer mac-usual pool.'

Still angry, the eel raised its head out of the water and hissed at the Boggart.

'Nivver mind, let me pass. Ah've brigands and lobster thieves tae catch.' Roary Borealis lunged towards the stepping stones.

The conger eel thrust its head high out of the water and made a swipe at him. The Boggart moved back smartly as the eel's jaws crashed together millimetres from his leg.

'LET ME PASS,' the angry Boggart bellowed. 'LET ME THROUGH!'

The conger eel swam round in a circle, keeping her beady eyes focused on the Boggart.

Roary made another attempt to move onto the first stepping stone but the razor-toothed head of the gigantic eel reared up between the Boggart and the stone. Roary Borealis roared in frustration and anger. He tried to grab the creature by the throat but it slipped under the water so quickly that he grasped nothing but air.

Realising that he was getting nowhere with this creature and that Mologan and the mac-visitors were carrying his prize possession further and further away, Roary Borealis took a deep breath and tried a different tactic. He knelt down at the edge of the pool.

'Mhairi-Anna,' he whispered in the nicest, most treacly–sweet voice he could muster.

He leered a sickly, dribbly smile into the mirror-like surface of the pool. The conger eel poked the top of her shiny brown head out of the water, exposing only her dark eyes and a ripple of dorsal fin.

'Mhairi-Anna, Ah've ken't ye fur a long time noo, Boggart an' Boggart-wain. Huv' Ah no?'

The conger eel stared at him and thrashed her tail.

'Aye, an' Ah've aye been guid tae ye. Huv Ah no fed ye wee scraps o' tasty scran ower the years an' kept ye aw the best bits o' the dolphin fins an' the rabbits' feet?'

The creature gurgled and raised its head, tilting it to one side in order to hear what the Boggart was saying.

'An didn't Ah gie ye such a mac-braw name when ye were jist a wee mac-elver? There's no many congers this side o' Ben Mhor wi' such a mac-special an' bonny name.'

Mhairi-Anna swam round in a circle calmly and thoughtfully but still eyed the Boggart with suspicion.

'Ah'll tell ye whit Ah'll do.' Roary Borealis was getting impatient. 'Ah'll gie ye a real mac-treat. Ah'll gie ye half o' wan o' thon theivin' mac-visitors when Ah catch them!'

Mhari-Anna slid quietly under the water, unimpressed.

'Weel, whit dae ye want then?' Roary Borealis was now standing, hopping from one foot to the other in exasperation. 'Ah'll chop it all up fur ye.'

Still no reaction.

'RIGHT, A WHOLE MAC-VISITOR THEN,' he bellowed.

Mhari-Anna's snout appeared, surrounded by black ripples. She thrashed her tail twice.

'NAW, AH'M NO GIE'IN' YE TWA MAC-VISITORS!' The Boggart stamped his huge foot, causing a small rock-fall at the side of the pool. The eel dived under the water to avoid the falling stones. When the ripples subsided Mhairi-Anna's tail poked straight out of the pool and splashed very forcefully on the surface two times.

'Ye mak a hard bargain fur a fush,' said Roary Borealis quietly. 'Twa mac-visitors it is. But Ah'm no choppin' them up fur ye. NOO LET ME BY.'

Mhairi-Anna's tail moved slowly around in an impatient circular motion.

Roary Borealis hesitated for a couple of seconds.

'RIGHT. TWA MAC-VISITORS. CHOPPED. CAN AH GO NOO?'

The eel lifted her head out of the pool, tilted it to one side and winked at the Boggart. Without losing any more precious time Roary Borealis sprinted across the stepping stones, his feet barely touching their slimy surface. He lumbered along the tunnel at a great speed, intent on catching up with the lobster raiders.

⌘

Mologan's bogling team had managed to put a considerable distance between them and their pursuer while Roary Borealis had been bargaining with the prettily named conger eel to cross the pool. The tunnel twisted and turned like a corkscrew, and in some places seemed to turn back in the direction they had come from. Presently the floor became steeper and they climbed upwards. The passage was now becoming lighter. Soon they could see the end of the tunnel. Breathlessly they ran towards the pale morning light but as they squeezed out of a small gap in a cliff face overlooking the sound they could hear a tremendous bellowing far behind them.

'LOBSTUR MARAUDERS! HE'S MINE!... HORACE! HORACE!'

'He's catching up with us,' Fin panted, bent over, hands on knees, glad to breathe fresh air again.

There was a massive roar from the passageway, followed by the sound of thumping and scraping and cursing.

'Ah think Roary's got stuck in yon narrow spat a wee bitty back,' Mologan chortled. 'That'll slow him doon.'

'Let's get going. We're nearly home now,' said Beth, gulping the sweet bog myrtle-scented air. 'We've only to cross the sound and we can dive into one of Mologan's tunnels. They're so narrow that Roary Borealis will never be able to follow us.'

They all nodded in agreement and relief. Mologan was examining his chewed bogling stick.

'Ah've had this stick fur a hunner an' ...'

'Look,' said Robbie, interrupting him. He pointed to the sound. It was flooded with water. 'The tide's come in.'

'We're cut off!' gasped Beth. 'How are we going to get back across to Craigmhor?'

'We could swim,' Fin suggested enthusiastically.

'Don't be so daft. The current's too strong,' Robbie snapped.

Mologan smiled and tapped the side of his nose.

A loud, squelchy, popping noise came from the tunnel, followed by the rumble of falling rocks, and heavy footsteps.

'Roary's escaping,' Fin cried.

'Follow on, mac-Boggarts,' called Mologan, diving into a small clump of stunted birches.

As Mologan's Boggarts pushed their way through low springy branches and tall bracken, Roary Borealis was close behind them, smashing the trees into crumpled sticks with his fists.

Coming out of the birch copse they ran up and down a heathery hillock, through a boggy patch and scrambled over a massive pile of jagged lichen-covered rocks.

'Come oan, Mac-Robbie, it's no' far,' Mologan encouraged him. Robbie was lagging behind the others.

'I'm coming as fast as I can,' Robbie called. 'It's a bit uneven here. I ... Ahhh!'

'What's up, Robbie?' Beth stopped and turned round.

Robbie was sitting on the ground rubbing his ankle.

'It's my ankle. I've twisted it.' He caught sight of Roary Borealis emerging from the bog cotton and tried to stand up. 'Ouch! I can't put my weight on this foot.'

Fin and Beth stumbled back over the rocks and helped Robbie to his feet, supporting him under his arms.

Mologan pointed to a small horizontal crack between two rocks. 'Squeeze in,' he ordered, 'Oan yer mac-tummies.' The crack looked very small. They could hear Roary's breathing close behind them. Quickly they squeezed through the hole and pulled Mologan in behind them – though only with difficulty as his well-rounded Boggart tummy was almost too big to squash into such a tight gap. He breathed in as deeply as he could and plopped into the small dry cave.

A blast of foul air blew into the cave and an ear-splitting roar knocked the bogling team to the ground, as a huge warty foot crashed through the narrow entrance.

'This mac-way.' Mologan led the team down a dry and fresh-smelling tunnel. Robbie hobbled along as best he could, leaning on what was left of Mologan's bogling stick, and supported by Beth and Fin at the widest parts of the passage. The roaring became gradually less distinct until they couldn't hear it at all.

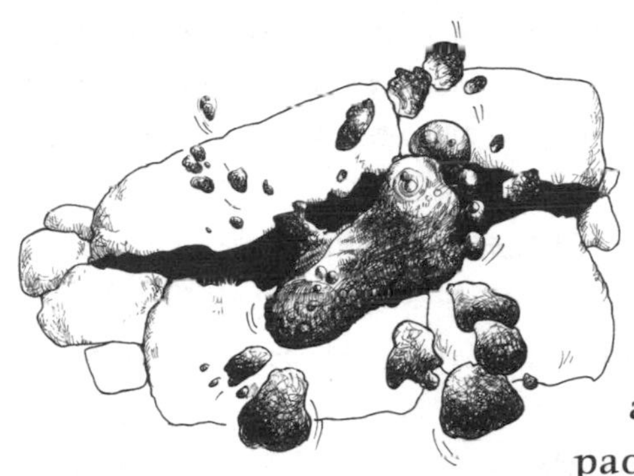

'I guess Roary has still got his foot stuck in the crack,' Beth laughed nervously, as they followed Mologan along the tunnel at a gentle walking pace.

'Perhaps his foot has swollen up like mine has and he'll be trapped there for weeks,' said Robbie, trying to take his mind off the pain in his ankle.

They continued walking for about ten minutes then the path climbed steeply upwards. Abruptly and unexpectedly they popped out into the fresh night air behind a hawthorn bush next to the Craigmhor boathouse.

Mologan, Fin, Beth and Robbie rested on the boathouse ramp. They lay on their backs staring up into the starry sky which was now streaked with a yellow dawn.

'You seem to have lost your peep-toed bogling trainer,' said Beth, nodding towards the wet and muddy fisherman's sock which Mologan was still wearing. 'I hope Roary Borealis can find a use for it.'

'Like falling over it and breaking his neck, or trying to eat it and choking to death,' Robbie suggested.

'Do you think Roary will swim over the sound after us when he manages to free his foot from the crack in the rock?' Fin asked.

'Naw, Fin Mac-visitor, dinnae be daft, it's nearly light,' Mologan laughed. 'An' Boggarts are mac-allergic tae watter. We're quite safe... fur the noo.' He turned to Robbie. 'How's thon ankle, Mac-Robbie? It looks gey mac-swollen.'

Robbie sat up and rubbed his ankle. 'Pretty sore. I think I've sprained it.'

Beth got up. 'I'll go and wet my scarf in the burn and you can use that as a cold compress.'

'Pity about your ankle,' Fin commiserated, 'but at least Mologan got the lobster.'

'Aye,' said Mologan, feeling around for his bogling bag. 'Ah'd better check that Horace is alright an' he's no suffa-mac-cated.' His hands scrabbled around. He stood up and scanned the ground, scratching his head. 'Whaur's ma boglin' bag?'

'You had the bogling bag in Roary's cave,' said Robbie. 'I put Horace into it before Roary came back.'

'Ah did that, Mac-Robbie,' Mologan agreed.

'Then what did you do with it?' Fin asked.

'Ah had it when Ah unfankle't youse frae the balin' twine.' Mologan screwed up his face thoughtfully. Then he shrugged and looked around his feet in despair as if expecting the bag to appear of its own accord.

'Think, Mologan,' Robbie rubbed his ankle and winced. 'What did you do with it when you untied us?'

The Boggart shrugged again.

Fin stood up and patted Mologan's hump kindly. 'Come on, shut your eyes and try to remember. You came into the cave and Robbie told you he had a pen knife and...?'

'Ah pit the boglin' bag doon so as tae get the mac-knife oot o' Mac-Robbie's pocket.'

'And...?' Fin encouraged.

'An' Ah cut the mac-twine, an', um... Ah cannae remember.'

Fin, Robbie and Mologan looked at each other in glum silence.

Robbie voiced their gloomy thoughts. 'We've lost Horace!'

CHAPTER 16

Horace the Green Lobster

'What's up?' said Beth brightly, returning with the damp scarf.

'It's the lobster,' Robbie began, 'in the bogling bag. It's um...'

'Here!' said Beth holding up Mologan's filthy bag. 'I gave Horace a splash about in the water when I was at the burn. I was worried he might have suffocated in the bag. He's fine.'

'But how...?' Mologan began.

'I picked the bag off the floor when we escaped from Roary's cave. I only remembered I had it on my back when it slipped round while I was leaning over the burn to soak my scarf.'

Fin, Robbie and Mologan sighed in unison, relieved. Beth applied the damp scarf to Robbie's ankle.

'Well done, Mac-Beth!' Mologan grinned, holding the bogling bag tightly. 'Mac-mission accomplished!'

They walked slowly up the track, supporting Robbie who was feeling the pain in his ankle more acutely now the excitement had passed. They had only climbed a few metres when Mologan turned sharply to the left and led them onto a narrow sheep path. The path followed a grassy ledge bordered by willows and stunted hazel trees. Stopping at a mossy mound next to a small stream Mologan said, 'Nearly mac-home,' and disappeared into a large burrow-like hole. The children followed wearily. A damp, earth-smelling passage led steeply downwards to a muddy cave. This cave had a very high ceiling. The children felt that they were standing at the bottom of a well.

Fin shone his torch around. Mologan was already beginning to climb a rickety ladder which led upwards into the gloom.

'Is this ladder safe?' Robbie asked, one foot on the bottom rung.

'Aye, it's the best o' stuff. The real McCoy. Teak, ye ken. Came oot o' a shipwreck, so it mac-did.' Mologan's voice echoed from high above them.

'Can you manage, Robbie?' said Beth, concerned.

But they had no choice but to climb the ladder. Robbie moved slowly and painfully, pulling himself up mainly by his arms. They reached a small ledge. There was another long ladder, and at the top of that there was a short, steep climb. Mologan pulled Robbie up the last few rocky steps into a wide tunnel and in a few moments they were back in the cosy familiarity of Mologan's cave. It seemed strangely homely and comfortable and hardly seemed to smell at all.

Robbie sat down gratefully on the Boggart's bed, his face chalk white. His ankle throbbed painfully. He felt like crying with the pain.

Mologan carefully rolled down the edges of his bogling bag and examined the lobster. Horace writhed and wriggled angrily. Fin picked up the lobster and carried him over to the water trough. He placed him

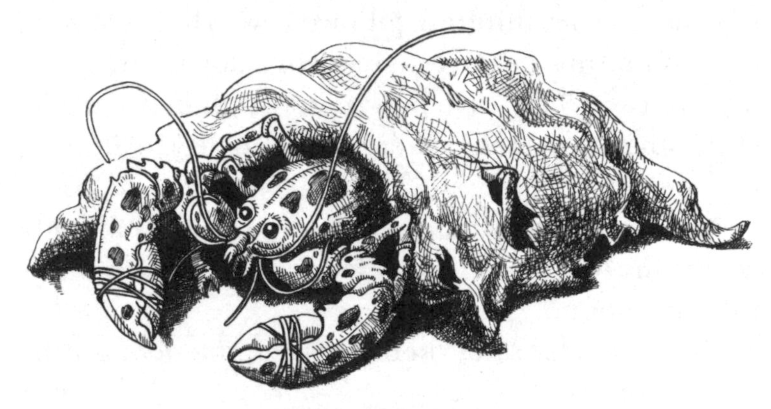

gently in the water. A few bubbles rose to the surface. Horace flicked his tail and swivelled his antennae around slowly. He stared at his captors for a second then began thrashing and splashing angrily.

'Good old Horace, back to his angry self,' said Fin. 'I think he's OK.'

'Well, another successful mac-mission for Mologan's Boggarts,' Mologan beamed contentedly. 'Yer mac-Chieftain is very mac-proud of youse.'

'That was the most dangerous bogling mission ever,' said Fin.

'It was that, Fin Mac-visitor. Ah'll be writin' it up in ma boglin' book later.' Mologan sighed wistfully. 'Aye, a historic bogle so it was. Boggarts are goin' tae talk about this mac-nificent bogle fur years tae come an Ah'm goin' tae be remember't as the great Boggart mac-Chieftain who led his brave team o' trainee Boggarts oan this successful mac-mission intae the daurk an' mac-dangerous caves o' Eilean Bodach. Ah think Ah'll call it "The Great Bodach Bogle", or, um,' he scratched his head, '"The Brilliant Borealis Bogle", or mibby "Mologan's Mac-nificent Mac-mission".'

'You weren't exaggerating when you said Roary Borealis was the meanest, mac-nastiest Boggart,' Beth interrupted Mologan's train of thought. 'He doesn't seem to stick to the bogling rules.'

'Rools?' Mologan growled and snorted fiercely. 'That thievin', mac-devious villain o' a Boggart doesnae ken whit rools is fur. He's bin boglin' oan ma mac-territory. Ah've got the proof. Did he no' bogle that fushin' box frae yer canoe at Boat Bay?' His face had turned blue with indignation. 'Ah huv the ancient boglin' rights tae Craigmhor. Ah'll no huv some devil o' a clamjamphrie rastler stealin' frae ma boglin' patch. Ah'm goin' tae mak' a complaint tae the Grand Boglin' Coort, so Ah am!'

'What about all those dead animals?' said Beth. 'That was the worst bit. Roary Borealis is killing and eating all sorts of animals. Did you see the seal's head and the otter's head?' she shivered and felt nauseous at the memory of the carnage in Roary Borealis's cave.

'Some of them were protected species, like otters,' Fin said.

'Yes, you're right Fin,' Beth agreed. 'If you're going to be an eco-warrior Boggart Chieftain, Mologan, maybe you should do something about stopping Roary from destroying the wildlife instead of moaning about ancient bogling rights and Roary stealing plastic fishing boxes from your bit of beach.'

Mologan crossed his arms and looked thoughtful.

'Ye're right, Mac-Beth. Ah've got tae protect the planet frae mac-nasty, cruel mac-criminal Boggarts. An eco-mac-warrior cannae sit back an' dae nothin'. He paced up and down. 'Ah'll, Ah'll, um... aye, Ah'll report Roary Borealis tae the Grand Boglin' Coort. That's whit Ah'll dae! He's breakin' aw the boglin' mac-rools.'

'How do you do that?' Robbie asked.

'Ah'll write a mac-letter.'

'How will it get to this Grand Bogling Court once you've written it? Do you have to deliver it?' Fin asked.

'Naw, there's the poglin'.'

The children looked blankly at Mologan.

'The poglin',' he repeated. 'The Boggart postal mac-service!'

'Do you have Boggart pogle-men, and pogle-boxes and Boggart stamps and things?' Beth asked.

'Aye, mac-zactly, Mac-Beth,' Mologan said. 'There's a pogle-hole unner the highest point of every Boggart's mac-territory. Mine is unner the cairn oan Mologan's Hill thonder.'

'I see,' said Beth. 'A pogle-Boggart comes round and picks up your mail from there?'

'Aye, it's a guid service. Very mac-regular. Auld Drouthie Mac-Scunner's bin the pogle-Boggart fur the past five hunner years. He's aye oan time, auld Drouthie. Ye could set yer mac-watch by him if ye had wan – every three years oan the dot.'

'Three years?' Fin laughed. 'You'd better hurry and get this letter written, Mologan, or you'll miss the post!'

⌘

'We'd better go, Mologan,' Robbie yawned. 'It'll be light outside.' He checked his watch. 'It's five o'clock.'

Fin picked up his rucksack and Beth helped Robbie to his feet.

'Wait,' said Mologan, 'What aboot ramorra'?'

'Tomorrow?' said Fin. 'What's happening tomorrow?'

'We've to take the bogle't mac-gredients tae Aggie, for the mac-potion, youse ken?'

Fin shuffled sleepily and looked at the others.

'Aggie said to come back in eight days,' Robbie said. 'I worked out that would be Saturday. What day is it today?'

They all shrugged. They had lost all sense of time.

'I think tomorrow's Friday. We'll go to the island on Saturday night. We can have a night off tomorrow to rest,' Beth said. 'Don't look so disappointed, Mologan, you don't have long to wait now.'

'It seems a long time tae me,' the Boggart said, his lip trembling. 'An whit am Ah gonnae eat? Ah cannae go oot, Ah've lost ma boglin' shoe.'

'Just like Cinderella,' Robbie said. 'But never mind, Mologan, you shall go to the ball!'

Mologan looked puzzled.

'What I mean is,' Robbie continued, 'We'll bring you something special to eat to cheer you up. You can spend the time you'd usually be out bogling writing the letter to the Grand Bogling Court and composing the epic story of our magnificent mac-mission in your bogling book. Then on Saturday we'll take you to Eilean nan Ron to get your potion. Will we need to bring anything for Horace to eat? What kind of things do lobsters eat?'

'Ah've some dried sea lice somewhere aboot. Ah can feed the wee craiturs. He'll like sea lice right enough.' Mologan pulled off his balaclava. Flakes of luminous green skin showered onto his shoulders like green dandruff and floated in the narrow shafts of pale sunlight now shining through cracks in the cave roof.

Mologan followed the children up the tunnel towards the secret door.

'Youse'll no forget the scran. Ah like thon potato mac-crisps an' the pink squidgy mac-bannocks,' he said, 'An' Ah really mac-fancy some pineapple chunks, an' some purridge wid be...'

But the children were already out of earshot.

'I think we'll have to go back to Roary Borealis's cave,' said Beth, zipping up her sleeping bag.

'Why?' Fin asked, horrified at the prospect.

'Because we bogled the lobster and didn't leave anything.'

'Mac-tough!' said Robbie, pulling his sleeping bag over his head.

CHAPTER 17

The Natural Laws of Bogling

Robbie returned from the cottage hospital with his ankle wrapped in a tight bandage.

'It's only a sprain,' Dad explained, as Mum fussed around making Robbie comfortable in the caravan. 'There's nothing broken. He'll be fine in a few days.'

'You were away for a long time,' said Mum. 'Coffee anyone?'

'It didn't take long at the hospital,' said Robbie. 'We came back through Clachnacala and went to the shop.'

'I wish you'd said you were going to the shop.' Mum poured hot water into the coffee cups. 'We're out of butter and orange juice. What did you buy?'

'Oh, just some fishing stuff,' said Dad nonchalantly.

'And some torch batteries and ice cream and a cook book.' Robbie said. '*Natural Foods from the Scottish Countryside*. There are some interesting recipes in it.'

'Where are Beth and Fin?' Dad asked.

'They went for a walk on the beach. They'll be back soon,' Mum said. 'I've made soup.'

'Aw, Mum. Not packet soup again,' Robbie moaned.

'No, it's homemade lentil soup made with real vegetables, and I've made soda scones.'

'Pity there's no butter,' Robbie grumbled.

'You know, Robbie, it's strange,' said Mum thoughtfully, stirring Dad's coffee, 'that you could sprain your ankle so easily between your tent and the toilet tent.'

'Oh, it can happen very easily. Just a small twist,' said Robbie. 'The doctor said so, didn't he, Dad?'

'Aye, it's easily done,' Dad agreed. 'The doctor told us about a woman who went over on her ankle on the edge of a hearth-rug and broke it. The ankle, I mean, not the hearth-rug!'

Mum laughed. 'But you've been climbing up and down cliffs and running along beaches all holidays, and you sprain your ankle on a tuft of grass!'

Robbie was beginning to doubt that the fibstane he had put in his mouth while explaining his injury to his parents had worked.

Just then, Beth and Fin arrived, panting and rosy-cheeked from their brisk climb up the steep shortcut.

'What's for lunch, Mum?' Fin called, sitting on the caravan step, taking off his muddy boots.

'It's starting to rain again,' said Beth stepping over her brother, 'You can see it coming over the sea.'

A dark cloud was moving from the horizon towards Craigmhor, obliterating the view of the islands. It suddenly became cooler as the first drops of rain plattered noisily on the roof of the caravan.

'A great day for fishing,' said Dad, rubbing the steamed up window with the back of his hand.

Mum groaned. She put two steaming bowls of soup on the table.

'When do you want to go?' Beth asked.

Dad stopped blowing on a spoonful of hot soup. 'Do you fancy coming fishing, Beth?'

'Yes, as long as I can take my personal CD player.'

'Fine,' Dad smiled. 'Anyone else coming? Fin?'

'No thanks, Dad,' said Fin, who really fancied a sleep. 'I'll keep Robbie company. Is there any butter for these scones?'

'I'll go to the shops and get some later since you'll all be occupied,' Mum said.

'Can you get some of those squidgy bannocks?' Beth asked.

Mum looked at Beth quizzically.

'Em, you know, those pink marshmallow biscuits.'

'But I thought you didn't like them.'

'Yes, but the boys do. Don't you, Fin, Robbie?' Beth kicked Fin under the table.

'Oh yes, Mum. Get lots.' Fin rubbed his leg and glared at Beth. 'Get some sausages and crisps as well... and could you get some pineapple chunks?'

Dad found a plastic container full of bits of string, pencil stubs, buttons, candles, dried up ball-point pens, flat batteries and other assorted odds and ends. He tipped the contents into a paper bag and stuffed it in a drawer. He put the new fishing lines, weights and feathers which he had bought at Clachnacala into the box and packed it into a rucksack, along with a flask of hot chocolate, two packets of crisps and some biscuits.

'Right, Beth. Are you ready?'

Dressed in waterproof jackets and woolly hats, Dad and Beth set off down the shortcut to Boat Bay. When they reached the canoe Dad pulled off the tarpaulin and folded it carefully. He wedged it into a gap between two rocks so that it didn't blow away. Returning to the canoe, he saw to his surprise the old red fishing box sitting on the seat.

'Crivens, Beth. Look at this.' Dad stood open-mouthed. 'It's the red fishing box!' He opened it, checking the contents. 'It's all here,' he said, astounded. 'Nothing's missing.'

'Perhaps someone borrowed it,' said Beth.

'Maybe,' said Dad thoughtfully, scratching his chin. 'Mmm, it definitely wasn't here yesterday. I looked all over for it.'

'Just like Mum's specs.'

'Aye, you're right, Beth. Very Fortean, as Auntie Morag would say.'

Beth smiled to herself. Bogling could be quite amusing sometimes. She and Fin had 'bogled back' the box earlier that day while Dad and Robbie were at the

Cottage Hospital. Looking up, she saw Fin at the top of the cliff, waving. She made a 'thumbs up' sign which Fin returned.

'Come on, Dad,' Beth said, 'let's get this canoe in the water. I fancy some barbecued mackerel for supper.'

Beth and Dad didn't catch anything and returned to the caravan damp and fed up. Guessing this would happen – Dad never caught any fish, no matter how many times he went fishing – Mum had bought some kippers in Clachnacala and Fin had begun to light the barbecue when they saw Dad and Beth paddling back into Boat Bay. It was drizzling slightly, but they didn't mind cooking outside. Mum set a table under the caravan awning and they sat comfortably watching the kippers spitting appetisingly on the barbecue.

They ate the kippers with fresh crusty bread and butter, some tasty Clachnacala tomatoes and strawberry milkshake. Dad put some bananas on the barbecue to roast in their skins and Mum made some caramel custard. There were no leftovers for Mologan.

During supper Dad went on and on about the fishing box.

'But how did it suddenly reappear when I'd looked for it several times and it definitely wasn't there?'

'Iona would tell you the Craigmhor Boggart had taken it,' said Mum. 'She says things like that happen all the time.'

'But why?' Dad was puzzled. 'Why do Boggarts take things and then put them back?'

'It's all part of the Boggart's job,' said Fin. 'A kind of service to the community. If he didn't bogle things, then who would?'

'You've got a good philosophical point, Fin,' Dad smiled. 'If it's an inevitable natural law that things go missing and reappear again then it must be someone or something's job in life to effect this natural phenomenon.'

'Um, yes.' Fin was a bit confused by the argument.

'Mmm,' said Dad, leaning back on his chair and putting his feet up on a fish-box. 'It's the same with dishes.'

Fin looked quizzically at Dad.

'Well, if it's also a natural law that dishes get greasy and dirty and need washing up then there must be someone whose job is to effect this natural phenomenon.' He looked at the children and raised his eyebrows.

'Oh, Dad...' Beth began.

'Whose turn is it tonight?' Dad laughed.

As Beth and Fin washed up Robbie investigated the contents of the food cupboard. 'I'm not sure what to give Mologan tonight,' he said. 'Mum'll notice if we take too much.'

'Why not look in the locker under the seats,' Beth suggested. 'Mum has had tins of things stored under there since last year or the year before. For emergencies, she says, but she's probably forgotten all about them.'

'Good thinking, Mac-Beth.' Robbie hobbled over to the other side of the caravan. He knelt down and lifted up the hinged lid under the foam seat cushion. In the dark recesses of the locker behind spare blankets, a broken thermos flask, a hammer, a large cooking pot and old wellies there were lots of neatly stacked tins.

Robbie investigated. Some of the tins were slightly rusty, having been stored for such a long time. He selected a couple which he thought Mologan would enjoy. 'Ravioli in tomato sauce and mandarin segments in syrup. He'll like these.' Robbie put the cushion back in place. 'They're both kind of squidgy mac-sluggy things.'

'I'm glad we've got tonight off,' said Beth, sliding into her sleeping bag. It was still light but the children were tired and had decided to have an early night. 'I wonder what Mologan's doing?'

⌘

In his cave below the camp Mologan had been hard at work composing his letter to the Grand Bogling Court. Wiping off the bits of ravioli and tomato sauce which had somehow smeared all over the seaweed parchment, he signed his name with a flourish and folded the letter carefully.

'Ah'll jist put this in the pogle-box the noo, in case Ah forget,' he thought.

Mologan dressed carefully in his cammy-mac-flag clothes and squeezed into his balaclava. He made his way along the tunnel which led to the far side of Mologan's Hill. The drizzle had stopped and the clouds were blowing in the direction of Ben Mhor, which looked dark and moody on the horizon. He reached the top of the hill and slipped his letter into the pogle-hole beneath the cairn.

Making his way back down the hill past some sleeping sheep Mologan realised he felt slightly peckish. The breakfast that the children had left him had been delicious, but not filling. He crept up to a huddle of sheep and lambs and sat down beside them. Very gently and meticulously he picked through their fleeces with his fingers, plucking out fat juicy sheep ticks and popping them into his mouth. Ticks were a particular favourite of Mologan's. He snacked happily until he could find no more.

Mologan decided to make his way back to his cave by way of the campsite just in case there was anything interesting waiting to be bogled. Conscious of his glowing green ears and face, Mologan was very cautious. He had a quick look in the bins at the croft and the holiday cottage and bogled some rotten fruit and a tub of mouldy cottage cheese.

A camper van had parked on the ledge earlier that evening. Mologan found some charred marshmallows beside an extinguished campfire and a half-full can of a fizzy drink which had attracted dozens of small brown slugs.

'Great boglin' tonight,' he thought, as he dropped a few beetles into a water container. He was tempted to let down one of the camper van's tyres but he wasn't sure if an eco-warrior Boggart would do that. He realised he was rather confused about what was good and what was bad bogling. Scratching his head, he moved silently on.

He smeared snot on some keys which had been left on the outside of a caravan door and raked through some more bins. Passing by the Douglas's caravan he peered in the window, leaving a green imprint of his

nose on the glass. He tapped slightly on the glass to scare the sleeping campers but they were deeply asleep and didn't hear him. Mologan nipped into Beth, Fin and Robbie's tent and left a bit of slime on each of their pillows as a friendly gesture to let them know their Chieftain had popped in. He bogled some charred banana skins and kipper heads out of the bin, then, humming his favourite bogling song, he headed back to his cave to write up 'Mologan's Mac-nificent Mac-mission' in his bogling book.

Before he went to bed Mologan gathered together all the bogled ingredients for the mixture. He placed them all on the table and methodically ticked off each one on Aggie Hagg-Boggart's list. He was suddenly overcome by a wave of excitement and relief. Tomorrow he would be cured. Things would get back to normal. A lifetime's happy bogling lay ahead of him. No more mac-green-ness and mac-luminous ears and no more Boggart training and mac-manoeuvres with Mac-Robbie and Fin Mac-visitor and Mac-Beth.

He swallowed hard, finding a lump in his throat. No more mac-visitors, or adventures, just ordinary bogling... well, eco-bogling, if he could understand how to do it... on his own.

Mologan suddenly felt very sad. After a hundred and forty seven years solitary bogling at Craigmhor, he realised how much he enjoyed company. What had Aggie said when she had read his chuckie stanes? He'd travel above and below water – well he'd done that. He'd get help from a creature with fernitcles. That was Mac-Beth of course, who had a braw fernitickled face. He'd become a great Chieftain. Aye, he had done that alright. Had he not led his own well-trained team of Boggarts on the most daring bogling mac-mission ever carried out this side of Ben Mhor?

He, Mologan the Boggart of Craigmhor had done all this. Mologan laughed a gurgly laugh.

'Aye, Mologan's Boggarts. The mac-finest boglin' team in the Western Isles,' he said out loud. 'Mibby the world?'

What an achievement for one Boggart in one lifetime. And he hadn't even reached maturity yet! Mologan beamed with pride and polished his fingernails on his plaid.

'Ah wunner if a could mac-instigate a team event at the National Bogling Compie-mac-tishun?' he fantasised, as he dropped off to sleep at dawn. 'Uch, naw, they're no real Boggarts. Ah keep forgettin'.'

CHAPTER 18

Sea-orange Cordial and a Magic Potion

'Of course you can't go to Eilean nan Ron, Robbie,' Beth whispered. 'You can hardly squeeze your swollen foot into a sandal, never mind your boots. And,' she continued, 'you're supposed to rest your ankle, not go hobbling around on cliffs and along slippery secret passages.'

'But we're going by canoe,' said Robbie, exasperated. 'There isn't much walking involved.'

'How would you get down the cliff onto the beach?'

'I could leave earlier and meet you there.'

'No, Robbie. I know you're disappointed but it would be stupid to do an expedition like this with a sprained ankle. Anyway it would be a tight squeeze. Four of us in the canoe. Maybe even dangerous. Perhaps it's for the best.'

'It's alright for you, Beth,' Robbie said huffily, 'I've been part of this mac-mission from the beginning and now I'm going to miss the end.'

'Shoosh, here's Mum.'

Robbie and Beth were sitting outside the caravan on sun loungers. Beth strummed her guitar. The family had decided to stay around the caravan that day to allow Robbie to rest his sprained ankle. Dad and Fin had wandered over to the croft to help Euan fix his tractor, and Mum was cleaning the caravan windows.

'What's that tune you're playing, Beth?' Mum said, rubbing vigorously at a green smudge on the glass.

'It's called "The Green Lobster Blues",' said Beth.

'Oh, very nice,' said Mum, distractedly, 'Who's it by?'

'Horace someone-or-other,' Beth grinned.

Robbie laughed.

'I'm sure there wasn't a green mark here yesterday.' Mum was oblivious to their laughter. She sprayed more glass cleaner onto the pane. 'It's so stubborn. Now it's smeared all over the window.'

Beth and Robbie looked at each other knowingly, remembering the green slime they had found on their pillows that morning.

⌘

Just before midnight Fin and Beth crept out of the tent. Robbie was very disappointed to be missing out on the final part of the mission, but his ankle hurt like hell when he put any weight on it and he knew that he would be a liability to the team.

'Don't forget this,' he whispered as Beth and Fin left. He handed them a small cardboard box. 'It's Mologan's supper. His last supper hopefully, before he gets back to normal and can bogle his own food. I've tried to make it a good one.'

Robbie had packed some left-over macaroni cheese, a boiled egg, a packet of prawn crackers, a tin of spaghetti hoops and six squidgy mac-bannocks.

'Good mac-luck,' he said, quietly.

There was a note under a small stone beside the secret door.

LET YERSELS IN
AT MIDNIT
AH WULL LEEV DORE OPEN
URE GRATE CHIEFTAIN

'I see Mologan's a great chieftain now,' Beth smiled as they read the note. 'He seems to have cheered up. He's back to his pompous old self.'

'The old Mologan that we know and love,' said Fin, as they let themselves in the secret door and made their way down the tunnel to Mologan's living-cave.

Mologan was dressed and ready to go. He had found another old wellie and had adapted it to fit his enormous left foot. 'Right mac-Boggarts, oor mac-mission tonight is tae deliver aw the mac-gredients...'

'We know,' said Fin, interrupting Mologan. 'Is everything ready?'

'Aye, in ma spare boglin' bag.'

'And Horace?' Beth asked.

'In the watter. We'll fush him oot afore we go.'

'You can fish him out,' said Fin, whose finger was still bruised from one of Horace's strong nips.

'I'll do it,' Beth volunteered. She grabbed Horace. The lobster struggled violently.

'Quick, mac-lastic bands,' said Mologan, and like a well-oiled machine Fin picked up two elastic bands, handed them to Mologan one at a time and the Boggart snapped them tightly onto Horace's claws.

'Weel done, mac-team,' Mologan beamed. 'Um, whaur's Mac-Robbie?'

'His ankle's too bad to come with us,' Beth explained. 'He sent you this, though.' She handed Mologan the box of food.

'Mac-shame,' Mologan mumbled, examining the food. 'Mibby Aggie would make him a mac-mixture?'

'Em, he'll be fine in a few days,' said Fin, imagining all the complications of bogling even more ingredients and acquiring another lobster for payment. 'We needn't bother Aggie.'

Dabberlocks was waiting in the bay. Before Fin and Beth had paddled far he popped up beside the canoe and barked softly. Mologan was sitting stiffly hunched, and grimly holding on to the sides of the canoe.

He said, 'Dabberlocks says he'll tow us. Throw him a mac-rope.'

Fin dropped the painter gently into the water. The seal dived and came up to the surface with the rope in his mouth. Beth and Fin put their paddles down and sat back to enjoy the ride. Mologan gripped the sides of the canoe more tightly and closed his eyes.

They moved off at a terrific pace and were soon through the lagoon and crossing the deep channel to the north of Eilean nan Ron. It was choppy here and the current was fast. Broch Tor loomed up to their left. The canoe bobbed and tossed. Beth and Fin were glad that Dabberlocks was towing them. It would have taken ages to paddle all this way in such a choppy sea. The seal slowed down and turned into the deep chasm which split Eilean nan Ron in two. He let go of the rope as the canoe drifted smoothly into the hidden cave entrance.

Beth was beside herself with excitement. Fin grinned. Mologan sat quietly, his back hunched, his eyes closed and his mouth clenched tightly shut. They guided the canoe through the sea tunnel by pulling on the seaweed growing on the walls and were soon in the mooring cavern. Beth tied the canoe to the rusty iron ring next to Aggie's coracle and Fin led the way up the sandy passage to Aggie Hagg-Boggart's cave.

A strong smell of boiled shellfish greeted them. Aggie Hagg-Boggart was feeding Dabberlocks with a fishy bannock when they arrived in the cave. He snorted and splashed in the pool.

'Come away in,' Aggie called warmly, in her deep croaky voice which reminded Beth of an old husky-voiced neighbour who smoked a lot of cigarettes. 'Come and warm yersels by the fire.'

The old Boggart witch poked at the fire with a long stick. The blue flames sprang to life, licking up the sides of the black, sooty and dented iron pot which hung over the fire, suspended from a rusty tripod. Yellow steam rose up from the bubbling liquid in the pot. Mologan leaned over it and sniffed.

'Is this the mac-mixture, Aggie?'

'Aye, Mologan ma boy, all mac-ready for the final mac-gredients. Did youse bogle everythin' oan the list?'

'We did that, Aggie. Ah had a guid mac-team.'

'Aye, Ah hear ye're a mac-Chieftain noo, Mologan.'

'Jist as ye predicted, Aggie. The Great Chieftain o' Mologan's Boggarts, the best Boggart patrol this side o' Ben Mhor.'

'Aye, it must be. It's certainly the only Boggart patrol this side o' Ben Mhor,' Aggie cackled. 'Ye must have mac-trained them weel, Mologan, tae have bogle't aw the mac-gredients in such a short time, and bogle't back ma wee Horace from thon evil Roary Borealis.'

Mologan swelled with pride.

Aggie gestured towards the children. 'An this must be the fernitickled craitur!'

'This is Mac-Beth,' Mologan smiled.

'Pleased tae make yer mac-quaintence, Mac-Beth,' said Aggie Hagg-Boggart, holding out a bony, withered hand.

Beth shook it politely. Her mouth felt dry.

'Sit youse doon.' Aggie gestured towards the seaweed-covered rocks. 'This mac-mixture might tak a whiley tae mac-feenish. Try ma sea-orange cordial. It's a mac-special recipe.' She hobbled towards them carrying the wheel-trim tray and put it down on the rock beside her barrel chair.

'Ah think youse'll like this,' she said, pouring out orangey brown liquid into a cracked glass. 'The warty-venus cockles add a pleasant piquancy to the taste.'

Fin screwed up his face, wondering what warty-venus cockles were. Beth was still speechless, trying to take everything in. She scanned the cave, wide-eyed.

'Ye'll try some Mac-Beth?' Aggie was proffering a glass of cordial.

'Em, yes, thanks,' said Beth, jolted out of her dwam.

Fin accepted the cracked, handle-less mug and was glad that Mologan had the '...ITTY ...UNKS' tin with the torn cat-food label.

Aggie held up the blue eye bath. 'Slangie-mac-var!' she said.

'Slangie-mac-var,' they repeated, toasting Aggie and taking a sip of the drink. It was quite nice. It tasted only vaguely of oranges. It was like salty, gingery mango with a hint of pepper and a slight aftertaste of shrimps.

Aggie passed round a scallop shell filled with small spherical crispy things. 'Spicy fish-egg mix, any-Boggart?'

Beth and Fin declined politely. Mologan scooped up a handful and shoved them all into his mouth.

'Dabberlocks tells me that Mac-Robbie has sprained his mac-ankle,' said Aggie, crunching spicy fish eggs. 'It's a mac-shame. Ah thought he'd have bin interested in helpin' me mix the mac-potion, wi' him sae keen oan recipes an' the like.'

'Yes, he was very disappointed,' said Beth. 'Robbie would have loved to... AARGH!' Beth squealed and jumped up, spilling her cordial. 'Ahhh... something slithered... it, it... touched my leg... it was slimy.' Beth hopped around, not sure where to stand. A dark, shiny shape slid across the cave floor.

'There it is,' said Fin, pointing at the creature slipped under the table.

Aggie pulled herself onto her feet, steadied by her stick. 'Uch, it's only wan o' these dammed mac-eels again. They're always jinkin' in here tae steal mac-food.' She rattled her stick under the table and banged on the floor. 'Oot, oot, shoo, ye wee mac-pest. Awa' wi' ye!' She poked the eel with her stick. 'Shoo, shoo!' The creature slithered across the cave floor, through the curtained door, and a few seconds later they heard a quiet splash.

'It's awa noo. They're an affie mac-bother. This cave is fu' o' them. A wee shoo mair cordial, Mac-Beth?'

Beth shook her head and sat down.

'Well, doon tae mac-business then.' Aggie Hagg-Boggart rubbed her bony hands. 'Where's ma wee greenichy lobstur?'

Beth, Fin and Mologan had almost forgotten about Horace. Mologan carefully opened the bogling bag and lifted out Aggie's lobster. He deftly slipped off the elastic bands from Horace's claws and quickly passed him to Aggie.

'Oh, my,' Aggie beamed, 'it's ma wee Horace. Whit a mac-lovely boy, so greenichy an' such mac-beautiful spots.' She held Horace to her cheek and hugged him. The lobster seemed placid and content. 'Ma own wee greenichy lobstur, the wee darlin'.'

Beth and Fin looked at each other, bemused.

'How did youse bogle him frae Eilean Bodach? It couldnae huv bin mac-easy.' Aggie kissed Horace's cold hard head.

'Well, we went up to Roary Borealis and poked him on the chest and said, "Give us Aggie's lobster and make it snappy!"' Beth said. But Aggie didn't hear. The lobster had begun to squirm and wriggle in her hand.

'Ye'll be wantin' a wee swim, Horace,' Aggie said and shuffled towards a shallow rock pool in a dark corner of the cave. She placed the lobster gently in the water. Horace splashed and blew bubbles and made happy gurgling noises. 'Look at him. So mac-happy.' Aggie crouched by the pool supported by her stick. She tickled Horace's head. 'Is wee Horacy-woracy happy mac-noo?' she said in a soft gravelly voice.

Fin stifled his giggles and Beth avoided looking at him in case she started to laugh. Mologan beamed and a tear ran down his face. He sniffed.

'Ah'm glad ye're pleased tae have Horace hame, Aggie. It's great tae see youse both so mac-happy.'

'Uch, dinnae be sae sentimental, Mologan, ye daft Boggart,' Aggie said, standing up. 'Pit the bogl't mac-gredients oan the boorden and we'll make a mac-stert oan the mac-mixture.'

Fin helped Mologan to empty the contents of the bogling bag and Aggie examined each of the items carefully.

'Rid biddie, aye, jist enough.' She frowned, holding the jar of wine up to the candle light to examine it.

'Three greenichy kail-wurums.' She tapped the jar of caterpillars with her long fingernail.

Fin unwrapped the goose egg which was wrapped in several metres of loo roll to protect it.

'Fine, a mac-lovely egg. Noo, whit's this?' Aggie held up a yellow rubber glove, a puzzled look on her face.

'Five yellow fingers,' said Beth.

Aggie frowned. 'That's nae use. Ah cannae mac-corporate cahouchy intae the mac-mixture. It willnae dissolve.'

'Ah,' said Fin, 'but we, trainee Boggarts, have used our mac-nishative!' He pulled the bunch of bananas out of a brown paper bag and held them aloft in a theatrical gesture. 'Da-daa!'

Aggie smiled toothlessly and croaked, 'Youse'll mak' fine Boggarts, so youse will. These yella' fingers are jist the very dab.' She squeezed a banana between her thumb and forefinger. 'Almost mac-perfect.'

Next, Aggie opened the gory bag of chicken innards. Expertly she picked out the gizzard and dropped it immediately into the bubbling liquid in the cooking pot. She tossed the remaining giblets towards Dabberlocks who was sniffing excitedly at the edge of his pool. He caught them adeptly in his mouth and barked his thanks.

Mologan counted out the ten puggie nuts and the seven grossets and Fin added the four rusty nails to the pile. Beth unwrapped the wiry dog hair and put it on the table. Aggie ticked each item off on her list and nodded in satisfaction. Mumbling to herself, she reached up and took a couple of jars down from a rickety shelf. 'Hen-pen, aye. Sea lice, here it is.'

Handing the jar of sea lice to Beth she said, 'Count oot twinty-five o' these, Mac-Beth.'

Beth opened the jar. It was covered with seaweed parchment stretched over the top of the jar and tied with twine. The sea lice had a strange smell, like aquarium food magnified a hundred times. Beth shook out a few lumps onto her palm, trying not to breathe onto them in case they blew away. She carefully counted twenty-five onto a cockle shell and replaced the seaweed parchment on the jar. Fin tied it neatly with the twine.

Aggie Hagg-Boggart consulted the list again.

'Where are the sting winkles?' she asked, re-arranging the items spread out on the table.

'Somewhere around, I expect,' said Fin. 'They're in a coffee jar.'

'Ah cannae mac-see them,' said Mologan, peering at the table.

They all looked again. Silence.

'Oh, no,' said Beth. 'We've forgotten them.'

'You said you'd packed everything,' said Fin accusingly, facing Mologan.

Mologan looked sulky. He shuffled his feet and pouted his huge mouth.

'What have you got to say for yourself, Mologan?' Aggie added, poking him on the chest. 'Ye big daft galoot! Aw this is just a mac-waste o' time noo. Youse'll have tae go back ben yer cave and get the sting winkles. Ah cannae mac-substitute anythin' else. They're a mac-portant ingredient.'

Mologan's nose flushed purple with embarrassment. Shocked at the prospect of extra sea trips and having to wait even longer to be cured he glowered and shuffled and scratched his ear and sighed. Gloom descended.

Beth picked up the bogling bag.

'We may as well go now, otherwise we'll waste time. The sooner we go...' She threw the bag over her shoulder. 'Ouch!' Something had hit her on the back.

Beth opened the bag. 'Look,' she said, pulling out a jar, 'the sting winkles! You hadn't unpacked them.'

'Poke the fire, Fin Mac-visitor,' Aggie rasped, rolling up her sleeves and adjusting her shawl. 'We're mac-ready!'

She approached Mologan brandishing a pair of rusty pruning shears.

'Noo, off wi' that bunnet, Mologan while Ah cut a wee bit o' yer mac-hair.'

Mologan winced. He pulled off his balaclava. Beth noticed that the pattern of the knitted wool was indented on his head. Aggie clipped a small piece of Mologan's wiry tuft and tied it in a small neat bundle with some pink twine. Returning to the table she peeled the bananas.

'We dinnae need this bit,' she said pushing aside the fruit.

'I'll eat some,' said Fin, 'if you only need to use the skin.'

'Yuch,' said Aggie. 'You mac-humans eat the mac-strangest things!'

Fin, Beth and Mologan munched the bananas while Aggie measured out the red biddie into a bowl and mixed it with the goose egg yolk. Mologan licked up the raw egg white. Aggie ground up all the other ingredients using a stone mortar and pestle and everything was carefully laid on a small flat stone next to the fire, ready to begin.

Fin helped Aggie to lift her huge 'Remedies' book onto the table. He turned to page 603. Aggie checked through the recipe instructions.

'Aye, we're ready noo,' she whispered. 'Blow oot thon candles Mac-Beth, an' we'll mac-stert.'

Now that the cave was lit only by the blue glow from the fire it seemed eerie and cold. Mologan's head and hands glowed spookily in the dark. Fin, Beth, Aggie and Mologan sat round the steaming cauldron. It was silent apart from the bubbling and splashing from Horace's pool. Aggie stirred the mixture slowly and began to hum very quietly. It was a low monotonous humming that was almost hypnotic. A shiver ran up Beth's spine.

'Hmmmmm... hmmmmm,' Aggie rocked slowly in her chair.

Suddenly the contents of the cauldron started bubbling furiously, and pale, greenish-yellow steam enveloped them all. Aggie rolled her eyes and tapped the floor three times with her stick. The steam subsided and Aggie smiled.

As if she were in a trance, Aggie picked up the red biddie and goose yolk mixture and poured it into the pot.

'WHOOM!' A flash of purple flames burst out of the cauldron. Beth, Fin and Mologan leaned back as far as they could from the fire. Aggie began to sing a soft, gentle song whose words were impossible to make out. Beth felt she was in a dream and Fin almost nodded off to sleep. Occasionally Aggie would add some more ingredients to the now foul-smelling mixture. When everything had been incorporated the steam gradually turned blue.

Aggie stood up and held her stick above her head.

Grosser, stoory, tapsulteerie,
Greengaw, foosty, gawky-leerie...

she chanted, and threw the bunch of Mologan's hair into the cauldron with a flourish. The blue steam subsided.

'That's it mac-feenished,' she said brightly, as if she had just knocked up an omelette. 'Ah'll reduce the broth a wee bit afore it's strained. More sea-orange cordial, young Boggarts?'

CHAPTER 19

Return of the Eco-warrior

Fin re-lit the candles using a smouldering stick from the fire.

When the mixture had cooled a little, Aggie strained it through an old knitted sock into a tall thin jar. Retrieving the bunch of Mologan's hair from the cauldron she popped it into the jar. She rummaged around in a box of old stoppers and corks until she found one to fit. Next, she dribbled candle-wax around the top of the jar to seal it and gave the blue-ish liquid a thorough shake.

Aggie then found a grubby, tattered luggage label and carefully crossed out 'veruca moss', turned it over, and wrote:

MOLOGANS MAC-MUXTUR
TAK HAF RAMORRA NIT
ON RIZIN AN HAF ON GAN
TAE BED

She tied the label neatly round the neck of the jar.

'Noo, read the mac-structions carefully, Mologan, an' Ah think it'll work mac-fine.' Aggie handed the jar to Mologan who accepted it solemnly.

'Thanks Aggie. Ah jist cannae wait tae get back tae mac-normal.'

'Ah ken, son.' Aggie patted Mologan's hump. 'It willnae be long noo. Dinnae be mac-tempted to take the mac-mixture afore ramorra. Bide yer time.'

Mologan was visibly moved.

⌘

'Say cheery-bye tae Horace,' said Aggie as they got ready to leave.

Beth, Fin and Mologan shuffled reluctantly but politely to the rock pool.

'Bye-bye, Horace,' they chorused. Fin knelt down to stroke the lobster's head but retracted his hand quickly as Horace splashed angrily and snappily towards him.

'Ach, Ah nearly forgot,' said Aggie, hirpling towards a cluttered shelf. 'Ah made youse a wee giftie.' She delved into a dilapidated and battered basket and pulled out a small parcel wrapped in a thick sheet of grey-brown seaweed parchment. 'Jist a wee bit o' ma famous cuttlefish fudge,' she said, beaming, handing the parcel to Beth. 'It might cheer up poor MacRobbie.

'I'm sure it will,' Beth smiled. 'Thanks Aggie, you're very kind.'

Mologan sniffed loudly. Beth, Fin and Aggie turned towards him.

'What's wrong, Mologan?' Aggie asked.

'Oh, nuthin',' he replied, pouting, and staring at the parcel of fudge. 'Ah used tae like yer cuttlefush fudge when Ah was a Boggart wain,' he stammered. 'Ah always said that Aggie Hagg-Boggart made the best cuttlefush fudge in the Western Isles.'

'Uch, stop mac-flatterin' me, Mologan. It'll get ye mac-nowhere!' Aggie poked Mologan's chest with a bony finger. 'Ah havnae forgotten thon time when when you and young Hector Mac-Snot swapped all yer holiday clamjamphrie for cuttlefush fudge an' youse were so mac-sick that youse boaked intae the Golden Quaich mac-trophy.'

Mologan frowned. His nose turned slightly purple with embarrassment, then he grinned. 'An' dae ye remember, Aggie, that Spewie Mac-Phlegm won the Boglin' Compie-mac-tishun that year? An' he thought it was pert o' the mac-prize and toasted every-Boggarts' health wi' it!'

'You mean he drank it?' Fin said.

Mologan nodded. He and Aggie laughed till the tears ran down their cheeks. Mologan's fangs glinted in the candle light.

Fin screwed up his face. 'Yuch!'

'Aye, thon were the mac-days,' Aggie choked, wiping her eyes with her seaweed shawl. She thrust a package which she had had hidden behind her back into Mologan's hand. 'There ye are, Mologan, ma boy. Do ye think Ah wid forget ma mac-favourite Boggart?'

Mologan snorted happily and tucked the fudge into his sporran.

Beth, Fin and Mologan said goodbye and made their way back down the passage to their canoe. Mologan clutched his precious jar of mixture close to his chest.

'Careful, Mologan, don't trip and fall in case you drop your potion,' Fin called.

'Shoosh, Fin. Don't tempt fate,' said Beth.

'Ah'm mac-fine,' said Mologan. 'It's too mac-valuable to drap. Ah'll be gey careful.'

'I like Aggie,' said Fin as he helped Mologan to squeeze into his lifejacket.

'Aye, she's a right guid Boggart witch,' Mologan agreed.

'Her chuckie-boord predictions all came true.' Fin held the canoe close to the rock ledge and Mologan nervously climbed in. 'I reckon her potion will cure you in no time, Mologan.'

'Ah've every mac-confidence in Aggie's magic. She's...'

'The oracle with the coracle!' Beth laughed.

⌘

Dabberlocks was waiting in the chasm. He barked a few words to Mologan.

'He says the weather's mac-changin' an' it's a bit choppy,' Mologan translated, 'an' we've tae hold on gey mac-tight. It'll be a rough mac-crossin'.' He gripped onto the canoe with one hand and clutched the jar of mixture in the other hand.

'Here's the rope, Dabberlocks.' Beth passed the painter to the waiting seal and they were off.

The canoe pitched and tossed. Mologan seemed to turn even greener. He sat rigid and silent.

'Don't worry, Mologan,' Fin called. 'The canoe's very buoyant, and you've got a lifejacket on. You'll be fine.'

Mologan screwed up his face and closed his eyes even tighter.

Dawn was breaking as they reached the lagoon. Now sheltered by Black Island, the sea was much calmer. Dabberlocks moved faster through the water, towing the canoe through the scatter of small rocky islands.

'Look,' Beth yelled, pointing towards the Craigmhor croft. 'There's Robbie.'

In the distance they saw a torch flash on and off at the top of the cliff.

'He can see us,' Fin called, and pulled out his torch to signal back to his brother. 'Look Mologan, It's Robbie. He's signalling to us.'

Dabberlocks was negotiating a tricky manoeuvre between two rocky islets. The canoe pitched suddenly to the right. As Mologan opened his eyes and looked up a wave splashed over the side of the canoe, soaking the Boggart's hand, arm and bottom.

'Ach, watter!' he howled, letting go of the sides of the canoe.

Just then, alarmed by Mologan's howl, a flock of oystercatchers rose into the air, screeching loudly.

Startled, Mologan suddenly stood up and turned round. The canoe rocked dangerously.

'Sit down, Mologan, or you'll capsize the...'

SPLASH!

Mologan was in the water.

Fin and Beth steadied the canoe and peered overboard.

'MOLOGAN!' they shouted in panic.

The Boggart bobbed up to the surface a few metres from the canoe.

'BOGGART OVERBOARD!' Beth cried.

Dabberlocks was beside Mologan instantly, gripping the straps of his lifejacket.

'Are you OK?' Fin shouted.

'Splutter, snort, gurgle.' Mologan thrashed around like an angry lobster.

Dabberlocks barked and winked.

'He's fine,' said Fin to Beth. 'Tow him over here, Dabberlocks.

The seal towed Mologan to the canoe. Fin and Beth gripped him under his arms and tried to pull him on board. The canoe tipped precariously.

Dabberlocks dived and pushed Mologan's bottom upwards with his head but they still could not pull the water-logged Boggart on board.

'He's too heavy,' said Beth, breathlessly. 'It's all these extra cammy-mac-flag clothes... and his kilt. They've soaked up too much water.'

'Well, at least his peep-toed wellies will drain quickly,' said Fin.

'This is no time for mac-jokes,' Mologan spluttered, 'Ah'm droonin'!'

'Calm down, Mologan. You're not drowning,' said Beth softly. 'We'll just have to think of a way to get you safely on board without capsizing the canoe.'

Dabberlocks barked, dived and surfaced at the back of the canoe. He nudged the stern with his head then tapped it with his flipper. He barked again.

'What's he saying?' Fin asked.

'Ah'm no doin' ony such thing!' Mologan whined.

Fin looked puzzled. 'Doing what? What is Dabberlocks saying?'

'He says tae mac-tie me tae the back o' the boat an' mac-tow me hame.' Mologan bobbed unhappily in the cold water.

'Great idea,' said Beth brusquely. 'If we don't get you back soon you'll chill to death.'

'And we don't want you to get hypo-mac-thermia, do we?' Fin patted Mologan's head.

'Grunt, snuffle.'

Beth tied a rope onto the stern of the canoe and slipped the other end into the water. Dabberlocks towed the reluctant and huffy Boggart into position, wound the rope under Mologan's arms and passed it back to Beth, who tied it securely.

Mologan made quiet whining and sniffling noises, but, resigned to his fate, he remained quite still and floated behind the canoe like a bloated whale.

'Full steam ahead, Dabberlocks!' Fin called.

Dabberlocks dived, caught the painter in his mouth and moved off at speed, pulling Mologan behind them like a fallen water skier. Beth talked reassuringly to Mologan who snuffled and snorted as water splashed up his nose and into his eyes.

Remembering that Robbie had been watching them from the cliff and had obviously witnessed Mologan's accident, Fin flashed his torch seven times towards Craigmhor. Robbie sent seven flashes in reply.

'Phew,' Fin sighed. 'I hoped Robbie would see we were OK. It would have been a disaster if he had panicked and wakened Mum and Dad.'

'He'll have seen Mologan's rescue with the binoculars,' said Beth. 'It's quite light now. Are you alright Mologan?'

'Grunt.'

⌘

Dabberlocks towed them into Boat Bay and helped Fin and Beth to release the grumpy, waterlogged Boggart.

'Thanks, Dabberlocks,' Fin said, patting the seal's head.

'Yeah, see you soon,' Beth called, as Dabberlocks

dived and swam off towards Eilean nan Ron. 'Come on, Mologan, let's get you home.'

Beth and Fin quickly put the canoe into its usual place and wrapped it in the tarpaulin. Mologan stood unhappily on the beach, moving from foot to foot, water trickling out of his peep-toed wellies and dripping from his sleeves and the hem of his kilt.

'Hurry up. Ah'm mac-drookit an' mac-freezin' an' Ah dinnae feel well,' he whined. 'Ah've probably got a cold an' hypo-mac-thermia forbye. Ah tell't youse that Boggarts are mac-allergic tae watter.'

The children bustled Mologan briskly across the machair and into the nearest secret tunnel and they were soon back in the Boggart's cave. They were surprised to find Robbie waiting for them.

'Here, I brought a towel,' he grinned, throwing a brightly coloured beach towel at Mologan. 'I thought you wouldn't have one.'

Mologan looked puzzled.

'It's for drying yourself,' Beth said.

Mologan stood, dripping water on the cave floor. He looked at the towel and shrugged.

'Take off your wet clothes and you'll feel better.' Robbie suggested.

'Ah cannae. No in front of...'

Beth was gently removing Mologan's gloves. Mologan, feeling embarrassed, shivered and buried his face in the towel.

'I saw what happened,' said Robbie, unzipping Mologan's cagoule, 'so I decided to limp down and see if you were alright. That's right, Mologan. Slip off the other sleeve now. Did you get the potion?'

'Oh, yes,' said Beth. 'Sit down on that box, Mologan, while I pull off your wellies.' Mologan sat down. Beth continued, 'Aggie brewed it there and then. It took ages. Mologan's to start taking the mixture tomorrow. Mologan, sit still. MOLOGAN!'

The Boggart had become rigid.

'Mologan? What's wrong? Can you hear me?' Beth shook his arm.

Mologan's nose flushed a very dark purple, he clenched his fists and covered his eyes. Then he looked round, jerking his head like a chicken from side to side and up and down.

'Mologan!' Fin gripped his shoulders. 'What's wrong?'

'Maybe it's a Boggart-type allergic reaction to sea water,' ventured Robbie. 'We'll have to get him dry.'

'It's, it's...' Mologan croaked, standing in a pool of water.

'Sit down again,' Beth coaxed him gently. 'You'll be fine when we get you dry.'

'Naw... it's the mac-mixture!' Mologan was breathing heavily. He began to shake all over.

'He's having a panic attack,' said Robbie, panicking.

'Calm down.' Beth gently stroked Mologan's forehead.

'But it's... oh no!' Mologan put his head in his hands. 'It's the mac-mixture, sniff, snort... it's mac-droonded!'

Fin, Beth and Robbie were dumbfounded.

Mologan sobbed and sniffed.

'You mean you lost the jar of mixture in the lagoon when you fell overboard?'

'Aye, Fin Mac-visitor. It's mac-lost.'

Fin put his arm around the wet Boggart. 'Never mind, Mologan, we'll go and look for it at low tide. Don't worry.'

'It'll be mac-ruined,' Mologan said, pessimistically.

'No it won't,' Beth reassured him. 'Aggie sealed it up with wax. It'll be fine.' She glanced at Fin who shrugged. 'Come on, lets get that balaclava off before it shrinks permanently to your head.'

'It may as weel,' Mologan sobbed. 'Ah'll probably have tae wear it fur ever, noo. Ouch, watch ma lugs.'

The balaclava peeled off the Boggart's head with a satisfying SCHLEP! Fin passed the towel to Mologan.

'Give your head a good rub,' said Robbie.

Mologan looked at the towel suspiciously.

'Like this.' Robbie threw the towel over Mologan's head and gently dried his hair. He dabbed round Mologan's eyes and nose carefully and rubbed behind his ears.

'Look how green this towel is.' Robbie peered at the towel curiously. They all examined it closely. Fin, Beth and Robbie stared at Mologan, grinning. 'Look, Mologan,' Robbie laughed, 'the mac-green-ness is coming off. It's on the towel!'

They dragged Mologan over to a shaft of sunlight that was streaming into the cave. Mologan stood in the light.

'Yes, It's coming off.' Beth snatched the towel and rubbed Mologan's arms. 'It's cleaning off.'

'The mac-green-ness must have *washed* off,' Fin observed, incredulous.

Mologan examined his arms and hands and beamed with delight. 'Ah'm un-mac-greenichied. Ah'm back tae mac-normal,' he grinned, peering into the water trough at the reflection of his grey, blotchy, lichen-coloured skin. 'Noo Ah can continue tae save the planet.' He puffed out his chest proudly and thrust his arm upwards triumphantly. 'The eco-warrior returns!'

Fin helped Mologan to take off his wellies. Then the children turned their backs discreetly while Mologan stripped off his T-shirt and kilt and wrapped himself in a couple of potato sacks.

'If the green-ness washed off,' said Robbie, thoughtfully, 'why didn't you discover this before?'

Mologan, bewildered by Robbie's question, shrugged and looked blankly at the children.

'I mean, if you were washing your hands or something,' Robbie continued, 'you'd see that the green-ness disappeared.'

'Ye ken Ah'm mac-allergic tae watter.' Mologan was confused. 'Ah dinnae ken whit ye mean.'

'When did you last touch water, Mologan? You know, have a wash.'

'Um,' Mologan looked thoughtful and scratched his chin. 'Um, Ah dinnae rightly ken. Mibby...' he counted on his fingers, mouthing the numbers silently to himself. 'Mibby, aboot a hunner an' forty–seven years.'

'What age did you say you were, Mologan?' Fin asked.

'A hunner an' forty-eight, next birthday.'

'Then,' said Fin, impressed, 'you've never washed?'

'Washed?' said Mologan rubbing his toes with the grubby green-stained towel, 'Mac-never!'

He glanced at his reflection again and smiled a wide, happy, fangy smile. 'This calls for a mac-celebration!'

'To celebrate your first wash for a hundred and forty-seven years?' said Fin. 'I'm all for that!'

'And the end of Mologan's Boggarts' sucessful mac-mission,' Robbie added.

'And I've got just the thing,' Beth grinned, pulling a small grey-brown package out of her pocket. 'Cuttle-fish fudge, any-Boggart?'

Glossary of Scots Words and Boggart-speak

A

Ablow below
Aboot about
Aff off
Affie awful
Afore before
Ahint behind
Alane alone
Alang along
Aroon around
Auld old
Aw all
Aye always
Ayne own

B

Bannocks biscuits
Baud bad
Ben in, inside
Biddie wine
Bide live, stay
Bide yer time wait patiently
Bin been
Birl spin, dance, turn round
Birsie wiry
Bitty small bit
Boaked vomited
Boggart a cave-dwelling creature who lives a solitary life in remote places

Bogle, boglin' to make mischief, spirit away discarded items or collect **clamjamphrie**

Bonny pretty

Boord board

Boorden table

Braw beautiful

Breenging rushing

Broch fort

Broon brown

Buddie person

Bunnet hat

Burds birds

C

Caddles nails

Cahouchy rubber

Canny cautious

Ceilidh party

Chuckies pebbles

Clabbydhus mussels

Clamjamphrie rubbish, junk collected and hoarded by Boggarts

Clouts cloths

Compie-mac-tishun competition

Coo cow

Coort court

Coracle small round boat

Crack chat

Craiturs creatures

Creel basket for carrying fish, or lobster pot (trap)

D

Dae do

Daurk dark

Dinnae don't

Divil devil

Do party

Doon down

Drap drop

Drookit soaking wet

Droonin' drowning

Dug dog

Dwam daydream

Dyke wall

E

Een eyes

Efter after

Elver baby eel

F

Fankled tangled

Fanklin' tangling
Feenish finish
Feenished finished
Ferniticles freckles
Fert fart
Flype upside down
Foosty musty, mouldy
Forbye as well
Fowk people, folk
Fower four
Frae from
Fur for
Furmented fermented
Fush fish
Fushin' fishing

G

Galoot idiot
Gey very
Gid, guid good
Gie give
Git get
Glowered glared
Greenichy green
Grossart, grosset gooseberry
Grumphie pig
Gruntle snout

H

Hale whole
Hap tarpaulin
Haud hold
Haud yer wheesht keep quiet
Hedger hedgehog
Heid head
Hirpling limping
Houlet owl
Hud had
Hunner hundred

I

Inpit contribution
Isnae isn't

J

Jinkin' moving quickly
Jist just
Jujubes soft sweets

K

Kail wurums caterpillars
Keek peek, look
Ken know
Kent knew

L

Lobstur lobster

Loup jump

M

Machair seaside pasture

Mair more

Maist most

Moldert rotted

Mony many

Muckle large

N

Nae, naw no

Neb nose

Nimpit tight

Nivver never

Noo now

O

Oan on

Oantae onto

Onybody anybody

Onythin anything

Onyways anyway

Oos fluff

Oot out

Ower over

Oxters armpit

P

Pert part

Pit put

Plaid a long piece of tartan cloth worn like a kilt

Poke bag

Puckle small amount

Puddock-stuil toadstool

Puggie-nits peanuts

Purridge porridge

Purvey selection of food

Q

Quaich cup, drinking bowl

R

Ramorra tomorrow

Rastler rustler

Rid red

Rools rules

Roosty rusty

Rummle feel (in your pocket), shake

Russlin' rustling

S

Sair sore
Scimpit small, measly
Scran food
Seeven seven
Sels selves
Sheilin' summer hut
Sherp sharp
Shoo bit, amount
Skedaddle run away
Skelfy splintered
Skiddled play aimlessly with something wet
Slangie-mac-var a Scots Boggart toast
Sleekit cunning
Sowel soul
Spat spot, place
Spoot razor clam
Sporran leather pouch worn with a kilt
Spreckled speckled
Squidgy soft and spongy
Stanes stones
Stert start
Stoor dust
Stoorie dusty
Stramash disturbance, clamour

T

Tae to, toe
Tap top
Tapsulteerie topsy-turvy, higgledy-piggledy
Tattie potato
Tell't told
Thereaboots thereabouts
Thole bear, put up with
Thon those
Thonder over there
Tor rocky hill
Twa two
Twinty twenty

U

Unco extremely, strange
Unco fowk Boggart word for humans
Unfankle untangle

W

Wain child

Wan one

Wance once

Wappin enormous

Watter water

Wee small

Weel well

Wheen large number, quantity

Wheesht! be quiet!

Whins gorse bushes

Whit what

Wifie woman

Windy-wallets flatulence

Wire in eat up

Wis was

Wrang wrong

Wull will

Wur'ni weren't

Y

Yane one

Yanes ones

Yased used

Yella yellow

Yersel' yourself

Yon that, those

Yonder over there

Youse you

Yun one